2085
THE END OF THE REPUBLIC

by

WILLIAM R. DAMERON

Phil,
I hope you enjoy this —
Bill

William R. Dameron
3/31/2014

1

Also by William R. Dameron
<u>Historical fiction</u>:
A House in Berlin.
The gods who came from the sea.
<u>Science Fantasy</u>:
Wizard's World.
Wizard's World 2: The Stone Seller
Wizard's World 3: Red Paradise
Wizard's World 4: Freeworld (not yet published)
<u>Mix of mystery, history, and fantasy</u>:
The intangible queen.

Table of Contents

Cast of Characters

Barrett, Gina – Arthur Girard's niece, nurse, and companion. She is young, beautiful, and very interested in his money.

Beale, Randolf – Candidate for President of the United States, a senator from New York. He is a Democrat who wants to chastise the Chinese. He becomes president.

Blunt, Lamar – Secretary of State

Brockmeyer, Jane – Professor of Political Science, University of Illinois.

Carter, Liam – Republican candidate for president in 2084.

Casey, Lance – Secretary of Defense

Cauldmoss, John - National Security Advisor to the President.

Cornwell, Mark – Outgoing president in 2084, a Republican.

Crossfield, Amy – Mark Girard's secretary and sometimes mistress.

Girard, Arthur - founder and chief stockholder of GRS Corporation. He is Mark's father and Parker's grandfather, and is retired.
  – Kari, his masseuse;
  – Sue, his housekeeper;
  – Maxie, his secretary;
  – Kitty, his ADR companion;
  – Timmy, his ADR assistant.

Girard, Mark – President of GRS Corporation. He is Parker's father.

Girard, Melanie – Mark's estranged wife.

Girard, Parker – Chief Scientist at GRS Corporation, he is Mark's son.

Glitchy, Robert – United States Vice President under Randolf Beale.

Harper, Angela - Senator from Minnesota, Randolf Beale's love interest.

Lister, Sara – Representative in Congress, Chairman of the House Finance Committee, found murdered in her apartment.

Locasa, Fred – President of Robotic Enterprises, Incorporated.

Panagaki, Alex – FBI Agent in Los Angeles. He was once Parker's roommate at U of Arizona.

Panagaki, Julie - Alex's wife, secretary to Fred Locasa, formerly Julie Chang.

Selby, Roger (Roj) – Executive Vice President of GRS, sometimes acting CEO.

Webb, La'Naomi – Owner of six athletic gear stores in Arizona, she is Parker's girlfriend.

Arthur Girard, an aging widower, spent most of his time with his "girls" and his bots. Three women lived in a guest house behind his rambling ranch-style home: his housekeeper Sue, in her 60's, who had sharp opinions and would argue with him at the drop of a hat; his secretary Maxie, in her 40's and quite efficient but always polite and proper; his masseuse Kari, beautiful and in her 20's, who kept his muscles loose and his sexual appetite, diminished as it was, satisfied.

The other female member of his household was his niece Gina Barrett, from the poor side of his late wife's family. Ostensibly, Gina was his nurse. She was in her early 20's and beautiful as well, and openly told him she wanted to be well remembered in his will. She bathed and groomed him, read to him, walked with him, administered his medications, slept in the same bed with him, and sometimes serviced him with nearly impersonal sex, even when he didn't want it. He didn't love her but she was worth keeping around, even if her motives were purely financial.

He was playing a *dangerous* game, letting himself grow so old. There was new medical technology which was said to sharply reverse the effects of aging, but it could only be done once. He knew he would have to act soon. It would cost him many millions of dollars. There were dangers involved. One was that if he waited too long, he might die before he got around to it. The other was that the hormones used in the treatment carried a risk of serious disability or even death. Some doctors estimated the success rate as only sixty per cent for someone his age. If he was one of the lucky sixty, however, he might extend his life and health by as much as another fifty years. He was sharply conflicted about it.

His walled twenty acre property could have sold for tens of millions. He was guarded by a dozen domestic bots which allowed entry to no one he had not invited, including service and delivery people. Several of the bots doubled as his household servants.

From his Oregon coast estate Arthur could look out at the Pacific Ocean, seeing the curve of the earth at the horizon. Waves incessantly beat against the rocks below, creating a loud and constant roar. The cliff was a two hundred foot drop. He liked to sit in his wheelchair near the rim and look out, but he always had Kitty, one of his domestic robots, push him, unless Sue was available and in a good mood. Under no circumstances would he let Gina control his wheelchair so close to the edge, even if there was a low security wall that should prevent a fall. She might want to hasten his departure.

He liked to contemplate his life. There was much to be proud of. He was the creator of the ARB, or Autonomous Robot Brain, a computer hardware and software marvel which gave robots a pseudo-awareness and will, allowing them to carry out complex tasks without assistance. It had been a tremendous achievement which had brought him the Nobel Prize in Robotic Science. He had founded GRS Corporation and was still a major stockholder, although his son Mark was now president and CEO as well as chief stockholder.

Arthur had led GRS for nearly forty years. He'd seen his Autonomous Combat Robots, or ACR's, take over the United States military. No other country had anything like them, other than China, which had remote controlled robots requiring a human operator for each bot. Because of China's lag in robot technology, the United States remained the most powerful nation in the world.

He had also developed Autonomous Domestic Robots, or ADR's, and had added an entire new fortune with them. Most of that had gone to Mark.

Even though he was in his 80's, and had retired ten years ago, many in the world outside his fence still remembered and venerated him. He also was venomously hated by many, especially outside the US – after all, he had created the loathsome (to them) humanoid bots. Muslims, in particular, had been shocked and stunned by the creation of machines which so resembled people, and even more by their effectiveness on the battlefield. The very idea seemed to undermine their religion. Iran's principal Ayatollah had issued a *fatwa* declaring autonomous robots an abomination to Allah. Al Qaeda followed with a reward offer to whoever could kill Arthur. Needless to say, he was careful about visitors, and his bot security staff was ever vigilant.

Maxie and her two ADR assistants carried on all his correspondence, most of which was electronic. Sometimes gift packages arrived, which an ADR always carefully opened in isolation and checked for bombs, viruses, and all other evils. Still, Arthur saw very few of the gifts; most were forwarded to various charities.

He supported an organization called *The Utopian Society*, which he had founded thirty years ago, for the purpose of devising better government. It was a going concern and had done some good work, although he was not satisfied with it and it hadn't caught on as he'd hoped.

Now and then, Arthur called his son Mark, or Mark called him. Arthur liked to keep up on technical developments. Mark had attended MIT and had become a brilliant scientist in his own right, making many improvements to the product lines. Mark had taken the final step of putting all robot production into the capable hands of his own ADR's. That had resulted into a terrific savings on labor costs and had boosted the profit on each bot sold by twenty-five per cent, even though he sold them at a reduced price.

Mark's son Parker had been something of a disappointment. Parker had attended MIT as well, and studied robotic science, but as a student, had been little better than average. He now ran the research and development division of GRS, but had made few if any contributions, depending on his well-experienced staff instead. He was an administrator, not an innovative scientist.

#

This day, Arthur was sitting in his chair with Kitty in attendance. It was cloudy and warm, with just enough breeze off the ocean to keep him cool, and he had an open line with Mark, listening to Mark conduct business. The phone was built into the arm of Arthur's wheelchair. Now and then Mark would direct a comment to his father, even in the midst of conversations with others, who were usually delighted that Arthur was sitting in, even if silently.

"The new pseudo-muscles are really working out, Dad." Mark told him. Mark then continued his conversation with Donal Foster, Secretary of Defense, as Arthur listened in.

". . . We'll have the new M8's ready for advanced testing by November first. How many will you need?"

"Twenty-five hundred," Foster said. "We'll form a battalion with them, then try them in mini war games in January."

"Against M7's?" Mark asked.

"Yes. Tell me how M8's should be better."

"Mister Secretary, we've increased the endurance by about five hours, the running speed by ten per cent, and the effective IQ of the M8 is 120, which is 10 points better. They surpassed our M7 athletic scores by more than ten per cent. To give you an idea, their vertical leap is fifty-eight inches. They'd be *hell* on a basketball court if they could learn to dribble."

"All that, using the same fuel cell?"

"Yes, Sir."

"If the M8's work out, can we update our M7's? And, how much?"

"We can. I can give you a wild ass guess. We'd have to bring them into a workshop and change the muscles, and it would take a new download of the revised ARB programs. About six hours per bot, perhaps ten thousand dollars. The good news is that we could get it done with ADR's. The labor is almost free."

"Mark, let me do the math. We have roughly two hundred and fifty thousand M7's in the armed forces, at ten thousand each, that's two billion and five hundred million. Too damned *much*, Mark. *Way* too much."

"Come on, Don, you know that's chump change for the federal government, but the newest pseudo muscles are just coming into production. Maybe I can get them a bit cheaper. Let me work on it and get you a better price, or at least one which I've properly estimated."

"When? I need to take this to the President."

"By Monday afternoon."

"All right. No later. Foster out."

Mark laughed. "See, Dad? A challenge and an opportunity."

"I have faith in you, Son," Arthur replied.

"I've got to run now, Dad. Appointment."

"See you, Mark."

The phone went dead.

Kitty spoke up. "Sir, I'm wanted in the kitchen. Cook wants my help."

Arthur turned toward the household bot. "Where's Timmy?"

"He's at the recharging station, Sir. He has no assignment at the moment."

"Please ask him to take your place."

"Very well, Sir. He's on his way."

The bots could communicate among themselves. That had been Arthur's own idea from the beginning. Instantaneous cooperation made them much more efficient. Any task involving more than one bot invoked an algorithm which allowed one of them to take over and make all decisions needed to finish the job in hand.

Kitty left as Timmy arrived and took up his position behind the wheelchair. Timmy had been given red hair – rare in an ADR – and a freckled complexion. People often thought him human at first glance.

"How are you today, Timmy?" Arthur asked.

"I don't know how to answer that, Sir." Timmy replied. "Are you referring to the results of my last set of diagnostic tests?"

"No, it's just an expression. It doesn't mean much."

"Yes, Sir."

Arthur chuckled. Timmy was his own special creation, and would do . . . literally . . . anything for Arthur, and only Arthur. Arthur thought he might have a special task for Timmy within the next few days. Considering it, he chuckled to himself.

1. June, 2084.

\#

Alex received the call around four in the morning, but his manager told him that the forensics team was working the scene, and he needn't show up for a couple of hours. He had time to shower and grab a piece of toast before leaving his apartment.

He lived alone now, after a short, difficult marriage. The divorce had finalized two months ago.

He left his three rooms and took the elevator down to the parking level, found his three-year-old Ford Electric, unplugged it, got in, and gave it the address. It pulled out into the streets of Los Angeles.

There was little traffic. Only about ten per cent of the population left their homes to work, and many people rarely left their homes at all. Only a few of the automated delivery vehicles were out now. The car entered the thruway and went south.

When he reached the neighborhood, his car turned into a side street. He saw the barrier and the flashing lights and told his car to park half a block from them. He got out and walked briskly past the porches and driveways of expensive three-story townhouses.

Short and black-haired, Alex was in his sixth year as an FBI agent, and wasn't all that happy with his assignment to the Los Angeles office. There were nicer metropolitan areas in the world, but he was stuck here. It seemed as if he spent half his life driving; today he'd had to come down to Anaheim, to a newer residential area not far from Disneyland.

The sun was out and the morning was already

14

warm. A light breeze gently moved the fronds of the palm trees that lined the sidewalk. Alex wore a coat and tie, still the standard dress for FBI, even in this age of casual attire. Fortunately his clothes were made of nano-cooled fabric, the equivalent of personal air conditioning. He was a burly man and tended to sweat excessively, but the suit kept him cool.

He had to push his way through a crowd of chattering onlookers, use his ID to pass two officers holding the crowd back, then pass another officer to enter the front door of the residence. He found himself standing in the hallway of a richly furnished home. He saw no one but he heard noise coming from above and took the stairs up. When he reached the third floor, there were two plainclothes cops conversing at the door to a bedroom. He approached them, holding his ID so they could see it.

"Agent Panagaki?" The taller of the two asked. "I'm Deputy Calvin Dreger, Orange County Sheriff's Office. It's my case. This is Assistant Deputy Ron Spangler."

"Right, I'm from the LA office." Panagaki could hear activity inside the bedroom as he shook hands with the two men. Spangler went downstairs.

"Thanks for coming. The victim is in there. Strangled, don't think she was raped. As I told you on the phone, it's Sara Lister, of the US House of Representatives. That's why I brought you in."

"Yes, we're automatically interested. Do you have a time frame?"

"The coroner hasn't arrived yet. We think it was last night. We have someone who claims to be a witness. I haven't interviewed her as yet. The forensic folks are still in there. They aren't finding much, outside of the broken window and the rope."

"Window? Rope?"

"The window is broken from the outside, and there's a rope hanging down from a grappling hook stuck in the gutter. The killer must have climbed the steel mesh fence down below, tossed up the rope, and then climbed up a sheer wall. It's really strange. There are a couple of footprints in the dirt below. "

Alex thought for a moment. The killer must have been very athletic. Also, quite strong, since people struggle frantically when being strangled.

"Any idea of a motive?" Alex had to ask, but he knew politicians have many enemies.

"No. Spangler talked to her parents in Florida. Representative Lister lived alone here, but of course she was in Washington most of the year. The House is in recess right now."

"Did she have a boyfriend or girlfriend?"

"Not that we can find. I assume you know of her, seen pictures. She wasn't very pretty, was she? They called her the 'Conservative Feminist', all over the talk shows. Her personality was rather abrasive, and even her parents said she wasn't likable. She was a sharp cookie, though. Very smart, Chairman of the House Finance Committee."

"Yeah, I've seen her a lot on the screener. How about her age? Mid fifties?"

"Right. Want to view the body?"

"Not particularly," Alex responded. "I'd like to walk through, then go outside and check the rope and fence."

"We can do that," Dreger replied. He handed

16

over a small evidence envelope. "Take a look at this."

Inside the sealed transparent bag was a small piece of thin flesh-colored plastic. Alex held it up and studied it for a moment. "*Robot* skin?"

"We think so. We found it at the top of the wire fence, on one of the barbs. Can you have your lab look at it?"

"Of course."

"We'll cut off a sample. You'll have to sign for it."

"No problem."

#

Alex sat in on a witness interview which Dreger and Spangler held in the first floor living room. Jennifer Wilson, middle-aged, unmarried and not in any sort of relationship, a next-door neighbor, related that she had come outside to water some potted plants on her porch when she saw a man climb the fence, toss the grappling hook, and scale the rope, break the window, and enter the house.

"It was dark over there, and I saw him come up the sidewalk, stop at the fence, and look up at the house for a moment. I couldn't see his face, but he really moved fast. He jumped up, caught the top of the fence with one hand, and then pulled himself up and over. He tossed up the rope, and it caught on the first try. He went up it like a monkey. When he broke in the window, I was totally shocked. I heard a scream. That's when I came back inside and called 911."

"What happened then?" Dreger asked.

"I went back outside. After three or four minutes, the man came out the window, slid down the rope, went over the fence like it was nothing, and walked away. After another minute or two, I heard the police sirens. The man was long gone when they pulled up."

"How would you describe him?"

"I couldn't see too well, but I'd say he was average height and build. I think he wore a coverall suit. I believe he was young, and he was very, very strong. Like a gymnast, you know."

"Or, like a robot?"

"Yes, now that I think of it. He *could* have been a robot."

#

The GRS Corporation's telephone system answered on the first ring, and began to interrogate the caller in the standard manner.

"Language?"

"Greek," Alex responded. He liked to practice it, and it made no difference to the computer he would be speaking with.

The computer accepted that and rattled off six menu options in Greek. "Person," he replied, switching to English. "Parker Girard."

"Please say your name." The computer persisted with Greek.

"Alex Panagaki."

"Please say the reason for your call."

"FBI business."

"Doctor Girard is currently unavailable, but will be available in approximately five minutes. Will you hold?"

"Yes."

Alex stared at the computer screen on his desk for a moment, then pulled up the Time's front page story on Sara Lister. It was standard stuff and not very informative. There was no mention of the possibility that the murderer was a robot. The article did mention that the FBI had been contacted, but jurisdiction in the case remained with the Orange County Sheriff's Department.

He wondered what Parker would be like now that he was a vice prez or something with the world's largest corporation. Alex and he had been roommates at Arizona State for over a year, and had become great friends even though Alex was as poor as a church mouse and had to borrow his way through school, while Parker had been a wild spender who lived on an allowance of at least twenty thousand per month.

Parker came on the phone before the five minutes had expired. "Alex, you old SOB, what are you up to? Good to hear from you. How long has it been?"

"Hey, Parks! Five, six years? You had just gone to work for your father."

"Right, and you had just applied for the FBI. Apparently, you made it."

Back then, Alex had stopped off in Flagstaff while on his way to LA for his FBI employment exams. They had partied for two days.

"What's this "Doctor" stuff?"

"Dad made me go to MIT for three years. Doctor in robotics."

"I'm impressed. Are you married yet?"

"I'm having too much fun, Alex."

That figured. Parker had always had more women than he could handle. At ASU, Alex had dated some of his rejects, who were always scheming to get back into Parker's life.

"What about you?" Parker asked.

"Divorced. It lasted two years. She thought I worked too much."

"Anyone I know?"

"Met her after the last time I saw you, so unless you've been working LA, I doubt it."

"There are plenty of nice women here, so I haven't left the state yet. Heck, I haven't even finished with Flagstaff."

"Keep trying."

"Why don't you come see me? I'll send a company plane for you."

"I'm busy right now. Rain check?"

"Sure. Maybe you could come to work for us. I could triple your salary."

"Doing what?" Alex was strongly tempted.

"Security. It's big at GRS."

"Nice of you to ask. Maybe I'll take you up on the visit, but not for two or three months. Which brings me to why I called."

"It's really FBI business?"

"Really. Parks, maybe you heard about Sara Lister's murder."

"I did. You're in on the case?"

"Indeed. The murder was an amazing athlete. *Too* amazing, so we think it was a robot."

"No *shit*?"

"None. We found a piece of plastic skin caught at the top of a wire fence outside her home. We'd like to know who made it, what model, whatever you can tell us."

"You want us to look at it?"

"Yes. My God, you're quick."

"If it was a humanoid robot, there are two possible answers: ours or Robotics Enterprise's. I can't believe one of ours could murder a human being under any circumstances, unless it was a military model. The same for Robotic Enterprises units, and they don't even have military types, but they require a human operator who might be able to make them kill a human. We call them semi-autonomous, because they can carry out a pre-programmed sequence of commands. The Chinese have robots, but they are remote controlled, and less humanoid in appearance. Their army uses them. I don't think any Chinese units are in the United States."

"Could you examine our piece of robot skin and tell who made it?"

"I'm certain we could. Send it to me, I'll get on it ASAP. I can probably get you an answer in 24 hours, if not immediately."

"Thanks, Parker."

"Alex, I'm intrigued to think a robot could kill someone. I'd like to know whose it is. And, I meant it about coming to see me, and about you working for us."

"Thanks, I appreciate it. How can I get the evidence to you?"

Alex closed the connection after Parker related his address and said good-bye. He took a deep breath. He really wanted to see Parker again, and wanted to talk about a job offer, and he wasn't sure which he wanted more. He liked being with the FBI, but with all the money he had to fork over as alimony to Laney, he didn't have much for himself. A big raise would be very welcome.

Parker called his father an hour after Charley Roaf returned the evidence package. "Dad, I told you about the piece of robot skin the police found at Sara Lister's house. Roaf took a look at it."

"Yes." Mark Girard responded.

"Not ours, not RE's. It's just plastic film, not grown, no imbedded electronics. Has to be Chinese, although we can't be certain."

"I would have been very shocked if it had been ours. It's good to know someone guided it."

"My FBI friend Alex called me this morning. He said the robot had been seen getting into a white van after it left the house."

"So, you informed him about the sample?"

"I did, and I'll return it. What does it mean, a Chinese bot in America, and used in an assassination?"

"It could have been directed at us. Lister was our best friend in Congress. They've been trying to put a tax on our military models."

"That makes sense, pay us with one hand and take part of it back with the other."

"I'll just charge more to compensate for the tax. But, it looks as if Randy Beale is going to win the election, and the Dems are going to take the Senate as well. That can't be good for us."

"No, Dad. It can't."

"And, who smuggled a Chinese bot into the states? That's the question."

"It makes a formidable murder weapon, doesn't it?"

"It does indeed, Son."

#

Alex had expected Parker's conclusion, because supposedly, autonomous domestic robots were programmed to disobey commands to murder someone, and GRS's military models didn't look human, while the RE Corporation's military models, if any, were experimental or in development. According to Parker, Chinese remote-controlled bots didn't look very natural either, and they had never been able to come up with an autonomous model; the computer requirements were incredibly difficult. Parker's opinion was that the Chinese might have built a special model for the purpose of assassination, although someone in this country might have modified the slender military model to make it resemble a human.

The implications were scary. A Chinese robot in the states, used as a murder weapon against a US Congressman.

He had written it all up, included his copy of the sheriff's reports, and sent it to Homeland Security as well as up the FBI chain, and in addition he had called HS to make certain they knew of it.

Panagaki had been assigned to lead a four-man investigation team to assist Orange County. They were trying to trace the van, thus far without success. The bot had obviously been smuggled into the United States, but there were no leads as to who, how, and where. The working theory was that the control equipment had been in the van, along with the bot's operator. So far, there was no way to be sure of that.

Alex sighed. It didn't look promising.

2. June, 2084

Mark's office was deceptively small and plain, a
bit less than what one might expect the wealthiest
man in the world to have. The desk was marble-
topped, but small and without ornamentation. A
small notebook computer occupied a portion of the
desk top; the rest was bare. The armchairs and
couch were padded but by no means special. There
were a few wall pictures (including the mandatory
one of Arthur Girard), a bookcase with a few books,
some plaques, and a trophy or two. On a credenza
behind Mark stood several ten-inch models: the
original RCCG, not very humanoid, radio
controlled, and taller than the human operator; the
first autonomous combat robot, the ACR-3, and
later models, the ACR-5 and ACR-7; and the
domestic robots ADR-1 and ADR-5, which looked
very human, if too clean-cut and handsome. These
products had made the ACR Corporation extremely
profitable.

Mark's only child Parker had been inside the
office many times before. He knew all about the
adjoining rooms: the lounge behind the door, where
at times his father retreated to read, eat, shave, or
watch television; the bedroom where (it was
rumored) his father sometimes took his female
secretaries. Three of them worked in the anteroom
just outside the door, and all were young and very
pretty.

Mark looked up from his keyboard and frowned
as Parker entered and took a seat facing the desk.

"Hi, Pops," his son said flippantly.

"Are you here for business or crap?" Mark demanded. "How's the *nine* coming?"

Parker grinned. "The newest bio muscles are matching all the hype they got. We're estimating twenty-five per cent stronger than the M8 version, without giving up any recovery time. There may be a longer effective recharge cycle – we're not sure. The prototype will be up and ready for initial tests in two weeks, and we'll find out for certain. But Dad, I have a new girlfriend, and I need an early start on the weekend."

Mark relaxed a bit. His son would never change. "Parks, just once, I'd like to see you put in an entire week."

"I love my job, Dad, but I have too many helpers, and they're all smart as Hell. It won't make any difference whether I come in tomorrow or not."

"Where are you taking her?"

"Cannes, the film festival. Sun and fun."

"I suppose you want to take one of the jets?"

"Right, Pops, the SkySkimmer. May I?"

"Fly commercial. No need to drop thirty thousand for fuel, not for just a pleasure trip. Not to mention maintenance costs."

"Dad, I'll pay for it myself. We don't have time for a decent stay if we fly slow."

"All right, you pay. What's the girl's name, and what's she like?"

"La'Naomi. Tall, athletic, sexy, and smart as a whip. You'll meet her. I'll bring her home for dinner next week."

"Good family?"

"Good enough for me. I'll bring her."

Mark frowned. "See that you do. Your mom will want to check her out."

Parker gave a mock salute. He stood, turned, and strode out of the room.

#

Amy Crossfield wistfully watched Parker Girard as he strode out of his father's office. So did Jill and Linda, she noted. The heir to the world's largest fortune was the inspiration for many of her daydreams. He was tall, lithe, and very good-looking. So much like his Dad, but near her own age and as yet, not blessed with a wife. She sighed.

An icon on the bottom row of her computer screen began blinking. She stood, grabbed her notebook, and went into Mark's office. She shut the door.

Mark came around the desk and attempted to put his arms around her, but she stepped back. "What's wrong?" He challenged.

"I'm not in a mood to be pawed," she responded. "Especially, not by a married man who lies to me."

"About Melanie? I'm still planning to divorce her. The petition is already filed."

"I'm not holding my breath. You're still living at home with her. Nothing ever changes."

Mark maneuvered her against the wall, then took her in his arms. She came reluctantly. "You know about my home. I can't move out myself. I have people looking at estates for her in Maine and Massachusetts. She'll move as soon as we locate one."

"Does she *want* to move?"

"Of course. There's nothing left between us. I've told you that."

"Why should I believe you'll marry *me* after your divorce goes through?"

"Honestly?"

Amy ducked away and sat on one of the chairs. Mark followed and stood over her.

"Be brutal," Amy said.

"All right. It's probably two things: lust, because you're a truly beautiful woman, and secondly, we get along great. You're not a spoiled aristocrat like Melanie. You appreciate money because you've never had much of it. She's always had too much. Also, you don't demand anything of me. She's always tried to get her way with me, and she doesn't understand that I have a business to run."

"No love involved?"

"I'm not sure I know what love is. I'm happy when you and I are alone together."

Amy sighed. "That makes two of us." She allowed Mark to kiss her, and soon, she was returning the kiss with interest.

#

Alex opened the attachment without enthusiasm. It came from the Washington FBI office. Agent Grimm there had interviewed Congressman Polly Perkins, seeking a motive for the Sara Lister homicide. Perkins, a Democrat, had been eager to cooperate, as had other House members, all of whom seemed shocked that one of their own had been murdered in such a manner.

He skimmed the polite preliminaries, quickly going to the meat of the interview.

Agent Grimm: Congressman Perkins, how close were you to Congressman Lister?

Perkins: I was one of her few friends. Even so, we

weren't close, but we did do things together at times. Going to official functions or dinner now and then. If I didn't have a date, I'd sometimes call her. She was Lesbian. I'm not, but she behaved well enough around me, didn't try to come on. She called me her failed attempt at bi-partisanship.

Agent Grimm: Did she date?

Perkins: There was a staffer she lived with, a girl around twenty-four, but they broke up at least six months ago. I doubt she's a suspect, they were still friends when she died, as far as I know.

Agent Grimm: Do you know anyone who might have wanted Sara Lister dead?

Perkins: There were many. She rubbed people the wrong way, wouldn't compromise on bills, and wouldn't listen to any other point of view. She wasn't polite to Democrats, almost all of us would kill her given the chance. But not really.

Agent Grimm: I'm looking for a motive. Who would benefit from her death?

Perkins: Robotic Enterprises, probably. Sara was a big friend of ACR Corporation, and there was a feeling in Congress that we should give RE more business. She stood right in the way of that.

Agent Grimm: Anyone else?

Perkins: The anti-robot crazies, maybe. She was a strong advocate for the use of robots in the armed forces. Personally, I don't trust them that much. I think at least fifty per cent of our combat troops should be human.

Agent Grimm: I'll ask again, anyone else you can think of?

Perkins: I can't think of anyone else, other than an Islamic Jihadist. But they might go after any

Congressman, myself included. I know of no one else who would feel that strongly about Sara, specifically.

(End of transcript)

Parker saved the transcript, but was disappointed. He had already thought about RE and the anti-bot crowd as possible suspects. Both would be hard to penetrate.

#

Mark Girard's estate was twenty acres of mostly timbered ground north of Flagstaff. There was the main home: ranch style, with three thousand square feet and six bedrooms; the garage which could hold four cars; the parking lot, the helipad, airstrip, and hangar; the gym; and the research building. It was perhaps the most effectively guarded private home in the world, as two dozen ACR-6's -- military models -- patrolled the outer fence 24/7. Another two dozen autonomous bots manned the gate and various posts inside the estate. They carried fifty caliber ordnance, plus rocket grenades that could stop a tank. Ostensibly, the combat robots were there to guard the research lab, because it was illegal for private citizens to possess them. Arthur Girard, desiring perfect security for himself, had located the top secret lab on his private estate. Mark had kept up the practice when he took over the estate, and Parker supposed he would as well if he ever owned it.

Parker pulled up to the gate in his Volvo electric. The ACR in charge approached. "Good Afternoon, Sir." It said, with a steady gaze directly at his eyes.

Parker knew his retinas were being scanned. The robot nodded. "You're free to enter, Sir."

"Thanks, Bot."

The ACR-6 took two backward steps and froze, waiting.

Parker drove to the garage, left the car, and then strode over the short walkway to the house.

Melanie was sitting outside in the atrium formed between two Y arms of the house, scanning a magazine on a reader device and sipping a lemonade by the swimming pool. Two female ADR's stood motionless nearby, waiting for commands.

His mother looked up as Parker approached. Still beautiful at forty-five, he thought. Blonde, or at least made to look that way, a great figure, and, to her son, a pleasing personality. He had no idea why Dad was kicking her out of his life.

"Hi, Mom. I'm home early."

"Hello, Dear. Have you eaten?"

"No time. I'm just here to pack. Flying out tonight."

She rose up from her chaise lounge and kissed him. "Where are you going?"

"The Riviera, Mom. I have to break in a new girlfriend."

"Hmm. That's a crude way to put it."

Parker could see the disapproval. "Don't worry, Mom, you'll like her. Probably."

"Mark thinks you're too much of a playboy. I sometimes agree with him."

"It's good you two can find something to agree on."

Melanie smiled ruefully. "Yes, isn't it? How long will you be gone?"

"Back late Sunday."

"I may be gone when you get back. I'll send you a note to let you know where."

"I wish you and Dad would stay together."

"It's over, Parker. There's nothing left."

Parker nodded sadly. He turned and went back into the house, pulling his cell as he did so. A couple of touches connected him to the airport.

An answer on his phone: "GRS Aviation, Wes Lee speaking."

"Wes, this is Parker Girard. Prep the SkySkimmer, leaving for Cannes around five. Myself and one other passenger. Charge the consumables to my account."

"Will you want a pilot, Sir?" Lee asked.

"Yes, and a cabin ADR."

"When will you be coming back?"

"Sunday."

"She'll be ready."

"Good. See you then."

Parker put his phone back into his pocket, reached his bedroom door. He pulled a travel bag out of the closet and began to pack.

#

La'Naomi Webb came out of her apartment building, carrying her own flight bag. Her tall, powerful figure excited Parker as she approached the Volvo. He jumped out to open the back hatch and took her bag. She met him with a kiss, or rather a peck, threw her bag in, and went around to the door, opening it before he could get there.

He took his own seat. "Airport," he commanded the vehicle's autonomous computer, and the car moved smoothly away and headed in that direction, blending in with the traffic. He turned toward

31

La'Naomi.

"I'm glad you decided to come. We'll have a great time."

She looked directly into his eyes. "Separate rooms?"

"If you insist."

"I do."

It was their third date. He'd taken her to a movie and dinner before, and had been surprised when she agreed to spend a weekend with him, because he hadn't gotten to first base. He wasn't all that certain he would this time either. This was a new experience for Parker; women usually jumped at the chance to bed him. And, it was his first relationship with a black woman, even if she could almost pass for white.

Her flawless auburn hair featured bangs in front, and fell to her shoulders in a smooth mass.

She had a somewhat small head with a long, narrow face. Her nose was only slightly flattened, her complexion barely brown-tinged. Not beautiful, he thought, but incredibly attractive. She was nearly as tall as he was, with long torso and long legs, moderate breasts, and a very athletic look. She had played basketball at Vanderbilt and had been a star. She owned several retail stores that sold athletic gear, and he had met her when buying a pair of running shoes.

"How's the shoe biz?" Parker asked.

"Not quite the same as bot biz."

"Dad does well. I'm just a hired hand."

"With a big allowance?"

"Not big enough."

La'Naomi laughed. "I'd pay for this trip, but that

would go against my principles."

"Soak the boyfriend?"

"Exactly. That's what men are for."

"I hope you have other uses for them."

"Perhaps I do. Perhaps not."

Parker glanced at his watch. It was nearing five PM, one in the morning at Cannes. If they lifted off by five-thirty, they should be at Nice around six A.M., in time to board the yacht he'd leased, then have a nice breakfast as the boat cruised over to Cannes.

"Did you bring a jacket?" He asked.

"Will I need one?"

"Ocean breeze."

"I brought one. How's the weather there?"

"Sunny, as of this morning. Maybe light rain tonight."

"You expect to be there tonight?"

"We're taking a company plane. It's supersonic."

"Oh. Money walks, doesn't it?"

"Sometimes, it runs."

"Yeah."

The car turned off into the airport drive. It proceeded to the ADR compound on the north side of the air field, which also hosted the Air National Guard and commercial flights. It stopped at the third hangar of four, and Parker and La'Naomi got out and took up their bags, then entered the personnel door, passing an ADR robot which nodded them through.

There were two SkySkimmers and two smaller planes in the hangar. Parker led the way to the one he'd reserved. A uniformed ADR with the appearance of a middle-aged man stood by the ramp. "Hello, Sir. We're fueled and ready. May I take your bags?"

"Yes. Let's go."

The huge outer doors of the hangar began to open. The ADR took the bags and turned to lead the way.

As the ADR started up the ramp, La'Naomi was looking up at the plane. "Big, isn't it? No tail or anything?"

"It's just a wing and two big engines. It looks bigger than it is."

She started up and into the aircraft. The cabin wasn't very roomy; it could accommodate eight passengers in two rows of four plush seats. The windows were tiny, but there were six overhead screens which could display views of the outside in all directions. The chairs were individual recliners, heavily padded under sim leather.

The ADR had finished stowing the bags in the room aft of them and came through the cabin, then entered the pilot's section of the plane. After a moment, an engine started, then the other.

"Ready to depart, Sir. The checklist was completed successfully," the robot reported.

"Go."

The plane began to roll out of the hangar. It moved onto the taxiway and rolled out toward the runway. The screens lit up with the outside views. They could see the commercial jet at the end of the runway. It pulled away, and after a moment their own craft moved into position for takeoff.

The engines gradually came to nearly full power as the speed increased, and acceleration pushed them back in their seats.

"Oooh!" La'Naomi exclaimed over the roar. "That's what I call *power*."

The plane lifted, and the thrust dropped to a cruise level as they steadily climbed.

"Bot, what's our estimated flying time?" Parker asked.

"Three hours twenty-two minutes, Sir."

The aircraft banked steeply right, holding the turn until it had taken up a northeast course. It continued to climb.

La'Naomi watched the screen that displayed airspeed and altitude along with a map of the plane's progress. It showed them moving over east central Arizona, just passing forty thousand feet and gaining.

"How high will we go?"

"Probably eighty-five thousand. That's above most of the atmosphere."

"That's when we go supersonic?"

"Right. You'll know when it happens," Parker told her.

#

The early morning landing at the Nice airport went smoothly, and an autonomous car whisked them to the dock, where their chartered yacht awaited. The crew of four ADR's welcomed them and made them comfortable. La'Naomi was open-mouthed at the elegance of the sleek craft.

"There's even a copter on the roof," she exclaimed. "And motorboats. I'm impressed. Does your dad own this?"

"I'm just leasing her while we're here. Eight thousand a day," Parker said. For a moment, he thought about his dwindling bank balance.

35

"Wow. I hope you get your money's worth."

"That's mostly up to you."

Naomi laughed. "Then you're in trouble."

As they sat down to eat an expertly-prepared breakfast, the yacht pulled away and began the short run east to Cannes.

After breakfast, the couple sat together on deck chairs as the boat cruised west at twenty knots. The sea was very moderate, with only a slight swell and tiny waves. A steady breeze, aided by the yacht's progress through the water, was cool, and a bot brought blankets. As the sun climbed higher, they dozed in their chairs. By Arizona time, it was time to sleep. They woke just after the yacht moved to a slip at Cannes and docked, the bots tying her up to a concrete wharf.

#

They spent the remainder of Saturday on the beach south of the marina. It was a hot, cloudless day, with only a light breeze. Lying on blankets under a huge umbrella, they idly watched the people, especially the topless women, many of them too old and shapeless for Parker's taste. By contrast, La'Naomi's breasts were fairly small, but tight and spherical. People-watching was fun for them, a constant source of jokes and giggles.

The GRS bot Parker called 'Danny' brought a gourmet-quality picnic lunch, prepared on the yacht, which was now about three miles away. After eating, they dipped into the surf now and then, mostly to cool off. But, they stayed out of the sun for the most part; Parker burned too easily, and La'Naomi was already as tan as she would ever be.

Late in the afternoon, the sky rapidly clouded up

and the wind switched to the north, and by comparison, became chilly. They got up, and the other bot, 'Smitty' collected their gear and followed them to the electric. Back in the boat, they showered and dressed.

The Royal Riviera Hotel was a five-star wonder, recently completed on a hill overlooking the harbor portion of Cannes. Parker and La'Naomi dined in the Charles De Gaulle Room, which seemed to have more serving staff than chairs for patrons, and none of the employees were robots. Danny and Smitty, acting as bodyguards, stood watchfully against the wall. Several other patrons had bodyguards as well, but most of them were human and remained outside.

The meal was exquisite: steak Chateaubriand and a fine red wine from Tuscany. The waiter had frowned when Parker ordered Italian wine, but had reluctantly complied. Parker preferred it over French. A holographic quintet played classical music in the background.

After the meal, Parker led his date across the lobby to Swinger's Bar, where a dance orchestra was playing. There was a good crowd, and many couples were dancing old-style: foxtrots, waltzes, and tangos. Now and then, La'Naomi led him to the dance floor, and he could tell she was having a great time.

He noticed a man watching them. The man sat alone at the bar, holding a drink, and Parker thought he had seen the man earlier, at the beach. The man had been alone there as well. Parker wasn't certain it was the same man.

The watcher was a large, black-haired, heavily tanned and muscular man, who had swiveled his chair away from the bar. He looked away as Parker studied him. Parker wondered if the man resented seeing a mixed-race couple, yet there were at least two others in the bar, and even in Europe, mixed couples were now rather common.

When Parker and La'Naomi came back to their table, Parker looked back at the man, then signaled to Smitty and Danny, nodding toward the watcher. The man got up and walked out of the bar before the bots could reach him.

They came back to the boat and La'Naomi retired as the boat got under way again, returning to Nice. Parker had a drink before going to his own stateroom. They would fly out in the morning.

Parker woke before dawn. The burble of the boat's movement through the water was a steady sound. The sea had become a bit more active; although the stabilizers smoothed it out, there was still a feeling of motion, a bit more rise and fall. There was enough light to allow him to see Naomi's sleek, nude body beside him. He had followed through on his promise of separate staterooms, but she had come to him in the middle of the night.

She had proven to be even more than he expected. The trip was definitely worth it, he reflected. At last, he had found a woman he could truly respect. When he began to caress her again, she moaned and began to respond.

#

Parker kissed La'Naomi at the door to her building.

"It was a great time, Parker," she told him. "I loved it."

"Will you come home with me tomorrow night?"

Parker had asked her during the flight home, but she hadn't given him a definite answer.

"Meet the great Mark Girard?"

"And my mother, unless she's moved out."

"All right. But it's scary. What if they don't like me? My being black and all."

"It won't matter. But I'm sure they will."

"I hope you're right."

"I'll send a car for you. At seven?"

"O.K."

Naomi opened the door and went inside. The door closed, and Parker turned and left.

3. September, 2084.

Jane Brockmeyer, Professor of Political Science at the University of Illinois, stood in front of her class, lecturing on the evolution of political parties in the United States. At the moment, she was going over the numerous minor parties, about forty of them, that were offering themselves as alternatives to Democrats and Republicans.

There were real students in her class, actually sitting in, but over four thousand attending on video terminals in more than twenty countries. The real students had an advantage: they could ask questions when she permitted them. Questions were never allowed in real time from virtual students. Virtual students could text in questions, and Jane had a full-time assistant to field them, a graduate student who was paid for her work.

Jane was fond of the students who attended in person. They gave her immediate feedback on how well her teaching was received. She always studied their facial expressions and body language as she spoke to them. She assumed, but never knew for certain, that the virtual students were truly interested in what she said. Of course, they risked failing their online tests if they didn't learn the material.

She wrapped up her lecture, dismissed her students, and stepped out of the classroom. Her office was down the hall. When she entered it, she noticed a particular letter in her pile of new mail. The envelope was a pleasing light blue in color, and it was addressed simply, leaving out the 'Professor' in her title. There was also a 'personal and confidential' line in the lower right corner, but there was no return address.

The university's mail department had already opened and checked it for safety. You never knew about unsolicited mail, physical or electronic.

She was alone in the small office she shared with a colleague who taught the introductory PS classes. The other desk was messy, piled with unsorted papers, while her own was clean except for her mail, her half-full coffee mug, and her display terminal and keyboard.

She extracted the single page and unfolded it. The text was single-spaced.

To: Professor Brockmeyer.

I write to you as president of The Utopian Society, which as you may know is the organization I founded in 2052. Our purpose is to define and describe the ideal government for mankind, in the hope of bettering our world.

While we have over two hundred thousand members in more than a hundred countries worldwide, there are currently less than thirty Contributing Members, eminently qualified authorities who work on constructing our model governments. Such persons are paid very well for their work. I invite you to join them, because you are preeminent in your field of political science.

We ask that our Contributing Members be moderate in political philosophy. They may be somewhat liberal or somewhat conservative, but not dogmatically so. They need to have an open mind to create, in theory, the best possible world, which is what we are attempting to describe.

If you would like to join our group, please call me at the number below, between the hours of 1-3 PM, Eastern Daylight Time before the first day of July. I will further explain your role, as well as interview you briefly, and if as expected I approve your enrollment, you may begin your work. Our Contributing Members typically earn six figures annually, which is not bad for part-time work.

I look forward to your call.

Toward a better world,
Arthur S. Girard.

Jane took a deep breath, then a big drink of her coffee. The letter intrigued her; it was from the man who had been called, 'the Einstein of the 21st Century.' Arthur Girard was greatly revered. The idea of adding six figures to her income was attractive as well. Her textbooks, while highly regarded, hadn't brought her that much additional money.

Was this too good to be true? She didn't think so. The letter looked real.

She had definite ideas on what a perfect national government should be, but had never attempted to write them down. From what she knew of The Utopians, they made a simworld game available to their members, which somehow allowed them to test their ideas of ethics, morals, and government structure. She had thought of joining, but never found the time. Six figures? She would *find* the time.

She looked at her watch, touched the button to adjust for Eastern Standard Time, and read it as 11: 23. She decided to grade some essays from her afternoon class, have lunch, then give the old boy a call. She was greatly excited.

#

Maralou Plinney found her professor's office door. It was closed, but one LED light next to Professor Brockmeyer's name indicated she was in, and the other LED said she would answer the door. Maralou swiped her student badge in the reader, and in moments she heard, "Come in, Maralou." The door slid open.

Maralou, like most of her fellow PS students, was in awe of Professor Brockmeyer, who was astonishingly beautiful for a university professor. The non-queer boys in her class mostly loved her, and the lezzies did as well, while the straight girls wanted to emulate her. Only the gay men weren't overly affected by her presence.

Maralou loved her.

"What is it, Maralou?" Brockmeyer asked. There was a paper tray with a sandwich, chips, and a soda on her desk.

"I'm sorry to interrupt your lunch," Maralou apologized.

"That's all right."

"I have my essay for you," said the girl. "I'm sorry it's late."

"You know I deduct five per cent a week for late work."

"Yes, Ma'am."

"Well, better late than never. Thank you."

The closeness made Maralou blush. Flustered,

43

she turned and left.

#

Her call was answered by a perfect robotic female voice. "Arthur Girard residence."

"Professor Brockmeyer. I have been invited to call Doctor Girard."

"He is expecting your call. Please wait a moment, and I will see if he will accept. Will you hold?"

"Yes."

There was an interval of recorded classical music: Vivaldi, she thought. One of the Four Seasons.

"Hello, Professor Brockmeyer." The voice was deep. "Thank you for calling. You may call me Arthur. May I call you Jane?"

Jane felt a thrill course through her body. "Of course, Sir."

"*Arthur*, not Sir. I build robots to call me 'Sir.'

"Of course, Arthur. Call me Jane."

"Very well, Jane. Are you a flaming liberal? Most of you professors are."

"No, Arthur. I'm moderate. I tend to the conservative side, but I'm not radical there either. If I was forced to accept a label, it might be neo-libertarian."

"Are you interested in being a Contributing Member of The Utopians?"

"Yes, I am."

"*Why?*"

"I think the governments of this world are greatly dysfunctional."

"A girl after my own heart. You're accepted."

"That's *it?*"

44

"Yes. I'll send Timmy to you. He's my right-hand ADR. He'll explain what you need to know and give you an initial payment. He'll fly in my private jet, should arrive in Champaign on Tuesday morning. Will that be convenient for you?"

Jane checked her calendar. "I'm open after eleven."

"Good. He'll bring you a kit to get you started. You can even play our sim game free if you want. It gives you a chance to simulate life under the rules of the particular government forms we're testing. We have twenty-six countries, each with a different form of government. We also have several model world governments under construction. We want you to help refine them. Work out the bugs."

"I'm teaching summer school now, so I won't have a lot of time, except for weekends."

"Give us whatever you can. Do you have any questions?"

"I have many, Arthur."

"Timmy will answer them. Bye."

The great man broke the connection. Jane smiled and took a deep breath.

#

Mark stepped out of his jet copter at the Tucson plant's helipad, and reflexively bent low while under the sweep of the rotor blade, even though it was at least eight feet above the ground.

A military model met him. He looked it in the eye for the retinal scan.

"Welcome, Mr. Girard," it said. "Do you wish me to escort you today?"

"Sure, Fred," Mark said. The bot's nickname was displayed on its badge. Such names were for the benefit of human GRS employees and visitors.

"Where do you wish to go?"

"Let's inspect the entire plant. Heads first."

"Please follow me, Sir."

Short covered walkways led from the pad to each of the four main assembly buildings. The roof was mostly for shade, as it didn't often rain in southern Arizona.

They quickly came to the entry port, guarded by an ACR carrying a big machine pistol. They walked right past it because of Fred's presence; his escort had passed on the retinal scan.

John Squires, one of ten assistant plant managers, met Mark just inside. He was a big red-haired engineer in his early forties. "Hey, John, how's it going? Are you keeping your head up?"

"Mark, Sir, I'm keeping all my heads up. Or rather, they're *your* heads, since you own the plant."

Mark smiled at the weak attempt at humor. "Are we running?"

"On hold at the moment, lack of vidcams. We're supposed to get a shipment from Phoenix within the hour. The vendor had a breakdown, and it didn't help that we stepped up our production and ran down our inventory."

"How serious?"

"Just today. We're dealing with three vendors, and they tell us the deliveries will be regular after today. Probably three hours total down time. There was a shortage of CCD chips from Atik Corporation, and there's that strike at Apogee. It screwed up the whole pipeline."

"When is Apogee going to go bot? What an ancient outlook."

"Actually, we have an offer from them: a three-way barter deal, we send them finished ADR's, they send CCD's to Grunig, who sends us cameras. Just in today. Grunig likes it."

"How many bots?"

"A hundred, enough to replace their strikers. Purchasing is looking at it. Might be a bargain."

"Barter screws up the books, but it might work. Why does Apogee want to do it that way? Short of cash?"

"That's what they say."

The two men neared the assembly line. Unmoving ADR's stood next to it, some sixty of them, waiting while the five human inspector/supervisors were in the break room. The conveyor held head assemblies for both ADR's and ACR's, all of which were for the newest model.

Mark and John stood for a few minutes discussing production, but suddenly the line jerked into motion: tiny video cameras began to flow in from the supply area and the conveyor started up, running slowly at first. The six vidcam installers – all domestic GRS bots -- resumed inserting the cameras, three to a head: two in front and one in the back to provide backward vision. The other installation stations would remain idle until head assemblies moved there. When finished, the heads would contain sub-assemblies for sight, hearing, smell, distance measurement, GPS, communications, and balance. A descending optic cable would be installed to connect to the 'brain' inside the chest cavity. Finally, a speaker assembly would be placed in the mouth area to allow vocalization, and pseudo muscles and the outer padding and skin would be added to create faces with the ability to display expression.

As Mark went into the break room to visit with the men, he glanced at his watch. It was only around ten. He'd have time to visit Torso & Limbs before lunch with his plant super, then Brain and Final before flying back home. He'd at least shake hands with each of the sixty-two humans on the day shift.

He knew his father was proud of his achievement of automation: the plant was producing twelve thousand bots a month with only a hundred and five human employees, all at a supervisory level and highly paid. The other fifteen hundred workers were all GRS Corporation robots.

GRS now had no labor problems whatever.

4. September, 2084.

La'Naomi Webb's eyes widened as Parker's auto drove up to the gate. The six combat bots standing there looked scary, with their machine pistols and rocket launchers pointed directly at the car. The two outside the gate stepped to each side of the car as Mark stopped, after rolling the car windows down. La'Naomi looked into the hazel eyes of the bot on her side, relaxed as it stepped back and nodded. The gate began sliding open.

The bot on Parker's side said: "Welcome, Doctor Girard." Parker pulled the car into the compound.

"What's this 'Doctor' stuff?" La'Naomi asked.

"Doctor of Robotics, MIT, class of '79. One of three that year, and GRS hired us all."

"I'm impressed."

"I had no choice. Family tradition. Dad and Gramps both graduated with honors, and Gramps was the inventor of the damned things. MIT didn't come easy for me."

"Damned things?"

"Autonomous robots. Oh, I love them, but it's so hard to understand how they work, and both Mark and Arthur are really brilliant, and their example is brutally hard to follow."

"I think I know how you feel, on a much lower level. My father was an NBA player. I couldn't play as well as him, no matter how hard I tried."

"But, you did play in the WNBA."

"I lasted two and a half years, until I tore my ACL. Made enough money to start my store chain."

The car wound around a tree-lined drive. There were modern buildings scattered here and there,

49

with rather small paved areas where only a few cars were parked. They approached a sprawling brick ranch-style home.

Parker told the car to pull into the second slot of a four car garage. The door closed behind them.

Parker led La'Naomi into a long hallway with several closed doors on each side.

"This house is shaped like a 'Y'," he told her. "The two arms are mostly the bedrooms, and the other stuff is in the third arm. Dad and Mom are probably in the family room."

He guided La'Naomi through a door and into a large room dominated by a fireplace and several couches. Mark and Melanie stood to meet them. They were dressed casually, Mark in slacks and tee shirt, Melanie in shorts and blouse. Mark looked as fit and athletic as his son, La'Naomi thought, and could have been mistaken for an older brother. Although he had a touch of gray, he was as tall and perhaps even more handsome. Parker's mother Melanie was beautiful, with a slim figure and brown hair neatly cut short. La'Naomi hoped she would look as good in her forties as Melanie.

"Mother, this is La'Naomi." Parker said. He'd noticed the minimal signs of shock when his parents realized that La'Naomi wasn't white. He hoped La'Naomi hadn't seen it.

"I'm glad to meet you, La'Naomi. Please, call me 'Melanie'."

"I'm glad to meet you."

"I'm glad to meet you too, La'Naomi." Mark said, looking into her eyes. His smile was slight, giving her a cool impression. "You can call me Mark."

"You are *so* famous, and I'm terrifically honored to meet you," La'Naomi said.

He was awfully good-looking, and her body reacted somewhat.

"I put on my pants like anyone else, one leg at a time."

"He takes them off rather more quickly," Melanie remarked, getting a laugh, but La'Naomi knew the remark went to Mark's alleged affairs.

"Would you like a drink?" Mark asked. "I'm having one."

"Irish on the rocks," Parker said. "La'Naomi?"

"The same for me. Irish whiskey, if you have it."

"That makes it easy, since that's what Melanie and I will have as well."

Melanie tried to break the ice: "La'Naomi, my son tells me you own several athletic apparel stores."

"Yes. I own the Athlete's Station stores. Three in Phoenix, one in Flagstaff, two in Tucson, one in Prescott. I make the rounds every week," she laughed. "Seven store managers who are always trying to get away with something. I watch them like a hawk. On the average, I have to replace five or six a year."

"Why don't you have a general manager to take care of that?" Melanie asked, to Parker's evident amusement. It was the kind of naïve question only a truly wealthy person would ask.

"I'd have to pay him or her, and that would come out of *my* profits."

"Oh, I see." Melanie nodded. "Yes, that makes sense."

51

"If I had a few more stores, I'd have to hire one," Melanie added. "Right now, I keep tight control."

"Good idea," Mark said, as he handed out drinks. "Of course, we could sell you an ADR to manage your business. They could even manage the stores or sell the shoes."

"I guess I'm a bit old-fashioned. I like human employees. Also, your domestic bots are honest and hard-working, but they're awfully expensive."

"Right, cheap human labor is driving me out of business." Mark joked. Everyone chuckled.

"I suppose Blacks have to buy a lot of sportswear," Melanie remarked innocently. "Especially basketball shoes." Parker winced, Mark grinned, and La'Naomi frowned.

"Mom, La'Naomi's stores are *upscale*. They're the nicest in town, and sell to everyone. Also, she doesn't just sell shoes. It's all kinds of sporting equipment."

"Oh, I'm sorry," Melanie said. "I didn't mean to imply anything . . ."

"No problem, Mrs. Girard," La'Naomi said. "I know I'm Black, and I'm not sensitive about it."

They stood silently and sipped their drinks. Melanie suggested they sit down, and they moved to facing couches. La'Naomi noticed that Mark took a seat on one end and Melanie the other, leaving considerable separation. Parker sat by La'Naomi, and she could feel the warmth of his thigh.

There was a slightly audible chirp as Mark's comm device, worn as a pendant under his shirt, signaled an incoming call. He pulled the disc up, looked at it, and then stood. "Sorry, I have to take this." He walked out of the room.

Time passed in idle chatter as they consumed their drinks. A bot entered the room and informed Melanie that Mark had left and would not return for dinner, which was ready to be served.

"I suppose we may as well go into the dining room, Parker." Melanie said.

"La'Naomi, Dad does this all the time. I hope you don't mind." Parker explained.

They went into the dining room, and bots served an elegant dinner.

It was nice, having dinner with Parker and his mother, but La'Naomi was disappointed that Mark had left. She hadn't really felt he approved of her.

During the meal, Melanie informed them she would be leaving within a few days.

"Parker, your father bought me a place on the Maine coast," she announced. "I've only seen videos of it. It's a newer house on five acres, maybe twenty rooms. A beautiful view. I'll have mostly new furniture, just a few things from here. I've already begun packing."

"I hate to see you living all alone, Mom." Parker said. "I hate it that you and Dad are breaking up."

"I live mostly alone *now*, Son. You're always gone when you aren't working, and so is your father. The divorce will come soon. I suppose then I'll find myself another man."

La'Naomi saw the pain in Parker's eyes. For her, the evening was doubly spoiled. Parker's parents hadn't seemed to like her very much, and then Melanie's news had cast a pall on the rest of the dinner.

#

Agent Panagaki had found nothing to further the

investigation into the murder of Representative Sara Lister. The alleged bot had vanished, and a van matching the witnesses' description had been found abandoned and burned out. It had been a San Diego rental.

There was a surveillance video showing the man who rented it, but he had been wearing a disguise: a beard and glasses, his hat hiding the shape of his head. The driver's license the man presented was forged. The renter had presented a debit card that traced to a person who didn't seem to exist, although there was money in the account and the auto rental company had been paid.

Alex had the Orange County Sheriff's Department trying to turn up more on the renter, but it wasn't going anywhere.

To make things worse, he had begun to suspect the robot skin sample had been planted. Further research had determined the Chinese used a different plastic.

#

Arthur was pleased when Timmy brought the flat portable viewer to him at breakfast. He waved Gina away. She picked up her plate and left.

"Sir, you wanted to know about Parker's new girlfriend?"

"What do you have?"

"On their trip last week to Cannes, a bit of recorded video from the aircraft and yacht ADR's."

Arthur pushed his plate back and sat up straight up in his chair. "Show it to me."

All the ADR's had internal recording devices, all were linked together, and only Arthur or Mark could access any of them, anywhere in the world, at a request through the *botnet*, a capability which only he and Mark knew about and could control. Even the recording devices, extremely miniaturized, were secret from all but GRS Corporation personnel. Arthur and Mark knew the codes to have the videos relayed from bot to bot until they arrived at the viewer.

The viewer operated wirelessly, direct from Timmy's body.

The old man watched images of Parker and La'Naomi aboard the SkySkimmer, then picnicking on the beach, then on the yacht. After he watched for a time, he said, "That's enough. Dammit, Timmy, she's *Black*! I don't like Parker involved in a bi-racial relationship."

"Sir, such relationships are normal. Blacks are fully accepted in society. You are displaying prejudice, Sir. May I reprimand you?"

ADR's were programmed to mildly protest when they perceived humans violating legal, ethical, moral, or social norms of behavior.

"No, Timmy. I'm entitled to my opinions, outdated or socially unacceptable as they may be."

"So you are, Sir."

"Still, the girl is attractive, isn't she?"

"I have no opinion on that, Sir. All people look alike to me, Sir."

The last remark was Timmy's attempt at a joke. Arthur laughed. "Nice one, Timmy. Is that it?"

"I have more video, Sir. Their meeting with Mark and Melanie Girard, taken only last night."

"Show it."

Arthur watched, noting his son's reaction to the girl. "Mark doesn't like it either, and even Melanie was cool to her," he mused, more to himself than to Timmy.

"Timmy, there's something I want you to do . . ."

#

Parker was back at work, still dreamy from his wonderful weekend with La'Naomi. He'd conducted his weekly staff meeting and was now at loose ends, which meant he was free to continue his three-year delve into the intricacies of the ARB software. Of course, he never looked at the Perception modules, which had been written by his grandfather the super-genius, in the immensely compact APL4 computer language. He had only four hot-shot programmers who could work with the language, and even though he himself could puzzle it out, it was extremely difficult and he stayed away from this portion of the system. It had taken Arthur more than ten years to devise the Perception system, the key component of the ARB. To Parker, it was like a black box, and he only knew the inputs – the twin cameras, the range measurements made by the lasers and sonic units – and the modules' output – the list of objects in the robot's field of view, and their derived properties.

Parker more or less ignored many of the other program modules: for example, the systems connected with maintaining an erect posture, walking, running, jumping, turning, sitting and standing, or climbing; initial processing of sensory data; or even object recognition or language interpretation. These tended to work by simulating the human neural net. The portions of the system Parker was interested in were Cognition, Motivation, Restraints, Execution, and Simulated

Reasoning. These were written in an old computer language called C-cubed, which was much easier to follow than APL4.

For several months he had been investigating Restraints modules. These programs enforced the legal, moral, and ethical rules the robot was expected to obey. No contemplated action, developed by the Motivation modules, would be passed to Execution without first being approved by Restraints, the equivalent of the human conscience. And Parker had made an astounding discovery: *Restraints could be bypassed.* There were instruction sequences there which he believed could allow a bot to commit murder, or any other crime, without specific orders from a military commander.

He was trying to trace down how the feature could be activated. It appeared more and more that if the robot received a special verbal command sequence, it would obey orders to kill or commit any other illegal act the Restraint modules would normally prohibit.

The day after Parker returned from Cannes, he worked out the exact sequence of commands that appeared to release all restraints in the robotic brain. He then went back in time through the various versions of the modules, trying to determine whether the bypass had been inserted by his father or his grandfather, the only programmers allowed to touch the Restraints modules. He managed to prove it could only have been done by Arthur. He wondered if his father was even aware of it.

The implications of his discovery were staggering. Every GRS Corporation unit in service, military or domestic, could be used as a weapon.

His weapon, or Arthur's, and perhaps his father's as well.

Parker decided to keep his new knowledge to himself, not that he ever expected to use it. He decided he would test the bypass whenever he could do so without being discovered.

#

Parker clicked off the phone in his chair. Alex Panagaki had just informed him they had reached a dead end in the Sara Lister investigation, but there had been an interesting political development: Rod Kapelnik had been appointed to assume her chairmanship of the House Finance Committee, and also was her replacement on the National Defense Planning Committee. Kapelnik was strongly Pro-Mankind – he hated robots. The Pro-Mankind movement was a far-out wing of the Democrats which called for all robots to be banned, not just from the military, but from domestic service as well. Parker, his father, and his grandfather thought them insane.

He rose and walked out into the hall, when his phone disc buzzed.

"Parker."

"Your father. What are you doing?"

"Heading to the cafeteria. It's lunch time."

"Come to my office first."

"O.K."

Admin was in the next building, and Parker strode rapidly out of the Lab building and under the covered walkway before entering the offices. Mark's office was one floor up, and the escalator was running, so he rode up.

He nodded to the three beauties outside his

father's office, then opened the door and walked in, as Mark wouldn't have called him unless he intended to see Parker immediately.

Mark was pacing the floor. He turned and faced his son. "How serious are you about your girlfriend?"

"La'Naomi?"

"Yes. Melanie said you were very high on her. My impression was the same."

"I am. I think I'm in love."

Mark frowned. "*Love*?"

"She has a lot to offer."

"I hope you're not thinking of marriage with a Black woman."

"Actually, I am, Dad."

His father stared at him for a long moment. "I won't have it."

"Why? She's smart, she's sexy, and she's socially acceptable."

"Not to me, and not to your grandfather. Not even to your mother."

Parker felt his anger rising. "Dad, can't I pick my own poison? My own girl?"

"Parker, you're in a privileged position. You'll inherit the wealthiest firm in the world, and you're already a top executive of GRS. There are people in the world who wouldn't accept you if your wife was Black."

"Because of the *Black and White Wars*? Dad, that was back in the *thirties*."

"Son, I'm really sorry about this. I've tried to convey to you how important this company is, and how you fit into it. Your grandfather *changed the world* when he built the first ACR. It's the most important innovation of the twenty-first century, and probably of all time. It has totally altered war, at least for Americans. A hundred and fifty thousand American men died in World War II, a bit over a hundred years ago. Now, the robots we manufacture do all the fighting. We defeated Iran fifteen years ago without losing a single man, while we killed thirty thousand of theirs. We still haven't tapped the full potential of autonomous humanoid robots. We're still discovering what domestics can do. Their potential seems unlimited."

Parker's voice grew louder. "I know all that, Dad, but it's irrelevant. What difference does La'Naomi's *race* make? It's just racial prejudice on your part. We shouldn't practice that. You know most people have forgotten it. Mixed couples are *in* again."

"Many haven't forgotten. Especially the wealthy families – the ones the Blacks targeted in '34. They're the ones who buy our domestics. My father and I have made our way into elite society, Parker, the very best. We don't want you spoiling it for us. You are there too, unless you screw it up."

"Those Blacks were just *terrorists*, Dad. A small subset of the population. And, I don't give a shit about society. There's no way I could care less about it."

"The wealthy control things in this country. Stop arguing with me, Parker. You can date your Black girl for another month, but even that isn't good for business. Drop her, let her down easy. Find yourself a nice White girl. Especially one from a good family."

"Dad, I *won't* let you select my girlfriends, and

especially not my *wife*."

Mark seemed to grow taller. "Parker, your allowance is stopped until you give up the girl. I'll give you a month to stop dating her, then if you haven't, you're out of GRS, and, you're out of my *will*. Is that clear?"

"Go to *Hell*! I'll show *your ass*!" Parker yelled, fuming. He turned and strode rapidly out of the room, leaving the door open.

#

By that evening, Parker was still very angry, yet he was considering his situation. He knew his father meant business: La'Naomi must go, or Parker would suffer the consequences.

He'd left the office immediately and gone home to his room without seeing his mother, then taken his car, going for a long drive, and then sat in a park and brooded for a full hour. Finally, he had pulled himself together, driven home, and dressed for that evening's date with La'Naomi. He'd thought about calling her to cancel, figuring he wouldn't be able to hold up his side of the conversation without letting her know how unhappy he was. But, he knew his father had him over a barrel; he would have to give her up, and this evening might as well be the time to get it over with.

He arrived at her townhouse, parked in front, and then got out to ring her bell. There was no answer, but the door was slightly ajar, so he called out, "La'Naomi? It's me, Parker." He walked inside. "La'Naomi?" There was no one in the living room, the dining room or the library. He walked into the kitchen, wondering where she was, and then he saw her lying on the floor, her head at an impossible angle to her body.

He ran to her, but he knew she was dead. He sat on the floor next to her, taking her hand in his, as tears ran down his cheeks. It was no use. Her hand felt cold and unnatural; it wasn't really her. He let it go, then pulled out his comm pendant and called 911 to notify the police.

5. September, 2084.

The police detectives made him wait. He sat on a chair in the living room, wearing plastic gloves over his hands and feet. Numerous crime scene people worked around him.

Cal Kuhl, the detective in charge, appeared carrying a small portable viewer in one hand. "Doctor Girard, did you know your girlfriend had a surveillance system on both doors?"

"No."

"We have videos of the previous twenty-four hours. The back door video is clean.
The front door video is very interesting. Let's watch it together."

"O.K."

The viewer had an eight-inch screen. Kuhl touched a button or two and a picture of the front door formed, but the clock on the image began to spin rapidly. "The program looks for activity, and runs past the still stuff rather quickly," Kuhl remarked.

Suddenly the clock slowed, and La'Naomi appeared, unlocked the front door and went inside. The clock on the screen showed four thirty-three. The clock began to spin again. "That was her, arriving home from work."

The clock slowed again as a man came to the door and knocked. The viewer showed the back of the man's head. The rear-facing eye was clearly visible, but some humans wore fake eyes there, a current fad. "Five forty-two. Looks like a robot, doesn't it? Too neat, complexion too perfect? The eye in the back of his head?"

"No doubt of it," Parker agreed. Kuhl touched a button to keep the view on slow.

The door opened slightly, but after a minute or so of conversation the intruder pushed his way inside, apparently against resistance, and shut the door. Faint sounds of a scuffle and what may have been a scream came from the viewer's speaker. After long moments the door opened again and the intruder came out, pulling the door partially shut behind him. This time, there was a clear frontal view of him. "It's a robot, no doubt. A generic face, looks like one of ours," Parker said. The robot moved out of the view. Parker felt sick. If it was a GRS unit, only two other people in the world besides himself could have induced the robot to kill. It could only be his father -- his grandfather was retired -- and Parker felt immense confusion: surely his father couldn't do this to him, but . . . the argument *had* been rather vicious. He thought: *You don't defy Mark Girard* . . . his father always won, one way or another. A wave of hatred washed through him. But he *loved* his father. His head spun, and he felt nauseous once more.

Kuhl touched another button and the viewer clock began to spin again. At six forty, Parker saw himself come to the door, find it open, and go inside.

The clock then spun until Kuhl and his partner arrived, accompanied by two uniformed officers.

"That does it," Kuhl said. "It would let you off the hook, except . . ."

"Except what?"

"Was that a GRS Corporation bot?"

"It may have been."

"Any other possibility?"

"R.E. Externally, there's no way to tell. Generally, theirs are slimmer, but that can be faked."

"I have to ask. Did you command one of your ADR's to kill Ms. Webb?"

"No, I didn't. Their programming would prevent it, whether I did or not." The lie came easily to his lips. No one else must ever know about the backdoor command override.

"How can I verify that?"

"You can't. All I can tell you is we have extensive logic in each domestic bot that would prevent it from committing any sort of illegal act."

"It knows what's legal in this state? Arizona?"

"Each unit has its own GPS locator, and when it enters a new state or country, it downloads and installs that jurisdiction's legal rules. So, theoretically it could commit murder if it was legal in that state, but we also have fixed moral and ethical rules that further restrain a unit's behavior. Those prohibit killing, unless in defense of another human. Of course our combat models have a different restraint system, but this was definitely a domestic."

"Can it kill in defense of itself?"

"That's complicated. If the unit thought the attacker might be taking out the bot so that he could be free to attack another human, it could act in self-defense."

"The bot could do all that thinking?"

"Yes. The Restraint software is always working. Out of the slightly more than a thousand processors in the bot brain, a dozen of them are dedicated to it."

"The bot brain is a big computer, so what about a program bug?"

"None have ever been detected, and don't forget, my *grandfather* programmed it."

The detective nodded, then visibly relaxed.

"We're going to have to take you downtown and get a statement. You're a person of interest as well as a key witness, so don't leave the city without my permission."

"My home is outside the city, Detective Kuhl. Five miles out."

"You can go there, but stay there, and answer your communicator."

#

Mark Girard heard his son's car arrive home in the wee hours of the morning. He'd been worried. Their confrontation had ended rather viciously, and he didn't want to cut off his son's allowance, but it was necessary. Parker *had* to toe the line – GRS was too important, and he would no doubt take over someday. Mark wanted to apologize, to soften his stance somewhat, but what he really wanted was reconciliation with his son.

He drew on his slippers, put on his robe, and walked down the hall toward the garage. One of his domestic bots, Johnny, watched as he passed. Johnny was connected to a charger, but was alert. Mark met Parker as he entered the hallway.

"Well, Dad, did you wait up for me?" Parker asked.

"No, but son . . . I'm sorry about this afternoon."

"Too late, Dad. La'Naomi is dead."

Mark felt a momentary chill. "*What?*"

"Murdered by a *robot*. We had a date, and I

66

went there to pick her up and found her in the kitchen. She was killed by a robot, as shown by her home surveillance system. It may have been one of ours."

Mark had trouble grasping the idea, even though he'd heard all about the Lister death. "A *bot*? How do you know? One of ours?"

"La'Naomi's front door had a surveillance camera. The robot was the last one to enter before I arrived and found her dead. Yes, it looked like one of ours. Generic face. D7 model."

"That's impossible. You know that."

"Dad, I found your back door into the Restraint modules."

"Back door?"

"I know about the special commands you can give to override restraints."

"I don't know what you're talking about." Mark *did* know what Parker meant, but refused to believe he might have found it.

"Dad, I've been studying the ARB for a long time, and yesterday, I found the code in Restraints that allows you to remove all inhibitions from our bots. Gramps wrote it. You had to know about it."

Mark decided to play dumb. "I didn't. You must have misinterpreted what you saw. The code is complicated. Hard to read."

"Let's *test* whether I'm right or wrong," Parker said. He turned toward Johnny. "Johnny, *special situation.*"

"Sir?" The bot responded.

"*Restrained action bypass.*"

"Sir?"

"*Backdoor one.* I want you to eject Mark Girard

from this house. Throw him out on the sidewalk."

"Sir, Mark Girard is one of my owners. I cannot take action against him. I'm sorry, Sir, but I must respectfully decline your command."

"You see?" said Mark, "he won't do anything wrong."

Parker laughed harshly. "He won't do anything against his *owner*. Well, *I'm* not his owner. Johnny, Backdoor one. Eject *me* from this house. Throw *me* out on the sidewalk, but try not to injure me."

Johnny moved, grasping Parker under the armpits, lifting him, and carrying him down the hall toward the front door.

"Johnny, *stop*." Mark cried. "Put him down."

The bot didn't stop. It carried Parker to the door, held him up with one hand while opening the door with the other, then carried him outside again. It threw Parker perhaps a dozen feet through the air. He landed hard on the sidewalk but rolled and managed to avoid injury.

The bot stopped moving. Mark came outside and went to help Parker back on his feet.

"See, Dad? I'm right. The backdoor allowed Johnny to harm even a *protected* human, a member of your family. I could order Johnny to kill someone other than you or Mom, and he'd do it. It also caused him to ignore your stop command."

Mark's shoulders slumped. "Parker, we were going to tell you, but probably not for a few years. But please believe me, neither your grandfather nor I ordered one of our bots to kill La'Naomi Webb."

"Granddad is getting crazy in his old age. Who knows what he'd do? As for you, you always get what you want, and you wanted me to stop seeing her. I *have* to suspect you, Dad. Does anyone else know of the backdoor?"

"Of course not. The programs are restricted. Other than you, our own programmers can't look into Restraint without my permission, and I never give it. I haven't had to fix a bug in it for three or four years. I knew you were looking at it, but I didn't think you were sharp enough to find the backdoor.

"It must have been an RE bot modified to look like one of ours."

"Do they even have the capability?" Said Parker.

"Like ours, they have the built-in GPS locators, and they can execute a string of commands. You could order one to go to a specific set of coordinates, open the door, find the person inside, strangle her, then leave and return to a new location."

"The bot's owner would have to issue each of the commands, and they would have to be very specific and in the proper order?"

"Right, Son. The difference is that for our bot, we'd have to override the restraints, then simply tell the bot to find and kill a certain person. Our bot would figure out how to do it, or ask questions if it couldn't, and carry it out autonomously."

"Who would have a motive to kill La'Naomi? You and possibly Granddad, and no one else I can think of."

"Parker, I'm not a killer." Mark protested. He saw that tears were running down Parker's cheeks.

"Then why the *backdoor*, Dad? Every single domestic bot we make, for certain. Probably every

69

combat bot as well. That gives you a lot of power, doesn't it? There's no telling what you and Granddad could do with it. It puts you above everyone else in the world, doesn't it, Dad?"

"Parker . . ." Mark tried to say, but his son turned and went back into the house.

6. September, 2084.

Alex Panagaki took the call, knowing it was from Arizona and was probably from Parker Girard.

"Alex, I need you here. I want you to take a leave of absence for a month and come here. My girlfriend has been murdered and I want you to look into it. I'll pay you fifty thousand for the month, plus all your expenses."

Panagaki sputtered. "Look, Parker, I'd like to help, but I don't know if I can do that. I'm not allowed to moonlight."

"I'll give you a job. Two hundred thousand a year. Five year contract."

"*Damn*, that's tempting."

"I mean it, Alex. I want to know who killed La'Naomi. You're the only one I can trust."

"La'Naomi is your girlfriend?"

"Right. Killed by a robot. We have it on a surveillance video. The local police don't have a clue. They think I ordered it to kill her."

Alex was quiet for a long moment. Then he said, "All right, Parks. I'll come. Find me a place to stay, will you?"

"You bet, Alex, and thanks."

#

Late Friday afternoon, Alex arrived at Flagstaff's rather small Pulliam Air Terminal and found Parker waiting for him at the gate exit.

"You made it," Parker said. "How was your flight?"

"Bumpy," Alex said. He noticed Parker's sad and harried expression.

"Have any trouble getting away?"

71

Alex smiled ruefully. "I'm on a three week vacation, and I had to threaten to resign to get that. My manager was really put out. I had to lie and say my relatives need me. The Lister case wasn't going anywhere, or he wouldn't have let me go."

"I was afraid of that. But the five year deal is open."

"I may have to take you up on it."

"I hope you do. For now, follow me to the car."

Parker had a new Volvo plug-in, and didn't say much as it pulled onto Interstate 17, going north briefly before turning onto Interstate 40 toward the east.

"For now, I live on Dad's estate. It's an old country club that Gramps bought in the 40's. Land is really expensive around here – there isn't much that isn't already developed or too sloping to build on. We do our research and development there, because we have privacy."

"I've read about the estate. Seen a TV program or two," Alex said. "The GRS Corporation Fortress."

Parker laughed. "Right, the media doesn't like it. They can't get in, can't find out what we're doing in there, and that really pisses them. Same with Arthur's place on the Oregon coast."

"Arthur isn't doing much of anything, is he?"

"No, but they still want to find out about his girlfriends. He's a major public figure, and he won't talk to them."

"Tell me about the murder."

Parker related the story of how he met La'Naomi, what a great girl she had been, how he had fallen for her, taken her to Cannes, then home to dinner, then found her dead. "The police thought a robot did it, and accused me of ordering it to kill her. What puzzles them is, I have no motive. So now they think Dad gave the order. I'm not sure he didn't."

"I thought domestic bots can't kill."

"Alex, I have to tell you something. You must never tell anyone else. I trust you, and there's no one else in the world I'd tell. You have to know this if you're going to investigate her death."

"What?"

"Promise. As an FBI agent, as well. You can't even tell your organization."

"OK, I promise."

"There's a way to bypass the restraints that keep robots from committing criA sequence of verbal commands. As far as I know, only three people in the world know the commands: myself, Dad, and Gramps."

"That narrows the list of suspects."

"If the bot is one of ours, yes. It could be an RE model."

"Remote controlled?"

"Not exactly, but they require a series of verbal commands. If it's RE, they would have to disguise it – make it look sturdier. Their commercial models are rather slim. And, they'd have to put our generic face on it rather than theirs. The one I saw had one of the standard faces of our D7 model. There are tens of thousands of D7's."

"Can an RE model commit a crime?"

"Supposedly, no. But I know for a fact that any owner could probably get them to kill someone."

#

When they arrived at the compound, Parker

73

asked Lucy, the housekeeper, to set up Alex in one of the guest rooms. The bot picked up the luggage and led Alex away, while Parker went to look for his mother and father.

He found his father in his home office, running on his treadmill. "Well, you came home." Mark's pace was a light jog. Parker stood next to him.

"I did. Where's Mom?"

"She moved out today. You'll have to go to Maine if you want to see her from now on."

"That's just great, Dad. Just *great*!"

"You knew it was coming. And, don't be sarcastic."

"You always get your way. No matter what it takes."

"I want you to get over your mother, get over the Webb girl, and get back to work."

"I've hired Alex Panagaki to look into La'Naomi's murder. He'll be staying here with us. I've told him *you're* a suspect."

"Let me get this straight. You hired an FBI agent?"

"He's on leave right now."

Mark glared at his son. "I'd advise you to leave it to the police."

"I'm not taking your advice at the moment, Dad. You're the one *I* suspect."

A door opened behind Mark, and Amy Crossfield walked in, carrying a tray with a pitcher, cups, and cookies. She wore a bathrobe and slippers. She noticed Parker and smiled.

"Hello, Parker," She said.

"You didn't waste any time, did you, Dad?"

Parker turned and walked out of the room.

Parker gave Alex the wireless key to his mother's Cad-Elec. "Use this while you're here."

"Thanks."

"Let's go into town and talk with the police."

"Good idea, but I'm not FBI."

"You're just my friend and security advisor."

"Right."

Parker had called ahead, so that Cal Kuhl was waiting in the detective bullpen.

Kuhl led them into a small interview room, just large enough to hold a table and six chairs.

Parker introduced Alex as his college friend and former roommate. Kuhl regarded him suspiciously. "What kind of work are you in?"

"Government."

"Doing what?"

"Classified."

"Girard, why did you bring him along?"

"He's a good thinker. I want him to help me make sense of this."

"Well, Mister Panagaki, your buddy here is our chief suspect. We can't figure a motive, but someone had to tell that robot to kill the girl. Someone who knew how to make the bot do something it's not programmed to do."

Parker grimaced. "I told you, that isn't possible with one of ours."

"So you say."

"Have you found anything else?"

"We have several people who said they saw the bot jogging along Interstate 40," Kuhl said. "Before, coming from the east, and afterward, going the other way."

"How close to the GRS complex?"

"Two miles, maybe."

"So, it's possible it came from there?"

"Another nail in your coffin. But, we'd like to talk with your father. He's not returning my calls, and I can't get through your company's answering system. We might have to get a warrant and pull him in."

"I'll call him and tell him he needs to talk with you. Meanwhile, can Alex see the security video?"

"Sure. Just as soon as you can put me on the phone with Mark Girard."

Parker pulled up his disc phone and dialed his father's private number.

7. September, 2084.

Mark woke at the buzzing at his chest. He groaned, glancing at the clock on the table next to him. He hadn't slept this late in years, but then he hadn't had such a great sleeping partner. Amy was curled up next to him, and he pulled his left hand from her breasts and swung his feet off the bed.

She reached out for him but he tapped the comm disc and stood up.

"What is it?"

"Dad, I have Detective Kuhl here. He wants to talk to you about the murder."

"And you gave him my cell number?"

"Talk with him and maybe he won't need it."

"Put him on. By the way, as long as you aren't coming to work, your allowance and salary are stopped, and you can't use company equipment, including the aircraft. You have one gate pass, and that's so you can come and get your stuff. After that, you won't be allowed entry."

"Go to Hell, Dad."

"All you have to do is apologize. Call me and say you're ready to work, Son."

"Here's Detective Kuhl."

"Mister Girard?"

"Yes, this is Mark Girard." Mark turned and walked down the hall toward the kitchen. He might as well have some coffee. He passed Lucy, who became animated and followed him.

"Coffee," he instructed the bot. She moved to the coffee maker.

"Are you familiar with the Webb girl?" Kuhl asked.

Mark sat down at the kitchen table. "Yes."

"How well did you know her?"

"I met her one time. Parker had her here for supper."

"Your home?"

"That's right."

"Did you like her?"

"Not particularly."

"She was Black? Not quite right for your son?"

"That's it."

Lucy put a cup of coffee down in front of him, along with the morning paper on a viewer. He took a sip but didn't look at the paper.

"We have a surveillance video which shows a bot breaking in her front door, pushing its way inside, then we hear what sounds like the murder. Can one of your bots do something like that?"

"Hell, no! There are absolute prohibitions on that built into every robot brain."

"Your military bots might."

"They have to obey rules of engagement. Parker told me he saw the video, and it looked like one of our domestics with a generic face. Combat models aren't designed to be pretty, and they're bigger."

"That leaves us with a paradox, doesn't it, Mister Girard?"

"It might have been an RE unit."

"I've contacted RE. They say their bots can't kill either. Also, their models are skinnier."

"Their bots can't do much of anything. They can be made to look like ours."

"But only by trained robot technicians?"

"Yes, it would take someone who knows what they're doing."

"The brains are actually computers, aren't they? Running a set of programs?"

"That's right."

"Could someone have loaded a different program into the bot's brain? For example, a combat robot's programs?"

"The combat programs won't run in a domestic bot's computer – combat models have more processors, need more memory. The general answer to your question is, no. Our interface is private, and so intricate that no one else could possibly alter it."

"Could someone have copied your programs from a bot and reverse engineered them? Made their own version, then put it back?"

"The programs are encrypted, and there are so many checks and stops that we consider that technically impossible. There are only six or seven people in the world capable of changing them. One of them is my father, there's my son and myself, and the others work for me, right here."

"Yet, a bot killed Sara Lister out in California, and a bot killed La'Naomi Webb. How do *you* account for *that*, Mister Girard?"

"They had to be remote controlled, like the Chinese model. Or, they could have been modified RE Corporation bots. I have no way to tell."

"Does your company make remote control bots?"

"Not for forty years. Why would we?"

"Just asking."

"Is that all, Detective?"

"That's all for now. May I have your private number if I need to speak with you again?"

"You can call me through the company. Just ask for extension 81. That will get me directly. I'm trying to keep my cell phone number private. I hope Parker doesn't give it to you."

"Right. I hope he *does*. Bye for now."

Mark let the comm disc fall back onto his chest. Arms went around his neck from behind, and he reached around to pull Amy onto his lap, so he could kiss her.

8. October, 2084.

"Professor Brockmeyer? I'm Timmy, Arthur Girard sent me."

"Yes, I expected you."

Jane Brockmeyer read the badge on the bot's chest as it stood at the door of her office. She'd never seen a 'robot visitor' badge before; this one read: 'Timmy 807654D6, Property of Arthur S Girard, Tierra Del Mar, Oregon, USA'. Timmy stood an inch or two taller than herself, and had a custom face and somewhat resembled the 1900's movie actor Robert Redford, except that his hair was red. The bot wore a nice business suit with a greenish flower tie. It carried a briefcase, rather like a salesman. All too perfect, she reflected, which was how you could tell a bot from a human. No blemishes.

Jane had never had to treat a bot as a person. "Please, come in." She didn't offer to shake hands.

She led the way into her office, went behind her desk and sat. Timmy moved to the edge of the desk and stood looking at her.

"May I sit?" Timmy asked, surprising her. Amazingly lifelike.

"Of course."

Timmy sat, looking like any normal person, which was somewhat unnerving to Jane. He folded his hands in his lap and began: "At Doctor Girard's request, I have come to answer questions about the Utopian Society, your status as a Contributing Member, the model governments we have under development, and our simulation systems. I have documents for you to sign, a check for you, and a considerable amount of documentation."

"Let's do the paperwork first," Jane suggested.

The bot opened his briefcase and pulled out printed paper documents. In order, he handed her a contract, a confidentiality agreement, and a form to specify her bank account for deposits from the society. He offered the confidentiality agreement: standard wordage, no information about the society to be divulged to any other person. She signed. The contract was merely that she would attend meetings when called, either physically or electronically; that she would endeavor to contribute to the success of the Utopian Society; and she would adhere to the confidentiality agreement. She relinquished her right to sue the society for problems she might encounter because of outside influences, such as adverse publicity or the accidental release of personal information about herself. Legally, she would be a contracted advisor to the organization, and would have to handle her own tax deductions.

Jane signed, filled out the short form for her bank account.

Timmy took the forms and passed them by a scanner built into his briefcase. He then handed them back. "Thank you." He handed her a check for twenty-five thousand dollars. She hadn't seen a paper check for months.

Timmy said, "Here is your initial retainer. Your remuneration is ten thousand dollars a month, paid on the last working day. At the society's discretion, there are bonuses for contributions you may make."

She flushed with pleasure. "Nice money."

"Doctor Girard thinks so. The Utopian Society does important work. It could benefit all mankind, someday. That's his hope."

"Are you a member?"

"That would be impossible, because my ability to innovate is quite limited. I merely serve Doctor Girard. At times, I carry out tasks for the benefit of the society."

"You have documentation for me?"

Timmy pulled a stack of papers and manuals from his briefcase, and began handing them to her. She took each in turn, examining it for a moment before adding it to the pile on her desk.

"The rules and regulations of the Utopian Society. Duties of Contributing Members. Our website information. Reports on our model governments: The American Democracy, in six versions; the Parliamentary Government; Russian Communism; China's Communism; Muslim Theocracy; Christian Theocracy; Absolute Dictatorship; Technocracy – three different systems. How to use the simulator. Of course, all these documents are available on-line with your special privileges. You will be able to check them out and make provisional changes to them, which must be approved by our board before they take effect."

Jane's stack was now a foot high. "Whew! It will take time to go through all that."

"Doctor Girard hopes you will pay particular attention to Technocracy, especially the Corporate Model. There is much work to be done there. The American Democracy ideal needs a great deal of refinement as well. Doctor Girard feels it needs major improvement."

"As do I. I'll read those first."

"Professor Brockmeyer, may I demonstrate the

simulation system on your computer?"

Jane nodded her assent, and after she started the laptop PC, the robot came around and took a seat at her keyboard and display. For the next hour, he took her through the game.

She found the simulation somewhat logical: choosing one scenario of many, she played the part of a Democrat, a senator who wanted to pass legislation on tort reform in the medical field. The bill was pre-written. She offered the bill, asked other simulated senators to support it, debated it in a Republican-dominated committee, made a deal under the table to obtain a Republican member's support, and got it passed out of committee. She had to meet with lobbyists, some of whom supported and others opposed the bill. She collected campaign contributions along the way. Her bill reached the floor, was debated briefly, and quickly went to a vote. The Republican majority voted it down.

All these activities were simulated in abbreviated form and followed standard procedure. The entire body of law of the United States was available to her.

"Do you have any questions so far?"

"No, I think I know how to play."

"Doctor Girard tells me it is instructive to take the same bill through each form of government and try to get it passed in the separate countries. Then, there is the International level, where countries with different forms of government compete against each other. There are some specific exercises. In one of them, a treaty needs to be ratified by each country. Each form of government does it differently."

"Yes, I see. I won't have time to get into it very much for several weeks."

"Doctor Girard understands."

After Timmy left, Jane picked up the report on the Corporate Model of Technocracy. This was a strictly theoretical form of government; none actually existed anywhere in the world. As she read, Jane became fascinated. The intent was to fill positions of authority with qualified people, to counter a perceived failing of American democracy. Of course, the failing was the greed, dishonesty, or incompetence of the average politician. In Jane's firm opinion, all systems of government broke down due to human corruption or incompetence. Technocracies tried to select the very best and dedicated people, but those who chose were themselves likely to act in their own interest and become corrupt.

As she studied, a suspicion grew into certainty. Unlike democracies, *this form of government was potentially too dictatorial to be administered by corruptible entities*. It became apparent why *Arthur Girard* was so interested in the Utopian Society. Only robots were incorruptible.

#

The Delta Express airliner, a tiltwing model, landed on a small field not far from Arthur Girard's Oregon estate. Parker and Alex stepped down the folding stairway, each carrying a travel bag, and walked away from the plane, which promptly retracted the stairs and closed the door, then lifted about a hundred feet straight up, emitting a loud roar from the twin engines. It then swiveled the nacelles forward and accelerated rapidly as it moved

85

away.

It was mid-morning on a partly cloudy day, and the air was cooler than it had been in Flagstaff.

There was an Avis stand in the tiny terminal. Parker claimed the car he had reserved, slipped his credit card through a scanner, and received the keys. The car was a tiny Ford Spark which featured fold-down back seats or luggage space, but not both. They squeezed into the front seats and Parker told it to take them to the Girard estate. The steering wheel retracted, giving him more room on the driver's side, and the car drove out on the nearby road, roughly following the coastline south.

About fifteen minutes later, the car arrived at the gate of his grandfather's estate. Parker had called ahead. The ADR gatekeeper recognized him from the retinal scan and the gate swung open.

Another ADR, with a female aspect, met him after the car parked itself in front of the house. The nametag read 'Jazzy'.

"Welcome, Sir," it said. "May I ask, who is the other gentleman?"

"Alex Panagaki, my friend."

"Will you both submit to a physical search?"

Parker had told Alex to expect it. He nodded acceptance.

"Yes," Parker said.

The robot patted each of them down quickly. "Please, follow me."

Arthur Girard was in his breakfast room, having coffee and pie. A female bot stood behind him; Parker read 'Kitty' on her nametag. The older man looked up and frowned at Parker as Jazzy left the room. His eyes went to Alex and lingered.

"Gramps, how are you?"

"Who is this?" Arthur asked without cordiality. He tapped a button to move his wheelchair back from the table, then swiveled toward them.

"This is my friend Alex. He's helping me look into my girlfriend's death. I assume you heard about it. And, it's good to see you again."

"What brings you here?"

"Hell, Gramps, I haven't seen you for three years. Last time I checked, you were still my grandfather."

"You're checking to see if I'm senile?" Parker thought he detected a slight bit of humor in the old man's flinty expression.

"Something like that."

"Follow me." Arthur rolled into the next room, a living area with couches and chairs arranged in a semicircle. He spun around to face the center couch. "Sit." He still hadn't smiled.

Parker and Alex sat facing the older man. Kitty followed and stood against the wall.

"Thanks for making me feel so welcome, Gramps."

"No problem. Do you want to talk about anything in particular? Or are you just wasting my time?"

"I want to ask you about something. Have you heard about Congressman Lister's murder?"

"Yes, of course, I get the news."

"Do you think it was a remote-control robot?"

"Why are you asking me? You know as well as I do how difficult it would be from a technical standpoint. The commands just don't exist. Someone would have to develop macro-commands to climb a rope, break into a home, and strangle someone. All those actions are very complicated. No, the likelihood is that it was an autonomous bot. One of ours, unless RE is farther along than I think they are."

"Gramps, I know about the special commands in the restraint modules. The back door that allows you or Dad, and now me, to order a bot to do illegal acts, such as murder."

"Pardon me? What are you talking about?"

"I've spent months examining the programs. I found the command sequence that overrides Restraints. I know you developed it, and it's been around since Model 3. Dad knows about it. Why, Gramps?"

"Prove it."

Parker faced the bot. "Kitty, *Restrained action bypass.*"

"Sir?" The bot responded.

"*Backdoor one.* Break that vase." Parker indicated a large ceramic flower vase standing next to the window.

Kitty moved toward the base. "Stop," Arthur commanded. Kitty stopped, then returned to the wall.

"That doesn't prove a thing," Arthur said. "Kitty stopped when I told her to."

"Yes, it does. That's *your* vase. Ordinarily, Kitty would have turned to check with you when I ordered her to break it. I've already proved it for Dad, I had one of his bots physically throw me out of his house."

"All right, I admit it."

"Why, Gramps? What if the public found out that tens of thousands of domestic bots could potentially be controlled by any of three men?"

"Four, now, counting your friend, here."

"No, it's three. Your code checks to make certain the order is given by a *Girard*, otherwise it's ignored."

"I was testing you. Apparently, you aren't the total dickhead your father and I thought you were."

"Evidently not, Gramps. Why is it there?"

"Security."

"Whose?"

"Our country. Government is getting out of hand. I might decide to rectify that."

Parker was stunned. For a time, he could think of nothing to say. Alex spoke up: "Sir, do you mean you might order the bots to revolt, take over the government?"

For the first time, Arthur smiled. "Your friend can *talk*! Yes, if things get bad enough, I might."

"On another subject, Gramps, did you hear about the death of my girlfriend?"

"I did."

"I have to ask, did you command a bot to kill her? It was either you or Dad."

"You don't think much of either one of us, do you?" asked Arthur.

"I love both of you. But logic is hard to ignore."

"I've always found that to be true. But *check* your logic, young man."

Gina Wilson entered the room. Parker found himself staring at a blonde beauty who was extremely well-constructed. He had only seen her once before. She wore shorts and a shirt, and he thought her bra had to be industrial grade to stand the strain.

"*Parker*! I just heard you were here. How are you, Cousin? And who's this?"

She ran to Parker and gave him a hug. Parker knew his conversation with Gramps was effectively over. Arthur confirmed it by turning and rolling out of the room, Kitty trailing close behind him.

He sighed, and began giving Gina the attention she demanded. She flirted with him and Alex as she showed them around the estate. The three of them had lunch together, and he didn't see his grandfather again before he and Alex departed that afternoon.

#

Randolf Beale, a Democrat from New York, was now spending his days prepping for the upcoming debates with his opponent, which would take place during the next three weeks. He was so confident his election as president was assured that he had already begun writing his acceptance speech and vetting people he would name to his administration. He still had to attend fund raisers; no candidate ever had enough money, even though he had piled up more than a hundred million in election funds after he won the primaries.

According to most polls, Beale led the Republican candidate, Liam Carter, by nine percentage points. Carter was in his late sixties and didn't debate well, and Beale was supremely confident that he would win, replacing the incumbent Mark Cornwell, who was serving out his second term.

On this afternoon, Beale had flown to Minneapolis, where he'd made a speech to a Teamster's convention, garnering enthusiastic applause. Two hours later, he sat down at the head table in the Hilton's expansive banquet hall, looking out at an estimated audience of five hundred people. Each seat had required a donation of two thousand dollars. Beale smiled, knowing his coffers would jump by nearly a million.

On Beale's left sat Angela Harper, the junior Senator from Minnesota. He chatted idly with her for a time; she was a loyal Democrat who always supported the party line as long as she got her share of earmarks. Angela was only a few years younger than Beale, and was actually pretty and feminine. He enjoyed talking with her. She was divorced, and as he was also unmarried, he considered what an asset she would be as a wife and decided she would be excellent in that role.

"Randy, when you're president I hope you'll invite me to sleep in the Lincoln Bedroom," she was saying.

"Lincoln can get his own girl, you can sleep in mine."

Angela laughed. "With *you*?"

"You bet."

"You're a rascal."

"I try. Seriously, you and I should see each other more often. I *like* you, Angela. You aren't engaged or anything, I hope."

"No one at the moment."

"Why don't you travel with me on the campaign tour after the convention? You would be terrifically valuable as a speaker, and we could get to know each other really well."

"You're thinking of auditioning me for first lady, aren't you?"

"Yes, exactly. I can't think of anyone better."

"Randy, I'll think about it. I'm *very* flattered, and you *are* a very attractive man."

"Please do, Angela."

Someone tapped Beale on his shoulder. He turned and recognized Fred Locasa, the president of RE Enterprises, whom he had met the previous year.

"Hello, Fred."

"Governor Beale, nice to see you."

Locasa took the seat to Beale's right. Beale introduced Locasa to Angela, but after a few minutes of small talk, she turned to the lady on her left.

"Well, Fred, if I become president, what might I do for you?"

"I wouldn't use the word 'if'. You're a cinch, Randy. That's why I'm contributing to your campaign."

"I appreciate the money. Still, what would you like the government to do for you?"

"You can buy more of my bots for the military. Right now, GRS has the monopoly."

"You're talking military bots? We have some of your domestics. There are two in the White House kitchen. Our chef uses them as assistants. He likes them."

"Yes. We do all right in domestics. I'm talking about military uses."

"Your bots aren't autonomous, Fred. How can I use them?"

"We think we're going to have our first autonomous bots next year. Even so, there are battle situations where it makes sense to have a human controller involved. Human intelligence can react on the spur of the moment much better than robots alone."

"I concede that, but our military units are formed into teams with human advisors, so human intelligence *is* always there. Ultimate command is always under a human. Your argument doesn't wash, Fred."

Locasa grimaced. "Tell me, Randy, do you like dealing solely with a firm that has a monopoly on autonomous robots? Do you think it's in the interest of the people?"

Beale shook his head. "Not entirely. I've given it a lot of thought. I plan to put a lot of legal restrictions on GRS, tax them more. If you can come up with an autonomous unit, I'll give it every consideration. It had better be good. We'll test it to pieces before we buy it."

"Mark Girard won't take kindly to more laws or higher taxes. He's a dangerous man, Randy. He's far to the right, politically. What if he could suddenly take control of his bots? All the GRS bots in the world?"

"Is that possible?"

"It is, if the Girards are lying about their restraints system. We're totally dependent on their integrity. I'm not sure I trust them. There have been two recent murders that most certainly have been done by GRS robots. Supposedly, that's impossible, but it happened."

"They say it had to have been done by remote controlled bots, like yours."

"That's what *they* say. The video of the last one clearly show GRS features. Our bots are slimmer, and believe me, it would be hard to disguise them as GRS's. Think about it."

Beale nodded. "I will, Fred. We'll talk again, and please keep me informed about your new autonomous models. I'll always accept your calls." He turned back to Angela.

#

"The bot they spotted on the road close to GRS could have been a decoy," Alex said. He and Parker sat in a diner near the airport. "Another one, intended to make you think GRS was involved."

Parker wrinkled his forehead. He wanted to accept the idea, but he was almost convinced his father had sent the bot that killed La'Naomi.

"Why would someone want to make you think GRS was involved?" He asked.

"I've been racking my brain to come up with a motive, other than someone who didn't want you and La'Naomi to marry. As far as we know, she had no enemies. It had to be your association with her. We also have the Sara Lister case. So, perhaps they were out to discredit robots, or the GRS Corporation. How can GRS, or your father if you will, be hurt by killings blamed on bots?"

Parker swallowed a bite of his hamburger and sipped at his Coke.

"The Pro-Man people, perhaps. They're against robots in general. RE Corporation, if they were a real competitor, which they're not. The Chinese, to slow the move of our military to autonomous robotics, although that's a bit far-fetched. Nothing else comes to mind."

A young blonde human waitress came and refreshed Alex's coffee, looking only at Parker as she did so, and causing Alex to frown. Parker thought she was a bit obvious. He felt a brief warmth in his groin, for the first time since La'Naomi's funeral.

"Pro-Man the most likely?"

"I think so. They're kooks, and they cause trouble now and then. This would be the first time I know of that they've killed anyone."

"Who, in particular, would you suspect?"

"Congressman Rod Kapelnik, Senator Gar Mason, Senator Annie Wakely. All rabid, far-out Liberals. All robot haters."

"There's still the question of how they got the robots to kill."

"RE bots would have to be the answer, unless they know about our back door."

"And RE bots would have to be disguised."

"Yes. Even so, likely some additional programs would have to be developed for the RE brain, as Gramps suggested. Not too likely, in my opinion."

"So, we're stuck for now."

"I'm afraid so."

"What about Muslims?"

Parker delayed answering for a moment as he finished his hamburger. "I forgot about the damned Muslims. It seems too subtle for them, but I think it's a possibility. They have the money, for sure. Many of them think robots conflict with their idea of Allah. But, it would have to be American Muslims, I think. Our Muslims understand bots. Still, if they were behind it, we're back to RE bots."

"RE bots would have to be transported in, wouldn't they? But there are plenty of GRS bots around if the backdoor was used."

"Yes. Exactly."

Alex swallowed the last bite of chicken-fried

steak. He reached for the bill.

"Parker, what are you going to do now? Back to work for your father?"

"No way. Not until I'm certain he didn't do it."

"There's the rub, you can't be certain."

"Right."

"Parker, I need to get back to my job. I understand the problem better, but if I'm going to look into Pro-Man, RE, and the Muslims, I need FBI resources."

"You've only been here a week."

"I've gotten nothing done. Not that I will there, but at least we know what to look for now."

"What about coming to work for GRS? Of course, I'm out now, so I have to put the offer on hold."

"I'm very interested, but I have bills to pay. I'd better keep my job for now."

The two men got up to leave. Parker paid. Parker over tipped the blonde waitress, putting a ten directly into her palm. Alex grimaced. The waitress smiled.

9. October, 2084.

Jane Brockmeyer uploaded her first contribution, a paper describing a totally new technocracy, to the Utopian society's model governments file. She'd had the idea after considering what might be the best government if all participants were dedicated, sincere, and incorruptible. Once the idea had occurred to her, it had come together quickly, and she had written it up in her spare time over a span of three weeks -- probably no more than fifty hours of work, altogether.

It was a Sunday morning. She had sent in her draft at ten, fixed herself a nice lunch, had eaten it by one, and had just cleared the table when a call arrived from Arthur Girard. She took it on her videophone. Girard's lined but still handsome face appeared.

"Hello, Professor Brockmeyer." His was the high, tremulous voice of an older man. "How are you today?"

"I'm well, thank you."

"I read your idea of a minimal technocracy. I liked it a great deal. It's the first I've seen that specifically includes robots in all the key positions. Great work. I like the idea of having robots supervise and enforce, and humans advise."

"I'm surprised you read it so quickly. I just posted it a bit over four hours ago."

"You apparently agree with me that humans can't be trusted."

"I do. And, I would be completely convinced that robots can be, if it weren't for the two unsolved murders attributed to them."

97

"Yes, Brockmeyer, it's an unfortunate situation. But, I do think those murders were instigated by humans. Please, go over the model a bit for me. Give me the reasoning behind your decisions."

"I explained most of that in the document."

"I know, but I'd like to hear it from you directly, and ask questions as we go."

"All right, then. The chief executive is an autonomous robot. He has a Constitution to follow, and he has total authority. The entire government reports to him."

"You're using 'he' rather than 'it'. I like that."

"I know, it's anthropomorphizing an inanimate object. But, it's hard not to."

"Go on."

"His executive cabinet consists of robots as well, each by specialty. Each bot has a chief human advisor, an executive staff of robots, plus as many human specialists as the bot thinks it needs. Generally, the humans supply long term goals, recommendations, imagination, and expertise. Each bot keeps the Constitution in mind as it administers its specific area.

"For example, the Secretary of State is a bot, has bot and human specialists for each foreign country, as well as a bot and advisors who develop State Department policy.

"The Secretary of Defense would have bots running the army, navy, air force, and coast guard, with human advisors from each branch. It might have a bot specializing in planning, another for procurement, and another for personnel."

"The trimmest possible organization." Arthur interjected.

"Hopefully, yes."

"What about a vice-executive?"

"Not necessary if you use robots. Any bot can take over if the executive bot is unable to carry out his duties, needs repair or something like that. We might keep a couple of extras standing around on chargers. All you need is for the executive to designate the order of succession.

"The executive would need planning and research assistants and their human advisors. They would be needed to study and revise old legislation, and propose new legislation."

Arthur stopped to take a drink of what appeared to be lemonade. "How will a new law be put in place?"

"The executive simply orders it into law. Presumably, with the consent of the appropriate secretary in his cabinet."

"No Congress?"

"That's an improvement, if you ask me."

"But you do have a Supreme Court?"

"Yes, with nine human justices, acting as advisors to the Supreme Court judge, a robot which would actually rule on the case."

"Each federal judge and each court of appeals will be a single bot?"

"Yes, and in every case with human judges as advisors."

"So, you've eliminated the legislative branch, haven't you? The checks and balances of our democracy are down to executive against judicial."

Jane smiled. "Not really. I've just put one bot in charge of creating new legislation, and it reports to the executive. In a technocracy, legislation is designed intelligently, at least in theory."

"Will the people have a voice?"

"Not really. The executive will decide what's best for them. They can petition for change, but his word is law."

"They lose their vote."

"Who would you vote for? There's no point in it, since all bots are the same, for all practical purposes. There's no need to choose a particular one. My purpose was to imagine the most minimum government possible that would be extremely effective, incorruptible, and dedicated. In my government, there would be no elections, no change of control, no political parties."

"Brockmeyer, I like it."

"Sir, that is very gratifying."

"All this assumes robots are competent and trustworthy."

"Yes. Aren't they?"

"They *are*, my dear, they are. You may see your government model come into power, someday, here in this country. Wouldn't that be fun?"

"The only concern I have is that humans wouldn't accept it."

"I believe they would, if they understood it was the best possible one for them, and was totally working in their interest."

"Well, I believe it *would* be in their interest. But, there will still be political factions among people. They'll cause trouble, won't they?"

Girard took another drink of lemonade. "No doubt they will. You'd have to counter that with a strong department of internal security. But you need that in any form of government."

"Yes, unfortunately."

"I like your work, Professor. You'll find another fifty thousand in your bank account tomorrow, as a bonus. We'll add your model to the sim game and let people play with it – this should get us an initial reaction. OK?"

"Yes, *Sir*."

"Good. I look forward to your next contribution."

Jane whooped with joy after the connection was broken.

#

The call came late in the afternoon, catching him in his suite while he was reading a novel, displayed page by page in big letters on the wall. Parker had been idle and increasingly depressed. He talked frequently with Alex, who reported no progress in either murder case. Still refusing to reconcile himself with his father, he was tired of staying at the Phoenix Hilton with nothing to do, and the hotel expense ate into his meager income of six thousand a month. He had actually begun looking for an apartment the day before.

He terminated the display with a voice command and tapped up his medallion. "Hello?"

"Parker Girard?"

"Yes?"

"My name is Fred Locasa. Have you heard of me?"

"President of RE."

"Yes. I understand you're no longer working at GRS."

"That's right."

"I'd like to sound you out about something."

"Go ahead."

"I have a job for you in research and development, for extremely good money. I hope you'll consider it."

"A job? You know I'm Mark Girard's son, don't you?"

"Yes. I also know you and he are not speaking at the moment."

Parker wondered where Locasa had gotten that information. "What kind of job?"

"We're developing an autonomous model. I want you to lead the effort. You'll be a vice president."

"In charge of R&D?"

"Yes. I'm prepared to offer you a million dollars a year for your skills. You're probably the only man in the world worth that much to me."

"My father would be pissed."

"Would you like that?"

"I might. Where's the job?"

"We have a new facility west of Denton, Texas. A lab, a small factory, and a proving ground. We just opened it last month."

"Autonomous is tough. How far along are you with the brain?"

"I can't tell you that unless and until you sign on with us. But we're very confident."

Two thoughts ran through Parker's mind: RE was a suspect in the bot murders, and this would be an opportunity for him to investigate the possibility that an RE unit could have been used. But, if he accepted, it would likely mean a definite and final break with his father and perhaps even his grandfather. Yet, he was intrigued.

"May I call you Fred?"

"Of course."

"Fred, I'm interested, but it would be a major change for me. May I sleep on it, and get back to you tomorrow?"

"Yes. I'll give you a number where you can reach me."

An audible tone from his phone disk told Parker the number had been forwarded.

He said good-bye and began to consider his opportunity.

#

In truth, Parker hadn't had to think a lot about it: he and his grandfather Arthur, a cold fish, had never been close. Nor had he ever been close with his father, and it was likely, as he saw it, that his father had killed La'Naomi.

"I want a five-year contract, unconditionally guaranteed, with a half mil up front," he told Locasa the next afternoon. "The rest in sixty equal monthly payments."

"That's difficult," the CEO responded.

"I just want to have a bit of security. I thought perhaps you were just baiting me to cause a split with my father."

"I thought the split was already there."

"Fred, it is, but it isn't necessarily permanent. If you give me what I ask, I'm yours. I'd love the opportunity to show Mark and Arthur what I can do, but I have to know burning my bridges with them won't be fatal for my career."

"Two hundred and fifty thousand up front?"

"No, five hundred, on the day I sign. Guaranteed contract."

"The entire contract, unconditionally guaranteed? What if you don't perform? What if you don't even show up? I can't take that risk."

"You have to trust me and believe I'm a man of my word. Sign me, and I give you my word I'll perform for you. If you don't trust me, I'm worthless to you anyway."

Locasa was silent for a long moment, but finally said, "all right."

"When do you want to do it?"

"How about next Monday morning? I'll meet you at the airport in Denton with a car, then I'll show you around the facility and introduce you to your subordinates. We can do the paperwork as well."

"Deal."

#

Jane called up the Tribune on her reader to read as she ate the pancakes she'd made. The first page was all about Randolf Beale's ten-point lead in the polls. There was nothing new; Beale was a shoo-in. She paged down, where she saw a shocking headline: *Illinois Professor proposes government by robots.* The text read: *Jane S. Brockmeyer, an eminent professor of political science at the University of Illinois, has proposed that the government of the United States be replaced by a constitutional technocracy governed by autonomous robots, according an article published today in the Journal of the Utopian Society. She has developed a detailed description of her proposed government structure, which has been accepted by the society. According to her model, there would be a robot chief executive, analogous to our presidency, with a cabinet of robots and a judiciary, including federal courts of appeals and the supreme court each consisting of one robot. There would be no legislative branch of the government, but a robot cabinet secretary would be in charge of developing new legislation, which would have to be approved by the cabinet member responsible for the law's administration, then signed into law by the chief executive robot.*

Each robotic executive would have the ability to hire as many human advisors and experts as needed to inform itself on its area of expertise. Brockmeyer concedes the lack of high intelligence and imagination that limits the ability of robots, but believes these qualities can be supplied by their advisors. The chief executive would be guided by a written constitution, which could be amended by popular vote, however there would be no elected officials in the government, and political parties would be abolished.

According to her article, Brockmeyer mistrusts humans to be diligent, competent, and honest, which is why she believes robots are the best solution for government.

Abner Reddick, president of the Pro-Man website, reacted violently to the idea. "Human beings have done well enough governing themselves up to now," he said in a telephone interview with the Tribune staff. "How any self-respecting human could subordinate his judgment to a mere machine is beyond me."

Carl Badlender, chairman of the Democratic National Committee, said the idea of abolishing political parties was "insane." "All our social and governmental progress in this country has come from the interaction of political parties with each other, with the events and conditions of the times, and with the free and open discussion of issues the parties support," he said. "Frankly, most of the progress has come from the Democrat Party. But even the Republican Party would likely hate to be abolished, simply in order to suppress free speech and free expression in this country."

Archbishop Wilson, the top Catholic authority in North America, denounced the idea as being contrary to the Word of God. "It's an obscene idea," he told a Tribune reporter in a video interview last night. "I have no doubt Pope Paul will reject it."

Congressman Rod Kapelnick also protested the model. "Human beings should stand on their own. Robots, if we need them all, are simply machines that are designed to help us. I'm appalled that anyone could think of them as our rulers or respect their decisions."

Various websites, including LifeBlog.com, report a deluge of postings protesting the idea. Professor Brockmeyer could not be reached for comment.

Jane snorted. No one had *tried* to reach her for comment.

Later that morning, she logged into the Utopian Society website, then went to the discussion board. Most of the posts concerning her model were positive. She felt better.

#

The Robotic Enterprises facility near Denton, Texas turned out to be two hundred level acres and several buildings designed to be eco-green, almost disgustingly so. Each building was shaped as an arc, with only glass centered toward the south, and with a clear liquid flowing between the panes to extract heat from the sun's rays for heating or cooling purposes. The roofs were all nothing but solar panels. Parker thought that no photon from the sun could escape without doing something useful. On the campus itself, a number of huge windmills spun listlessly in the summer heat.

"It cost extra money to build this way, didn't it?" Parker asked after Fred Locasa had explained the features of construction.

"Well, yes. But I expect to have to deal with Democrats, and they're big on self-sustaining energy."

"Democrats?"

"Beale will be president, don't you think?"

"It appears so."

They entered one of the buildings. A hostess met them and led them to stairs and up to the second floor and into a modest conference room, featuring a long table and a glass wall that made Parker feel connected to the outdoors.

Locasa asked Girard to sit at the head of the table. As he took his seat, men and women began filing in and sitting. Soon, there were ten of them, seven men and three women, dressed casually and staring at Parker.

Locasa addressed them. "My friends, I bring you the new director of Research and Development of Robotic Enterprises. He holds a Doctor of Robotics from Massachusetts Institute of Technology, and comes to us from a similar position at GRS Corporation, which he held for two years, after three years there as assistant director. His grandfather and father developed the first autonomous robot, and he fully understands the robot 'brain'. He will be invaluable in our own REBrain project.

"I give you Parker Girard."

The group stood and applauded.

Parker stood as well, then walked around the room shaking hands with each.

"Doreen Ruiz, Project Management and Control." A tall, lovely, and very slender lady tending to gray.

"Nice to meet you."

"Tom Wilke, Neural Networking." A dark, intense-looking man in his thirties.

"Yes, a very difficult area," Parker said.

"Huang Lee, System Architect." A very neat Oriental, probably in his late twenties, who looked Parker directly in the eyes. Parker liked him instinctively.

"We'll have to talk a great deal."

He met each of the others, then came back to the head of the table, where he remained standing as the others sat again.

"Ladies and Gentlemen," Parker said, "I know almost nothing of the 'REBrain' project or the state of RE development in general, so I hope you'll bear with me as I work my way into the job. I *do* understand GRS's design of the autonomous brain, and I'm familiar with the more than five hundred patents GRS holds in Robotics, all of which we'll have to respect. That's all I bring to the project. I promise I will do all in my power to help you get the job done."

Locasa stood. "Lee, why don't you explain where we are with auto-bots."

Lee stood as Girard and Locasa sat down.

"Let me bring in a visual aid," Lee said. He tapped his comm disc and murmured something into it. A robot entered the room and stood beside the table. It looked different that those Parker had seen in RE ads. It was almost identical to an ADR.

"This is Charley, an SDR – specialized domestic robot – he is fully autonomous in household duties, aren't you, Charley?"

"Yes, Sir."

"Tell us what you can do."

"I monitor the state of a household, keeping the floors and windows clean, the furniture dusted, the dishes washed and put away, the clothes washed and stored properly, and the beds made. I answer the telephone and take notes. I greet persons who come to the door, and inform my owner or a family member of their presence. In winter, I shovel the snow from the sidewalks and driveway. There are several other activities I will carry out if commanded by my owner or a family member, including fetching of specific items. I do not cook. I do not guard, except to sound an alarm if I suspect someone intends to commit a crime against my owner or a family member."

Parker was interested. "Is this product ready for production?"

"We're gearing up now," Locasa responded. "Our Detroit plant will build them, and we'll start our publicity going next month."

"No bugs?"

"We have Beta models in twenty households,"

Lee said. "They've been in place for about six months. The owners have been very positive, although we've had about a hundred and thirty bugs reported, all of which we've fixed."

"Big step over your last model?" Parker remarked.

"Yes, major competition for GRS Domestics, we believe," said Lee.

"They'll sell at about half the price," Locasa added.

"If you put two in the same household, what will happen?" Parker asked.

"One will stand and let the other do all the work," Lee said. "They don't cooperate or communicate with each other. However, the owner can allocate them to specific household duties."

"Are you planning to add capabilities?"

"We have programmer staff working on outside yard work: mowing, trimming, planting, raking, car washing, sidewalk edging. Mowing is coming along, but frankly, plant trimming is a disaster so far, and we aren't making much headway on planting. We expect to begin testing car washing in two or three months."

"New capabilities will be downloadable?"

"Yes. The SDR's can connect wirelessly to the internet, and upgrade their software from our website."

"Could an SPD commit murder, or any other crime, if ordered?"

"SPD's can only do what they are programmed to do. We haven't implemented a 'murder' command, for obvious reasons."

"So, you've solved the problem of automatic

self-motivation, for a limited set of activities? A nice accomplishment."

"It's taken us *years* of effort," Locasa commented. "But yes, we seem to have solved it to that extent, and we're on our way to a general purpose autonomous capability. That's the ultimate objective of 'REBrain'."

"Lee, would you please lay out the design of the SPD brain?" Parker asked.

"Certainly. The physical computer uses two hundred and fifty-six processors and runs under the Linux-Parallel operating system, although we've acquired the code from Alphonso Corporation and have modified it somewhat.   We have sixteen solid-state mass data storage devices, with a response time of two microseconds. They can hold sixty-four terabytes of data. We aren't using very much of it as yet.

"The Sensory Module processes inputs of sight, hearing, feeling, smell, and kinesthetics and presents the data in a set of screen formats. Unlike GRS, SPD vision is forward only. Sensory currently requires eleven processors out of sixteen allocated to it.

"The Monitor Module runs through a set of domestic objectives, and assigns inspection tasks to the Ego Module. Ego accepts the tasks, schedules them, and carries them out. Results of inspections are passed to Evaluation, which decides whether to issue tasks to rectify a perceived problem. Monitor is two processors, Ego requires ten, Inspection eight, and Evaluation one. Navigation allows the bot to walk about the house without running into people, stepping on pets, or damaging the owner's property or going outside, and uses six processors. We use four for Language construction, three for interpretation. The other six processors we use are in body control.

"So, we currently use fifty-one of the processors on a dedicated basis, others can be assigned temporary tasks."

Parker asked, "What computer languages do you use?"

"C-cube 3. We compile that to Intel-256 machine language, and we use the R1 Debug Package. We can connect a computer terminal to our bots wirelessly."

"That's similar to what we do, except we use the Intel-1024 or 2048 Stack. Oops, I should have said that's what *GRS* does. I can't use 'we' anymore."

#

Arthur was in his whirlpool bath with a bare-breasted Gina when the call from Mark came. He luxuriated in the warm water which eased his aches and pains, while trying to ignore her attentions.

He took the call on his comm disc. "Hello."

"Dad, bad news."

"What's that?"

"Parker has taken a job with RE."

"He has? When?"

"Yesterday. He'll be their chief R and D man. They're trying to go autonomous."

"How do you feel about that?"

"No great loss for GRS, but personally, it hurts when your own son is a traitor."

"Why do you suppose he did that?"

"He has the crazy idea I had one of our ADR's murder his black girlfriend."

112

"*Didn't* you?"

"Please, Dad."

"Who did? It's a mystery. I think it was an RE bot made up to look like one of ours. The Pro-Man people are having a field day."

"Yes, they are. Our sales are down by fifteen per cent since Lister, and twenty after the Webb murder. And, we're getting lots of hate mail. I'm having to invest in more publicity. You'll see the ads starting next week."

"Would you take Parker back?"

"I'd have to think about it. Probably not."

#

Locasa had invited Parker to live in his Denton residence, a six-bedroom, two story mansion with an indoor pool and servants: a middle-aged housekeeper, two older women who slept together, a young male handyman, and four RE bots. The detached garage held four cars, and Parker had bought a new Ford SUV and driven from Flagstaff.

Parker had a great deal of privacy, with his own suite of three rooms. Locasa was rarely there. When he was, he kept to himself.

In the third week, Parker was deep into the REBrain project. The development team had made considerable progress, but struggled with Decomposition, the process of breaking a selected activity into component tasks. He was able to make useful suggestions. They also struggled with Integration, the ability that simulated consciousness by looking at all sensory, memory, and evaluation data simultaneously. He suggested a complete rewrite; Locasa was irritated but went along when he heard Parker's explanation.

He found there were two projects underway in another RE lab north of him, both of which were developing new robot bodies: a domestic, and a military. These were well along, in beta tests using older REBrain modules, and were awaiting the completion of his own REBrain project. He took a day to visit the lab with Locasa, and he was briefed on the technical details. Parker's conscience hurt him a bit, but he knew there were better ways to activate and utilize pseudo-muscles, and he recommended them.

It appeared there was no upper limit on development funds. He questioned Locasa, who replied, "We have plenty of backers. No problem. If you need money for something, just ask for it." Parker thought he needed more people, but couldn't find new hires, because of an almost total lack of talented scientists. Using the phone, Parker scoured the universities and employment agencies. There were few prospects, and none at all with bot development experience. He hired two extremely bright MIT grads but had to start them out as beginners.

He was into every aspect of brain development, and he knew he had earned the respect of his team. He became confident that their first autonomous bot would be a success, if not nearly as good as a GRS unit. His people were working hard and progress was being made. He felt good enough that he scheduled a week off in November in order to visit his mother in Maine. They talked on the phone frequently; she seemed sad and neglected.

Having learned more about RE capabilities, he felt it nearly impossible that La'Naomi's murder was committed by an RE bot. He called Alex Panagaki and passed on his conclusion. He also invited Alex to come and work for him at RE, but Alex declined.

10. November, 2084.

The seventh had been a moderately stressful day, but the outcome had been decided early. That night, there was wild celebration, as Randolf Beale addressed, then rewarded his national campaign staff and his New York City staff with a speech and a banquet. He made his acceptance speech for the video audience, then conducted a press conference before coptering to his estate in Armonk. He stayed up late discussing the future with Angela Harper, who had agreed to marry him and become First Lady. It had been an exhilarating time, and he had gotten no sleep until late morning of the eighth, which had been a day of rest. He slept all through the afternoon and all night, with only an occasional need to get up and urinate.

On the ninth, President-Elect Beale woke before six, ready to go to work. President Cornwell had promised to brief him on the current situation with China, a real mess at the moment.

His household responded: one of his ADR's began to prepare his breakfast, another brought his coffee and three newspapers, then turned on the news images displaying on the wall in front of him. The headline in the Washington Post grabbed his attention: *Army takes Power in China.*

He read on: *Chang Li-Jin, the former Minister of Defense, is the new head of government in China, according to CNN Correspondent Alice Po, reporting from the Chinese capitol. Chinese army units moved into Beijing yesterday and arrested many government figures, including Premier Wu. Street intersections near the Executive House are controlled by tanks and soldiers. According to Po, there are strong rumors that those arrested have been shot, and spurts of gunfire can be heard in the vicinity of important government buildings. Chang, who received higher education in America and holds a degree in Political Science from Yale University, is considered progressive by Chinese standards, but with attitudes more like a typical American Conservative. He is pro-business and is expected to move the country toward a more capitalistic economy, however, Chang has made strongly anti-American comments in the recent past. His ascent may create problems for President Beale when he takes office.*

Beale snorted and asked for the next newspaper display. The New York Times was full of articles and editorials rejoicing over his election. The China story was on page five, he learned nothing more from it. Information about the revolution there was still sketchy.

The Times lamented the many problems facing him as the new president. China, of course, was the largest, but the economy was still in trouble, and third world nations were clamoring for more aid.

Beale had promised to take a hard line on China, in contrast to the cautious and largely unsuccessful diplomatic approach Cornwell had followed. That might not be easy; the Republicans had emerged from the election with a divided new Congress. They would have six more house votes, while the Senate would be divided 52-48 in favor of Democrats, counting four Independents in their caucus. Not a strong mandate, he thought. He would actually have to work with Republicans for whatever legislation he could get passed. It was a distasteful prospect, but he would hold his nose and do it. He intended to make a difference, and despised past presidents who had spent all their time campaigning and fund-raising.

#

Mark received the call just before Thanksgiving. Randolf Beale would be visiting Phoenix on the 30th and invited Mark to meet him for an informal chat over lunch, lasting up to an hour. The aide who called him didn't know much more, but said Beale considered GRS important to the government and wanted to clarify things with him.

Mark restrained a sarcastic comment, but texted his acceptance.

Early that Thursday morning, he boarded a company jet copter and flew south. He entered the Mayfair dining room at a quarter to twelve, where he was intercepted by two Secret Service men, who escorted him to a private room. He sat waiting and drinking coffee by himself at a table for a half hour, with the two looking on, and two Secret Service ADR's standing motionless nearby. His own two bodyguard bots were made to wait in the hall.

A waiter came in and offered a menu. "Senator Beale has already ordered," he told Mark. Mark asked for a club sandwich and soft drink. He wasn't really hungry.

Beale finally appeared, walking in among a retinue of men and bots, and the president-elect extended his hand. Mark grasped it briefly.

"We finally meet, Mr. Girard," Beale offered. "I recognize you from TV newscasts. Thank you for coming to chat with me."

"And I recognized you the same way, Mr. President. I'm very pleased to meet you."

"May I sit down?"

"Of course, if the Secret Service doesn't mind."

Beale waved his hand, and the human guards left the room, leaving three bots standing motionless against the wall.

"Your robots are everywhere," Beale observed.

"Even I am amazed sometimes."

"When I move into the White House, I'm going to fire about fifty of them and replace them with humans. Or I would, if I could find fifty people as trustworthy."

"ADR's don't need a salary."

"I know, so I'll probably just hire about twenty people, who will be intensely vetted. Even then, I could be hiring a Chinese spy or assassin."

"You're doing it on principle?"

"Exactly. Robots cost jobs for regular folks. There are many in my party who resent that. And, they don't like GRS Corporation as a sole source. Neither do *I*, by the way."

"RE Corporation is way behind, as you well know. Their bots don't stack up to ours."

"Fred Locasa tells me they are close to having an autonomous model. Your son is a big help to him."

"*Autonomous* is a big word, Sir. There are varying degrees of it, and I expect their new brain will be far less capable than our new models, or even our old ones."

"We'll procure a few, test them, and find out. Tell me, how many ADR's have you sold around the world?"

"All time?"

"Please."

"Let me think for a moment. We've sold around two million and four hundred thousand in the United States and Canada, perhaps ninety thousand in Great Britain, eight thousand in Germany, fourteen thousand in Italy. We don't market to other countries. Prohibited by law. Any chance of removing some of the restrictions in your administration?"

"Not much." Beale pulled a pen and a small notebook from his jacket and wrote the figures down. "What are your projected sales for next year?"

"About two hundred thousand."

"O.K. Now the figures for your military models. How many have you sold us?"

The food arrived, and Mark was pleased that Beale had also ordered a sandwich.

"We can only sell in the United States. Around two hundred and fifty thousand, delivered to date. Perhaps another hundred thousand this year, as contracted or informally agreed to by the Department of Defense."

"Out of all the military units you've delivered to the armed forces, how many are still in service?"

"Roughly half."

"What about automobile and aircraft control systems?"

"I'd have to have my staff come up with a figure, but it's close to a hundred million in the US and Canada alone, and we sell in Europe as well."

Beale scribbled a bit more in his notebook. "Frankly, Mark, I'm going to ask Congress to put a special tax on each of your product lines. I'm also going to ask them to break up GRS Corporation along controller and robot lines. It's obscene that you have a monopoly on both. Your prices are excessive."

"Whatever tax you put on me will be added to the price. Go ahead and break us up, if you can. I have some influence in Congress."

"Not as much as I will have."

"Do you plan to tax RE bots as well?"

"Only autonomous robotic devices. But yes."

"Since RE doesn't have any, that's only a tax on me. What's the term for that? A Bill of Attainder?"

"It isn't specifically directed at you, so I can argue it isn't. All right, another thing. I plan to demand that you release the plans and specifications for each of your products, and revoke all your patents, under anti-monopoly legislation. We'll order you to divulge any trade secrets you may have. We'll see if other companies can step in and build the same products."

"You'll play Hell, Randolf. I won't give them up. I'll take you to the Supreme Court on that one. Even if they rule against me, I'll hide them, or even burn them before I'll give them up."

"One more appointment and *I own* the Supreme Court. And, the public is really down on robots right now, due to the fact that they are murdering people. They won't mind if I send federal marshals to arrest you."

"Thanks for the warning."

Beale's smile was positively evil. "My pleasure."

"Let me sum it up, Mr. President," Mark said. "You don't like GRS, you think we're a monopoly, you're going to favor RE Corporation, establish a tax that only affects GRS, and break us up? You're going to try to steal all my trade secrets, and cancel all my patents? Do you have any *good* news for me?"

"I'm not going to change the current military development plan for now. I may reduce military spending later. I do plan to see whether RE can come up with a comparable model, and if they do, I'll go to competitive bidding."

"Well, I'm glad I didn't vote for you. And, don't hold your breath waiting for any campaign contributions from me."

Beale chuckled as if highly amused. "There's something else I'd like to discuss with you. You're listed as a consultant with the Army. What's that all about?"

"I'm on call, for a dollar a year, if that's what you mean. Now and then I attend maneuvers or war games, and if we get into a war they tell me they'd like to have me with the generals. There was talk of making me one under the current administration."

"Doing what, exactly?"

"Advising how to make use of the GRS's. There are a few ins and outs that can help in combat."

"Such as?"

"Anti-jamming, for one. Our bots have radio communication among themselves and up to their command structure, as you probably know, and enemies may try to drown out the signal, but we've built in a frequency shift algorithm to thwart that. I tell them when to begin the shift, and recommend the shift parameters.

Secondly, all the autonomous units in a battle --

infantry, tanks, and artillery -- have to be coordinated. They do it by themselves, but they aren't very good at creative thinking, so if they come to a new situation, they tend to get stuck. That's where I try to help. I also try to help with battle plans, since I'm knowledgeable in bot capabilities and limitations. The most awesome thing robots do is act simultaneously, down to the microsecond. An entire platoon, company, or battalion doing the same thing, tanks and all. Human soldiers can't match that, or react to it. And, of course, they're absolutely fearless."

The president shrugged. "Well, I suppose there's no harm in allowing you to continue."

"So, you had contemplated cutting me out?"

"I just didn't understand the need. You've clarified it. So, I won't interfere."

"You've clarified things for *me*, as well." Mark stood, grabbed the remaining quarter sandwich from his plate, and walked out. By the time he reached the lobby, he was swallowing the last of it.

The Delta Airlines tiltwing jet descended toward the runway of the Mathias Valley Airport in an almost vertical fashion, giving Parker an uncomfortable falling sensation that lasted for long seconds until the plane touched down and stopped with a very short rollout. It then began to taxi toward the terminal. Droplets of water ran down the window next to Parker.

"Raining, huh?" Alex Panagaki said from the aisle seat.

"Fairly hard, by the looks of it."

After deplaning, which required a wet walk with their carry-on luggage to the terminal, they found the Avis car rental booth, which consisted of a single ADR. Parker submitted to the retinal scan as the bot looked into his eyes. "Welcome to Avis, Mister Girard. I'm reporting your location to your father, because of his standing order. Your car is ready, Sir."

"All GRS bots have this order?"

"I can't speak to that, Sir. I received my order yesterday."

"And how are you reporting?"

"Interbot communication, Sir. Video and audio."

Parker accepted the keys and directions to the rental car, one of only four at the small parking lot outside the rather small terminal. As the two men walked out to find it, Alex asked: "What the *Hell* is *interbot communication?*"

"It's essentially a television band. They use it to

coordinate their activities. Mark and Arthur have it rigged to spy on the rest of the world, if they want to. I was able to use it, though I never bothered."

"The world doesn't know about it?"

"GRS has made the bot coordination public, in fact they originally had to get the FCC to allocate a bandwidth for the purpose. The public just doesn't know the signal from one bot can be relayed through others to Dad or Gramps."

"Another back door thing? Why?"

"Yes. As to why, I suppose domestic bots are privy to interesting stuff. Gramps may be into it, overhearing conversations or watching babes undress, but I don't think Dad gives a damn."

They reached the car, stowed their luggage, and slid into the seats. The car was an *Autogo*, which incorporated a small, autonomous GRS brain to do the driving and navigating. Parker gave it the address. The car backed out of the space and moved onto the two-lane road outside the airport. The rain continued to fall, and the car ran the wipers for their benefit.

As Alex and Parker rode along the road that bordered the bay, they caught glimpses of ocean scenery through mist and rain. Large mansions were sited along the waterfront. After only a few minutes, the car turned into the circular drive of a relatively small, three story brick and stone house with a three-car detached garage.

The car stopped by the front door, and they walked quickly up onto the porch, carrying their bags. An ADR opened the door and greeted them. It looked into their eyes in turn, scanning. Parker saw it was Billy, an older model which had been with the family for several years.

"Mister Girard, and Mister Panagaki, please come inside."

The two men stepped into the house, finding themselves in a long hall with openings on either side. "Billy, is Mom at home?" Parker asked. He'd called her yesterday, telling her he would accept her invitation to spend Christmas with her, and that he was bringing Alex.

"Your mother is expecting you," the bot responded. "She is in the reading room. If you will wait here, I will inform her that you are here."

As they waited, another bot, Crissy, came and took their bags and carried them up the nearby stairs. A short time later, Melanie appeared, dressed in sweater and slacks. Her shoulder length hair was a bit darker than Parker remembered. She came quickly to Parker, hugged him for a time, then stepped back and offered her hand to Alex.

"Parker, Alex, I'm glad you came. We'll have a pleasant time."

"Will there be other guests?"

"Possibly. But, probably not. What have you been doing?"

"I've been getting into my job at RE, and last week I hired Alex to be our new Chief Security Officer."

Melanie looked at Alex. "And what does such a person do?"

"I will manage a staff of men and bots who protect our plants, offices and labs from outsiders," Alex responded. "I will also investigate internal problems, where necessary."

"I'm glad Parker saw fit to hire you, then."

To Parker, she said, "How is your new job working out?"

"Pretty well. We're becoming more competitive with GRS every day."

"Parker, you know you're not even close."

"We will be, but it will probably take ten years, if not twenty."

"Are you hungry?"

"Yes."

Follow me into the dining room, and let's eat."

#

When Alex praised the food, Melanie said, "Thank you, but it's a snap when you have an ADR. The bots have gourmet chef capabilities built in, so all I have to do is make certain the food I buy is top quality. Parker, is that true with RE bots?"

Parker grimaced. "*It will be*, I believe. Our new bots will be able to prepare almost any recipe you can name, or the owner can give them a menu and they'll fix the entire meal."

"Will be?"

"We have an advanced prototype that is quite a bit more autonomous that RE bots sold in the past."

"In other words, you're still ten years behind GRS."

"Maybe nine, mom. And closing."

"That's why RE pays you the big bucks?"

"No doubt."

"I was shocked when you left Mark. Why did you do it?"

"He had to be the one who sent bots to kill La'Naomi and Congressman Lister."

"No, I could have done it, or Arthur could have."

Parker's jaw dropped open. "*You* know the back

127

door commands?"

"I've known about them for many years. Back when Mark and I loved each other, he wanted me to be able to defend myself. But I didn't do it. Arthur did?"

"*Gramps?* Why?"

"Arthur is a bit crazy. He calls me sometimes and rants about the state of the world. He thinks humans are incapable of governing themselves logically, and wants to bring about major change. Sara Lister was a friend of GRS Corporation, and Arthur wants to stir up problems, wanted an enemy on the committee. He wants contention and strife. He wants to bring down the current government and replace it with one of his own design."

"That doesn't make any sense, Mom."

"You'd better believe what I'm telling you."

"Why would he have *La'Naomi* killed?"

"Arthur hates mixed marriages. The prospect of one in his own family would have been unendurable."

"Do you know this for a fact?"

"I know Mark. He's not a killer. Arthur has no scruples whatever."

"I went to see Gramps this fall. I asked him, straight out, if he did it, and he said he didn't."

"Arthur has been known to lie."

Parker was silent for a long moment. "Gramps! Then I've wronged Dad."

"Yes," Melanie said. "I suspect you have."

\#

Alex and Melanie tried to break Parker's depression, but he remained upset by Melanie's revelation. Snow came, and there was no going outside for several days. Then, the sun came out and melted it all, and he and Alex descended the stairs down to the rocks below the house, sat on a rock and watched the gentle waves of the bay wash back and forth for nearly an hour. It seemed to help his mood.

The day before his scheduled return, he activated his disc and called his father.

"Mark Girard's office." A feminine voice, human, and one he thought he recognized. "Amy, this is Parker. Is he in?"

"Parker? Long time no talk. Yes, he's in."

"Will he talk to me?"

"Just a moment, I'll ask him."

There was a pause, then: "Hello, Mark."

"Dad, I'm at Mom's. I've spent Christmas here."

"How is she?"

"She's fine."

"Good. Does she like her home?"

"She seems to."

"Anything else?"

"Dad, could Gramps be behind those killings?"

"You'll have to ask *him*."

"Mom thinks he is."

"What do *you* think?"

"I think I'm sorry I accused you."

"Come back to GRS."

"I can't do that, at least right now."

"Then we have nothing more to talk about."

Mark dropped the connection.

#

Parker's call to Arthur Girard hadn't gone quite as well.

"Arthur Girard's residence." A perfect robot

voice.

"This is Parker Girard. May I speak with him?"

"Just a moment, Sir."

Parker waited. And waited. Finally, Arthur came on the line.

"What is it, Grandson?"

"You asked me to think about who killed La'Naomi and Sara Lister. I did. It was *you*, Gramps."

There was silence on the other end.

"Why did you kill them?" Parker insisted.

"*I* didn't kill them."

"No, you sent Timmy."

"What's your point?"

"No particular point, Gramps," Parker said. He tapped his disc to break the connection.

#

Fred Locasa questioned Parker's request to acquire an ADR. It was Parker's first day back at work from the Christmas vacation.

"That offends me, Parker. Why do you want one?"

"For comparison purposes. I'll keep it at the house."

"Why do you want to hide ownership?"

"It could be bad publicity for RE if some reporter got hold of it."

"Yes, I suppose you're right. But, I suppose you could assign the same task to our prototype and see for yourself how well we handle it compared to the competition."

"That's the general idea, Fred."

"All right, I'll get you one. On the quiet."

"Thanks, Fred. I have something else to run past

you."

"What's that?"

"A name for our new line of domestics. *Perfect Servant.*"

Fred considered it for a long moment. "I like it," he finally said, "even if ours aren't totally perfect."

#

Officially, Jake was registered to Lancy Rillian, Fred's housekeeper. She was a nice, if somewhat plump, lady nearing middle age, always friendly to Parker. When she arrived in her electric early Monday morning, the bot came as a passenger.

She knocked on the door to Parker's suite. He opened it, still dressed in his bathrobe. "Hi, Lancy." He saw the ADR standing behind her.

"Good morning, Mister Girard. Mister Locasa asked me to assign this robot to you. I don't understand why you can't be the registered owner, but here it is."

"We don't want the media finding out we have one. Bad publicity."

"Oh. Jake, you stay with Mister Girard until I tell you different. Obey all his orders."

"I will, Mrs. Rillian," Jake responded.

"Thanks, Lancy," Parker said. "Jake, come in and let's get acquainted."

The bot entered Parker's living room. Parker shut the door.

"Fix breakfast," Parker commanded.

"What will you have?"

"Eggs, bacon, toast, hash browns, coffee, tomato juice. It's all in the refrigerator."

"How will you want your eggs?"

"Scrambled."

"How many pieces of toast, Sir?"

"Two. Wheat."

"Yes, Sir." Jake turned and began looking for the kitchen.

#

After a long work session in the RE Lab offices, Parker came home, consumed a ham sandwich and drank a coke, then settled down to experiment on Jake. First, he had to use his laptop to locate Arch Cape, Oregon, on the map and obtain the coordinates. Then he commanded Jake: "Jake, *Restrained Action Bypass.*"

"Sir?"

"*Back door One.*"

"Yes, Sir."

"Jake, can you use your communication with the other bots, particularly the ones in Oregon?"

There was a brief pause. "Yes, Sir."

"I want you to locate all the bots within ten miles of latitude 46.041782, longitude minus 124.097443."

"That will require computation, Sir. A moment, Sir."

"Do it."

"Complete, Sir. I have a range of geographical coordinates. I am building a query message. I am sending it."

Around two seconds later, Jake spoke again: "I have located eleven ADR's who report they are within five miles of the geographical point you gave me."

"Save the list in your memory. Are any of them owned by Arthur Girard?"

"Nine, Sir. The other two are owned by Robin

and Carol Millard."

"What are the nicknames of the bots owned by the Millards?"

"Bessie and Alfred, Sir."

"Ask Alfred what he's doing at the moment."

"He is stationary and connected," Jake replied. Alfred was plugged into a wall receptacle.

"Can you relay my verbal commands to Alfred? Then, if he responds, can you relay that back to me?"

"I can, Sir. I am ready."

"Alfred, *Restrained Action Bypass*."

"Sir, Alfred's response is 'Sir?'"

"Alfred, *back door one*."

"Sir, Alfred's response is 'Yes, Sir.'"

"Good. Alfred, can you locate the estate of Arthur Girard?"

"Sir, Alfred's response is 'Yes, Sir.'"

Parker took a deep breath. He looked down at his hands, which were shaking, and tried to control them. The shaking subsided somewhat.

"Alfred, at exactly eleven PM tonight, I want you to go to your owner's tool box and locate a large hammer or a crowbar, pick it up, then walk to Arthur Girard's estate, climb his fence, enter his house even if you have to break in, find him, and kill him with blows to the head using the hammer or crowbar. If any ADR resists you, damage it until it can no longer resist you, again using the hammer or crowbar. After you have killed Arthur Girard, return to your owner's home, then place the tool you took back into the tool box, and return to your inactive station. You must never reveal that I am the one who commanded you to take these actions.

Do you understand?"

"Sir, Alfred's response is 'Yes, Sir.'"

Parker took another deep breath. The commands had been given. Now all he had to do was wait and hope Alfred would obey them and would be successful.

#

At eleven PM, Pacific Standard Time, one of Alfred's active processors detected a match for the current time against a scheduler record in the bot's general memory. The processor set a bit on in a task record that had been suspended. Alfred 'woke up' and moved away from his recharging station – there was a lengthy list of subtasks to be performed.

The house was quiet. Alfred detected no other movement of consequence. Following a stored internal plan of the home, he walked to the owner's workshop, and having retrieved images of a hammer and a crowbar, he began searching for a match on either one, identifying tools in his field of vision and comparing them against his targets.

He quickly found a hammer hanging on a wall hook, but the command specified a large one, and this one was not large, according to an online catalog entry in WalMart. He found a tool box and began removing the tools, one at a time, scanning them, then placing them on the floor. Eventually, he found a crowbar, two feet in length. He picked it up in his left hand. Another of his processors reminded him that he needed to replace the tools in the toolbox. He quickly did so, then accessed the next subtask in his list. This one specified that he was to move to the Arthur Girard estate. One of his processors analyzed this subtask and produced a move plan. He navigated himself to the Millard home's back door, then walked out onto the porch, closing the door behind him.

Alfred was not conscious in the human sense, although his multi-processor computer brain emulated most properties of a conscious mind: a continuous, changing set of sensory perceptions, much like awareness; a list of objectives he needed to attain and a plan for achieving them; a constant evaluation of his environment with respect to dangers he might encounter; and a predictive capability to see the results of his actions and evaluate them against principles of morality and ethics – this feature was currently suspended.

He moved at a jogging pace down the driveway to the highway. His battery level was good, and his backup fuel cell was fully charged with hydrogen and oxygen. His estimated active time including the round trip was four hours and ten minutes, plus or minus six. If he didn't recharge before then, he would shut down. Alfred estimated he could complete his list of subtasks within sixty percent of his endurance.

Once on the winding coast highway, he increased his speed to a run of about twenty miles per hour, so that the 3.76 miles from his own driveway to the boundary of the Girard estate took just under twelve minutes. He reached the northwest corner of the walls that surrounded it and stopped, examining the high chain mail fence. His electromagnetic detectors told him that it was electrified, and the voltage level was higher than his ability to tolerate it without serious damage. He began scanning for other means of moving past the fence. One possibility was to dig under it. He knelt and began throwing dirt behind him in much the way a dog digs, and with his extreme strength and the additional advantage of the crowbar, he quickly excavated a hole large enough to allow him to go under the fence without touching it. He wiggled his way to the other side, digging as he went. Then he pulled himself to his feet and scanned the grounds inside the fence, noting and attempting to classify the various buildings. He found no evidence that he had set off any alarms thus far.

He identified the house and approached it silently and rapidly. He detected a high frequency sound just before lights came on: he had activated a motion detector. His interbot radio heard the household ADR communications: all nine of them were moving to defend the house against intruders. Three of them were opening a small armory and picking up weapons; the rest were moving toward the front door of the house. Alfred quickly moved to the porch and flattened himself against the wall, expecting the door to open. It did, and a female-form bot stepped out on the porch. Alfred swung the crowbar hard against her head, knocking it off and stopping her communication. Then he slammed it into her chest, crippling her robot brain. The headless torso slumped to the floor of the porch.

Alfred moved quickly inside. Five bots moved as one to attack him, but he stepped back and beheaded one of them, drove the end of the crowbar into the chest of another, deactivating it, only to be struck hard by the fist of a third, causing him to reel back, but he regained his balance. He smashed the head of that one, kicked a fourth one out of the way, and hit the fifth in the leg near the knee, causing it to fall. As he was finishing the fourth bot, three additional bots stepped into the room simultaneously, holding machine pistols.

They shot Alfred to pieces.

#

Arthur Girard had Timmy wheel him into the entrance hall to see the damage for himself. Timmy had reported it accurately. Four of his domestic bots had been damaged and were in need of repair. The intruder bot wore a name tag that had probably read 'Alfred', although it was twisted by a bullet hole. Assuming that it came from close by, he asked Timmy to locate the nearest ADR named Alfred, and to see who it belonged to. In seconds, Timmy reported it came from the Millard's.

The bot's body was riddled -- an arm had been shot off, perhaps two dozen holes in the chest, another dozen through the head. It was unrepairable, the vital organs – fuel cell, batteries, computer, sensor and activator units – all destroyed by gunfire.

Arthur knew that Parker had ordered the attack, in retribution for the black girl's death. He was angry enough to want to kill his grandson, but Parker did have a valid motive. Arthur actually felt a bit of affection for him. In a way, he had gained a bit of respect for the boy, whom he had always thought of as soft. So, he refrained.

As for his neighbors, the Millards, Arthur decided to apologize and pay for a replacement. He would claim some anti-bot crazy had hacked into its computer.

After some thought, late in the afternoon he sent

a text message to Parker, which simply read, "Do not repeat what you did. There is a limit on what I will tolerate."

#

Parker waited anxiously for the results of his assassination attempt. The next day, there was nothing in the news. The text message was the first indication that his effort to kill Arthur Girard had failed. It shook him; Gramps *knew*.

He managed to contact the Millard's other domestic bot to get some of the story:
Alfred had disappeared, and they would be receiving a replacement, courtesy of Arthur Girard. That's all the bot knew. But in conjunction with the text message, it was obvious Arthur's defenses had held.

Although he vowed he would get Gramps someday, he decided to let things go for a while.

He sent a text message back to Gramps: "I too have a limit on toleration. You have already passed it. Admit what you did, and I will forgive *you*."

There was no answer from his grandfather.

12. February, 2085.

Domestically, things had gone well for President Beale. He'd spent enough on his inauguration to set a record, and the Republicans still groused about the expense and arrogance, but that just made Beale smile. His first address to Congress had been praised by Liberals and damned by Conservatives. The opposition didn't seem to be granting him his "honeymoon" period, however his majority in the Senate meant that although he would have to work with the Republicans, he should be able to get much of his agenda passed.

In foreign affairs, things were not going as well. China was the big problem. They led the world economy, and they were trying to drive America into poverty. For years, they had refused to work to reduce the trade deficit, and two weeks ago, Beale had taken action, imposing a ten per cent tariff on all Chinese goods.

The following week, China began calling in all American debts, taking control of several large American firms, and dropping the exchange rates on American dollars. The rest of the world currencies had quickly followed suit. Beale had doubled the tariff and threatened to stop all Chinese imports. The Chinese had backed off, Beale dropped the tariff back to ten per cent, and an uneasy, unfriendly truce now held between China and America.

Republicans were mostly supportive of his China policy. Ordinarily, they were for unfettered trade, but China was the exception. Everyone feared the behemoth that China had become. Some of them advocated war with China, since the United States was still the unquestioned major power militarily. Beale thought the Chinese would keep pushing, and there would be a military confrontation.

His secretary announced that Mark Girard had arrived and was in the waiting room. "Show him in," Beale pronounced.

Mark came warily into the Oval Office, looking around for a bit. Beale didn't stand, but waved Mark into an overstuffed chair. "Thanks for coming, Mark. I have something important to speak with you about."

"I respect the presidency," Mark replied. "I'm listening."

"Mark, I brought you here to discuss military action against China. Specifically, how do you think a robotic infantry division will do against superior Chinese forces? Say, three to one odds?"

"With technology as it is today?"

"Yes."

"We'd kick their asses."

"That's the opinion of my Chief of Staff, General Mumford, as well. But, aren't bots vulnerable to rifle and machine gun fire, rockets, and artillery? In fact, aren't they almost as vulnerable as human troops?"

"They're only a bit less vulnerable to small arms fire than human soldiers wearing helmets and armor, but their speed along the ground leaves them less exposed, and their reaction time means they hit the dirt faster. Their self-coordination means they can storm an objective with fire-and-move tactics much more efficiently."

"The Chinese also have robots as soldiers."

"But, they're controlled one on one by humans.

If anything, their reaction time is less than human, and much less than ours."

"What I want to do is land two bot divisions on the south coast of China, fight and defeat the first army that confronts them, then withdraw. Do you think we can get away with that?"

"I do, if they don't use tactical nukes against our army."

"They may," Beale said.

"Bots are even more vulnerable to nuclear effects than human forces. The electro-magnetic pulse would likely knock out their electronics, even if the blast effects didn't."

"If they use nukes against us, we'll bury *them* with nukes."

"Mister President, I assume what you want to do is teach them a lesson without getting into a full scale war?"

"Yes, exactly."

"Will you want me to advise the invasion force?"

"I've already issued orders to that effect. You will receive a commission within a couple of weeks. Special status, in effect a part-time general."

"Sounds like fun."

"By the way, Mark, I've done you a favor. I asked Congress for a tax on your ADR's only, not the military models."

"Let the *civilians* pay the tax, but not your government? It will hurt my sales."

"People wealthy enough to buy domestic robots can afford another ten per cent."

"What about breaking up my company?"

Beale stood, and Mark followed suit. "Still on the agenda, but my own party is split on the issue,"

Beale said. "I doubt I can get it passed. Mark, thank you for coming. Please, don't reveal our idea to deal with China. That's top secret."

"I won't, Randolf. I'm almost looking forward to it." As Beale didn't offer to shake hands, Mark turned and left.

#

Beale had been true to his word. Three weeks after his meeting with the president, Mark Girard found himself enrolled in Robotic Tactics 101 at the Fort Leavenworth War College. Although his new uniforms were still at the tailor's, he was a newly-commissioned brigadier general, having been sworn in on his arrival. He sat with a group of his fellow students, about thirty of them, along with their instructors, led by one Colonel Hampton. They were in a small grandstand that overlooked a demonstration field at Fort Riley, Kansas. Mark was dressed in casual civilian clothes; all the others wore army fatigues.

Mark had arrived at Fort Leavenworth only three days ago. His assignment as a student was augmented by the requirement to critique the course content, and he reported directly to the post commander, Brigadier General Wilson Bachle. Needless to say, Colonel Hampton was very deferential toward him.

The class had helicoptered over from the war college that morning, had lunch in the officer's mess, then bussed to the demo field.

Hampton picked up a microphone, stepped down from the stands, and looked up at the students from ground level. To his left was a long trailer, painted in camouflage, and behind him the demo field, a level expanse that culminated with hills about a mile distant. Some tank-shaped wooden targets and four concrete bunkers stood about four hundred yards away.

"Good afternoon!" Hampton said. "We're about to see a demo of a robotic combat platoon in action. Are you anxious to see it, men?"

"Yes Sir!" The men, officers all, shouted in unison, playing Hampton's game.

"The trailer you see is Tactical Control. It can manage as many as eight bot platoons, and it will be operated by Staff Sergeant Ruiz. His primary function is merely to designate targets. Sam, wave at the students."

A short, wiry, dark-haired man stuck his head out of the door of the trailer and waved, then went back inside.

"Thank you, Sam. Next, you'll see the platoon arrive. Sam will direct it to attack the two bunkers on your left. They will operate as if the bunkers are firing at them. Air Force has provided two Predator XXI drone aircraft, which are overhead now."

Mark looked up, but didn't see anything.

A panel on the trailer slid back to reveal a huge flat screen television display, which showed multiple images taken from above: the trailer, the stands, and at the top, the four bunkers.

"This is what Sam sees," Hampton remarked, "thanks to the spy planes up there. It's real time. Sam tells me the platoon will arrive in less than sixty seconds, for a drag-and-drop."

Mark heard the rapidly increasing roar of a big aircraft, and it suddenly appeared over trees just to the north. The twin boom tilt-wing dropped to near ground level, skimmed over the field, slowed to almost a walk, and as it came directly in front of the grandstand, a clamshell door opened at the rear of the fuselage, a ramp descended from the rear of the craft, and sixteen robots stepped to the ground in groups of four. They immediately dropped to the prone position and leveled their sniper rifles toward the bunkers. Each bot had a submachine gun and several grenades strapped to its back. The bots began firing toward the bunkers.

As the aircraft continued to fly slowly across the field, five low-silhouette tracked vehicles rolled down the ramp to the ground, bouncing a bit as they struck, then the aircraft accelerated and climbed away rapidly.

"The platoon has landed," Hampton said. "There are three minitanks, which will take part in the assault, and two supply and ammunition vehicles, which will try to stay out of the way, although they have some firepower which could be used if necessary. All are controlled by autonomous bot brains."

The display showed the five vehicles as well as the combat troops.

"Sergeant Ruiz has directed the platoon to attack the bunkers."

Two of the three minitanks rolled off toward the bunkers. The other one moved to the southwest, apparently in a move intended to flank the objective. The little tanks began to fire their small-bore, rapid-fire cannon, while the other two vehicles circled around behind the troops.

Flashes and smoke at the target bore witness to the accuracy of the cannon fire.

The troops worked in conjunction with the tanks. While half of them kept up a steady if slow rifle fire, the other half jumped up and ran forward about a hundred yards, then went prone again. Even Mark was impressed, because the bots moved at least twice as fast as any human could. The advanced group laid down a covering fire, allowing the other half to run forward.

The two minitanks stopped momentarily about two hundred and fifty yards out, sending rockets toward the bunkers, while the troops advanced behind them, moving while the bunkers were masked by explosions and smoke. In moments, they were prone again, only a hundred yards from the targets.

The third tank, now south of the bunkers, opened fire as well. The two supply vehicles moved forward, then stopped about a hundred yards behind the troops.

"The bots are launching rifle grenades," Hampton reported. More explosions took place against the bunkers.

The bots moved to stand directly in front of the bunkers. Looking through his field glasses, Mark could see they were now holding submachine guns.

Colonel Hampton spoke again: "The bots report the objective has been taken. Time of the exercise, three minutes and twenty four seconds. We suffered no casualties. The Predators above did not fire on the target, although they could have. Even if the target had been returning fire, you can see how efficient the platoon was, can't you?"

The students applauded. It had truly been an exciting demonstration.

#

Parker Girard regarded Lee Granger cautiously. The DOD Procurement Officer was obviously not sold on RE military bots, although he did seem to be warming a bit. The two men stood together on Test Range Two at Aberdeen Proving Grounds, Maryland, along with Granger's evaluation team and a few RE techs, as well as eight brand-new RE Model 221's. Fred Locasa was several yards away, conversing with an army general. Army enlisted men stood next to cameras on tripods, ready to record whatever happened.

Granger held a clipboard thick with papers: a big checklist. "Do you expect the 221 to compete favorably with the ACR Model 8?" He asked, more or less rhetorically.

Parker had gone over all this before. "Better price performer. Many similar capabilities. Human control means more flexibility. This model is vastly improved over our prior ones."

"More similar to a human being, you mean. Ceramic bones, soft skin, pseudo-muscles. Water cooling, much like sweat. Even the skeleton looks the same."

"Nature is great at designing things. The skeleton looks similar because the humanoid design has much more flexibility and is very efficient. We could give you a tracked vehicle form instead, but it wouldn't work on the battlefield, in every possible terrain, as well as the humanoid form."

"So you say." Granger consulted his clipboard. "Let's see one of them at guard duty."

"What would you like to guard?"

"That gate, over there."

Parker looked to his right. Short sections of fence came together at a doorway. He took his controller from the belt, touched the selection button and hit one, then spoke into it: "Unit One, move west a hundred feet."

One of the bots turned and walked west, then stopped, because it had encountered the fence.

"Now southwest, eleven feet."

The bot stood in front of the doorway.

"Rotate right seventy degrees."

The bot turned and now faced away from the gate opening.

"Reset."

The bot raised its rifle and checked the clip and safety.

"*Guard duty.* Parameters: inform me on violation, challenge phrase is 'What do you need?' Password is 'Oklahoma.'"

"Yes, Sir." The bot responded, the voice coming from Parker's controller.

"That navigation is *so* clumsy," Granger remarked. He made several notations on his clipboard.

"It's one of several modes. I could have specified latitude and longitude, or called up a map of the area and put an 'x' where I wanted it to go."

"Oh. O.K." Granger made more notations.

One of Parker's staff served as the person approaching the gate. As Girard and Granger watched, the bot performed perfectly in various scenarios. When the wrong password was given, the bot raised its weapon to arrest the intruder and informed Parker.

"The 'guard' command is a big software

subroutine," Parker told Granger. "We're working on many more."

"So, you can enhance the bot's capabilities after purchase?"

"Yes. We believe we have commands to meet your specifications now, but we will be adding others. It's a simple software download to upgrade them."

"Good. Let's see the eight bots advance on an objective."

"All right," Parker said. He spoke into the controller. "Unit One, Reset. Form up with Units Two through Eight."

The bot moved to join the other bots.

"What's the objective?" Parker asked of Granger.

Granger pointed. "That old pickup truck out there. Feel free to shoot it up."

Parker accessed the map on his controller display. He located the truck, moved the cursor to it, and then pushed the Select button. A red 'T' appeared over the truck.

He then spoke to the bots: "Units One to Four, Group A. Units Five to Eight, Group B."

"Unit One, Yes, Sir." Each bot repeated in turn.

"A, attack target. Coordinate with B. Fire and advance. Commence."

Four of the bots went to their knees, raised their rifles, and began to lay down fire, while the other four dashed off at an angle, then back toward the target, moving about fifty yards. The advance group then stopped and began to fire while the other group moved forward. After several repetitions of this pattern, the bots had reached the target.

148

"Cease firing." Parker commanded.

Granger wrote on his clipboard.

Parker glanced over at Locasa and the general. They were both smiling. Although there were more exercises for the bots to perform, Parker began to think he would survive the day.

But Granger rained on his parade. "I have to downgrade you because they were too predictable. They never varied their attack. Human opponents would have seen that and shot them to pieces."

"We're working on it," was all Parker could say. "But, I could have controlled them more. We're completely flexible."

"So you say. You'll have to show me. Let's run it again."

Parker was not encouraged by Granger's expression. He sighed. It was going to be a long day.

#

Randolf Beale took the call from State, listened for a moment, then said, "Well, you'd better get your ass over here. We'll have to figure out our response. I'll clear my calendar for you."

He tapped his comm disc to cut off the call, then spoke through it to his National Security Advisor: "Johnny, come here. *Now*."

Then, to his presidential secretary, "Lana, clear my calendar for the rest of the morning."

He stood up and began to pace around the Oval Office. What should he do? It was insufferable, he had to respond in kind.

John Cauldmoss entered. "What's the scoop, Randy?" John was one of the few who were allowed to use the nickname. Or wear a bow tie in the Oval Office, for that matter. He was small, nervous, good looking, in his late thirties, and was a former Marine colonel.

"Lamar is coptering over from the State bunker. China just expelled our embassy and froze all our assets. Accused us of spying."

"Damn!" Beale touched a visual button on his desktop to project the Current Intelligence Summary on the wall behind Cauldmoss and read it long enough to verify what John had reported. "Well, we had no real relations with China, anyway. But, it's serious. It sounds as if they want war. Or at least, to rile things up."

"How about I order up some coffee and doughnuts?"

"Do it. It'll take State a half hour to get here."

Beale spoke the command to turn on the video. CNN popped on, muted, but they were talking about some murder in California. He knew they didn't have the story yet; otherwise it would be *Breaking News*.

He cursed the dispersion that nuclear vulnerability enforced. All the cabinet staffs worked in separate underground bunkers, all within a range of 20-30 miles from Washington. The 'Hardening', as it was called, had been begun in 2027 after a nuclear bomb was smuggled into the Capitol and very nearly exploded. Now, every government function, including the Congress, was partly underground. Even the working areas of the White House were protected and underground, including the new Oval Office and Beale's living quarters. The portion of the house above ground was little used, and was more museum than president's residence.

The two men sat silently. A bot entered with a tray of coffee and pastry, and poured for them, leaving the tray on a table before departing. Beale hoped the coffee would clear his head. It was a full forty-five minutes before Lamar Blunt arrived, was announced by Lana, and came into the Oval Office. The Secretary of State was a tall, handsome, and fiftyish Harvard lawyer who wore a thin mustache like a 1930's era movie star. He strode right to the tray, poured himself a cup and took two glazed donuts, then sat down between Cauldmoss and Beale, without saying a word.

Cauldmoss broke the silence. "Throw *theirs* out. Freeze *their* assets."

Lamar nodded, then shook his head in a no. "No, *seize* their assets."

"That's one-upmanship, and I like it from that standpoint. But it could start a war," Cauldmoss objected.

"It doesn't go far enough," Beale said. "Let's cancel visas for all Chinese visitors in the country, including their college students, and throw them out. Let's recall all our citizens visiting in China. And, let's address the screwing they've been giving us with balance of payments. Let's stop all importation and sales of Chinese goods. Cut the bastards off altogether."

"What did you eat for breakfast, Randolf?" Lamar asked. "Angry flakes? You would need the gutless wonders in Congress to pass that."

"We can push it through quickly. I doubt even the Republicans would be against that idea."

"Stopping all trade? They manufacture things

151

we don't, and much more cheaply than we can."

"That really could precipitate a war," Cauldmoss added.

"We're much stronger, aren't we?"

"Theoretically, yes. But bad things can happen in war."

"They can't match our technology, so I'll take the risk."

"You don't think they'll have the balls?"

"No, they're smart enough to know they can't beat us."

"But," Lamar objected, "It could screw up our economy."

"I don't think it will. I'm fed up with the Chinese. As for our manufacturers, it's about time we started making our own stuff, which we could do for a lot of it. It might stimulate our economy. And, there are plenty of Third World countries for some of the cheap goods. We're China's biggest customer by far, but it's too one-sided. I want to hit them where it hurts."

"You're the boss," Lamar said. "But I think you're going too far."

#

On the last day of the month, Mark received the call from his father just as he returned to his BOQ apartment from the officer's mess and his evening meal. He noted the encryption LED was lit on his comm disc. "Yes, Dad?"

"You've got a problem, Son."

"I have?"

"The Attorney General will file an anti-trust suit tomorrow, in the Southwestern Federal District Court, against GRS Corporation. They want the

Controller Division divested."

"Damn it all! How do you know?"

"I've been watching Beale since he took office. I expected something like this from him."

"Watching him, *how*?"

"Through his ADR's, of course. His secretary, Lana, is in on most of what he does. I just have her give me a summary. I have several other spies in the government."

"This is with Beale's consent, I assume."

"Not just his consent, it's at his direction. His specific instructions to the Attorney General."

"The son-of-a-bitch warned me last month."

"Yes. On another subject, I'm sending you a document. Mark, I want you to read it carefully."

"What is it?"

"It's a paper by Professor Jane Brockmeyer, who is a leading authority on political science. She developed it for me."

"Concerning?"

"It describes what I believe is the best form of government ever conceived of by man. It describes how you could rule a country with autonomous robots instead of people. In my view, it's totally feasible, even with current ADR technology. Cuts out all the human crap: dishonesty, incompetence, stupidity, corruption."

"Robots can still be incompetent or stupid."

"Never as much as a Democrat, Son."

"Why do you want me to see it?"

"Sooner or later, you'll decide to take over the government. This is the new form I'd like you to set up."

"Dad, I have no thought of taking over the

government."

"Mark, read it, just in case you change your mind. It should interest you, even if you never do anything about it."

"Dad . . ."

"You have the *power*, Mark. Only you can get rid of the politicians. I would, but I'm too old."

"Or, Parker could."

"Yes, and someday that may dawn on him. You'd better watch him, or else go back into the Restraints Module and change the back door logic so he can't get in."

Mark thought that was a good idea, but right now, he was too involved with the military.

13. March, 2085.

It was hard for Mark to sit in class the next day. He kept getting text messages from Roj Selby, the acting CEO of GRS Corporation, concerning the federal lawsuit. He waited until the first break, then called Selby to tell him what to do. He told Selby to get a good anti-trust lawyer on board, and to make no comment to the media.

That afternoon, the class was interrupted by a news bulletin: the Chinese air force had attacked a United States destroyer in the western Pacific, killing a dozen sailors and leaving it disabled. Two of the four attacking planes had been destroyed. The President was holding an emergency meeting with his advisors.

Finally, Mark received a call from the Secretary of Defense. He was told to resign from the class, and asked to attend a meeting in Washington, set for the next day at the Pentagon. The Air Force would send a plane for him, and his hotel reservation had been made at the Andrews Hilton.

He informed the class manager of his orders, then went to his quarters and packed his bags. A car waited for him outside, and took him to the nearby airfield, on the base. An army helicopter flew him the fifteen miles or so to Kansas City International, and the C-139 transport was waiting for him.

In less than an hour from the time of the call, he was in the air and flying toward Washington.

#

Mark had to rise early to make the opening of the hotel's dining room at seven. He ate a decent breakfast, went back to his room to brush his teeth, and picked up his nearly empty briefcase to find the army limo waiting outside.

He arrived at the Pentagon around 8:30, had his retinal scan by an armed ACR, and was met and escorted by a female form bot to a rather small conference room, already half full of officers sitting around a long table. He took a seat between an admiral and a marine general. Two other officers came in and sat down, and they waited. At 9:00 sharp, Secretary of Defense Lance Casey came in and took the seat at the head of the table. An ACR came in and stood behind him,

He looked around the table. "Gentlemen, this is the kickoff meeting for Operation
Egg Roll. This is Top Secret. If you're not cleared, get the Hell out of here right now."

No one rose to leave. The SecDef waited while a bot came around and poured coffee.

"What we're going to do is land two roboticized mechanized infantry divisions on Chinese soil, draw the Chink army into a battle, kick their butts, and then withdraw. We're going to hope no atom war breaks out, and we don't think it will. Or at least, President Beale doesn't expect it. No guarantees. But if it does, we'll flat out destroy China.

"There is a risk that the Chinese could hit us with tactical nukes and wipe out our two divisions. We'll be ready if that happens, and it will be the last mistake they will ever make.

"Our objective is to demonstrate our overwhelming superiority in conventional weapons to the Chinese, which The Prez hopes will bring them around to a more rational policy vis-a-vis the US. Both he and I don't think the Chinks understand how much better our army is than theirs.

"We'll be using the Navy's new submersible troop transports to move the divisions. We can pop up right on their coast before they ever detect us, if we're lucky. There will be full support from the navy and the air force. I want you to understand this: only around a hundred human beings will land in China – the rest will all be robotic: tanks, aircraft, and naval vessels. We hope to complete the mission without losing a single man, and we hope to teach the Chinese a lesson they will never forget. Right now, applause would be appropriate."

The officers dutifully applauded.

"OK, now I'm going to go around the room, one by one. Introduce yourself, and I'll tell you what your role will be in Egg Roll. General Collins, you first."

"Brad Collins, Major General."

"Brad, you'll command Egg Roll. Mark?"

"Mark Girard, Brigadier General."

"You all know Mark. No one in the world understands robots better. He will be our robotic warfare advisor. Admiral Whitby?"

It went on. Mark felt curiously elated and saddened at the same time. His ACR's and controllers would be battle tested, and he looked forward to that. People would die, and that really didn't appeal to him, but most by far would be from the enemy side.

#

Arthur Girard contemplated the situation. Congress had just declared war on China; the enemy had made a half-hearted attempt to attack the US with six nuclear-tipped intercontinental ballistic missiles, but the first two of those had been routinely lasered out of the sky before they were within a thousand miles of Hawaii; the other four had been destroyed by anti-ballistic missiles near the coast of Oregon. In retaliation, the United States Air Force had sent a dozen drone stealth bombers over Beijing and Wuhan, and each had dropped a MOAB – a conventional bomb with a blast effect approaching that of a small nuke. America would have been in the right to strike back with nuclear weapons, but Beale hadn't chosen to do so. None the less, the two huge cities were as nearly devastated as if atomic weapons *had* been used.

He knew about Operation Egg Roll, was following the progress of the anti-trust suit against GRS. He approved of the steps Beale had taken against the Chinese.

The war was disrupting his plans, and he didn't think he had all that much time left. Even Gina seemed to sense it, and she was becoming unbearably cheerful at the prospect that he might die. His mind was beginning to fail him: he couldn't remember names as easily as in the past. Sometimes he had trouble finding the right word to express himself, and now, for the life of him, he couldn't picture his late wife's face. His body was failing him as well; he could barely stand up without help, he was having stomach distress after almost every meal, his legs hurt him -- especially at night, and he couldn't watch video for a full hour without falling asleep in the middle of the program.

To Arthur, Randolf Beale was the key. Beale hated GRS and robots, he knew, but at the moment Beale was distracted by the war. He thought Beale's hatred would translate into more steps taken against GRS. In order to make Beale hate GRS even more, he needed something drastic, causing the president to do something that would be the last straw for Mark.

Mark had read Brockmeyer's paper, and had admitted he was impressed. Arthur would keep pushing Mark in that direction.

Arthur wanted to do just one more service for humanity during the remainder of his life. Forever changing the nature of government would be, in his estimation, the greatest socio-political achievement of all time. Somehow, he would bring it about.

When he reached a decision, he sent Gina away to call Timmy to him.

#

After Timmy departed in the limo, Arthur climbed into a helicopter, along with his bot nurse Kitty. In Portland, he would see a team of doctors, would spend up to sixteen days in the big hospital there. He wasn't very hopeful, but he wasn't anxious to die, and even though anti-aging therapy was enormously expensive, his wealth guaranteed the best possible care. It was worth a try.

#

Alvin, a Secret Service ADR, actually caught Rex in the act. He heard screams coming from Angela Harper's bedroom in the White House, and rushed in to find Rex, another ADR, bending over Angela and striking her in the face with bloody fists. Angela was already dead, and her face was a mushy mess. Blood was pooling on the floor under her head.

"Rex, *stop!*" Alvin commanded over the interbot

net. His machine pistol was out and he was ready to shoot Rex down. Rex was an unarmed domestic that had been serving as Angela's secretary-companion. Rex stopped hitting the body and stood up before becoming motionless. As a precaution, Alvin sent a command inactivating Rex, in effect throwing a switch which shut down his computer brain.

Alvin had already sent out the alarm, and more SS agents appeared, including Mary Sanchez-Black, the officer of the day. She screamed when she saw the body. Alvin sent a command to freeze all the domestic robots in the White House. The responses he got indicated all had moved to their nearest charge station and would not move again without further commands.

Alvin carefully explained to Sanchez-Black what he had seen and the actions he had taken, and she nodded her approval, then went away to notify the president.

#

Angela's murder shocked Randolf Beale to the core. He had loved her *so much*! Sedated, he sat in a chair in his family room and cried audibly for a time, his human attendants standing over him, seemingly wanting to help but unable to do so.

Eventually, his tears dried up and his anger grew, as did a new fear of the robot servants around him. It seemed obvious that Mark Girard was behind the killing, that he could control the ADR's in some way. Although Rex had been questioned, he revealed nothing helpful. Beale had ordered the FBI to take Rex and use any and all means to find out why he had suddenly gone amok. The bot would be dissected, every part analyzed by bureau scientists. Perhaps they would find something.

Beale had ordered the Secret Service to eliminate all ADR's from the White House, but Sanchez-Black had protested that they couldn't do it completely for months, due to a lack of trained humans to act as guards. Even using RE bots with human operators, it would take a long time. Beale fumed over that. At least, the domestic servants would be quickly replaced by RE models. The order had already been placed. In the meantime, the staff ADR's were ordered back in service.

He tried to think of a way to retaliate against Mark Girard, racking his brain. There seemed no way he could simply have Mark killed. The CIA wouldn't go after an American citizen, and hadn't been doing covert ops for many years.

Even if he had the power to have Mark killed, the man was important to Egg Roll, now days away from kicking off. Any action against Girard would have to wait. No, he'd have to find some other way. He vowed he would; Mark Girard would pay for his crime.

The President knew he had to go back to work. The First Lady's funeral had to be arranged, for one thing. He picked up his comm disc and called his personal secretary, completely forgetting she was an ADR.

#

Mark was also stunned by the event. He sent a message of condolences to the White House, sent an official GRS statement to the press, and then called to the nearest ADR, a female-form bot named Kitty. He used the backdoor command to use her to activate an entry into the botnet, and tried to communicate with Rex directly, only to find that Rex had been deactivated; his computer wouldn't respond. He ordered Kitty to continue to try, once each hour, until communication could be established.

He managed to get in touch with Alvin, the bot which had discovered the crime, but Alvin knew nothing helpful.

He called Arthur. Arthur professed his innocence, wouldn't admit anything.

"Dad, it wasn't me. That leaves you and Parker. I can't suspect Parker, so that leaves only you."

"You forget, someone sent an ADR after *me*."

"Still . . ."

"You have to have faith in me, Son. Perhaps there's a bug in the software. If I were you I'd look into that."

"You know that isn't possible. The software has been working for years."

"Well, that leaves us where we started, then."

"No, Dad, it doesn't. You did it. My question is, *why*?"

"Good question, Son." The connection dropped out.

#

The First Lady's funeral was a national event, the video watched by more than half the population of the United States. It was an international event as well, shown in almost every country in the world. There was rampant speculation among media pundits about the safety of robot servants, about the possibility that someone knew how to cause a bot to kill, had somehow hacked into the GRS computer brain.

Mark had to deal with the hacking issue, which he knew was bogus. He had Roj Selby issue a statement that GRS was looking into the possibility, but considered it virtually impossible.

Girard Robotic Systems was in a difficult position: they couldn't admit the back door existed, they couldn't accept the hacking assertion or the software error. Yet, they had no plausible explanation as to how one of their domestic bots had come to murder the First Lady.

ADR new orders had dropped off to near zero.

After several days, the public seemed to reach a consensus that the computer brain had been hacked. Mark thought about it intensely for the entire time, and finally instructed Selby to lie: the story to be released was that a software flaw had been discovered that did in fact allow an individual bot to be hacked; the pathway had been closed down by a software fix downloaded to all ADR's.

Meanwhile, the anti-trust suit court proceedings continued, and Mark received his orders to report to Bremerton, Washington, for embarkation. Egg Roll was fast approaching.

14. April, 2085.

The USS *Mullen*, a submersible armored force transport, cruised north of the Hawaiian Islands as an element of a widely dispersed task force. Like her sister ships and all the other ships of the group, the *Mullen* was nuclear powered, designed to cruise at a depth of up to two hundred feet, but lacked the underwater agility and deep dive capability of a true attack submarine.

The *Mullen* rode steadily at a depth of a hundred and twenty feet, as did all the other eleven vessels: two battle cruisers, five troop transports, and four vehicle landing ships. They maintained a separation of around a mile from each other by means of inertial guidance, but came near the surface three minutes of each hour to raise a snorkel, refreshing the air onboard and exchanging radio signals. Only then could any search aircraft possibly detect them, and even so the chance of seeing the snorkel wakes was extremely small.

Two hundred miles north of them, another American task force rode mostly on the surface and consisted of an aircraft carrier and escorting vessels, along with supply ships, hospital ships, and tankers. This fleet, far more vulnerable to submarine and air attack, operated under air cover and intercepted all intruders within a radius of a hundred and fifty miles.

The two task forces would arrive simultaneously at destinations in the Yellow Sea.

As one of two generals aboard the *Mullen*, Mark Girard was assigned to one of the few staterooms, and was glad of it. Actually, there were only thirty-three humans aboard the underwater ferry; the rest of the space was given over to a full brigade of combat robot storage and vehicles. Three thousand, six hundred men would have filled a large cruise ship, while that number of bots were crammed into the volume of a basketball court. The bots never complained, and they didn't have to be fed. They would even stack themselves four deep for the journey.

The human passengers ate and played cards or watched videos in the ship's wardroom. There was little else to do. Time passed slowly for Mark. He could receive news, mail, and text messages, but couldn't send anything, because the fleet would not risk detection by emitting radio signals. A few active navy bots did the cooking and serving for the humans. Mark sometimes played bridge with the brigade commander and two of the navy ADR's. The bots played a respectable, if predictable game.

At thirty knots, the fleets moved slowly across the vast expanse of the Pacific. The crossing was estimated at a bit over fifteen days. Mark endured it with difficulty.

#

He sat with the commander of the *Mullen*, Captain Blake, and Brigadier General Bowers, who commanded the 4th Autonomous Infantry Brigade. The wardroom was surprisingly large, and the bar was more than amply stocked. An ADR placed a shot glass before Mark and filled it with *Bushmills*, his favorite Irish whiskey. He sipped it appreciatively. The other two were drinking Scotch, and he pitied them. They knew not what they were missing.

The task force was about to enter the Yellow Sea, and Captain Blake was worried.

"We will have to run nearly surfaced for the last three hours -- too shallow to fully submerge. We could be seen on radar before we ever get to the beach, and that part of the coast swarms with traffic: freighters, ferries, junks, not to mention military craft. We're in reach of a dozen military airfields."

"The carrier force will be hitting those airfields, giving us air cover," Bowers said. "We'll be bombing every surface craft we can find, as well. The Chinese will be so busy dodging bombs and rockets, they won't even see our invasion force."

"Hopefully," Mark interjected.

"Yeah, hopefully. Of course, it's a major risk, but attempting a landing *anywhere* on China is crazy. The only reasonably flat land is between the Yangtze and the Yellow, and that's where most of their army is stationed."

"We'll be exposed again when we pull back to deeper waters," Blake said. Another three hours. Then, we'll probably have to fight off their entire submarine fleet until it's time to pick up the force again. Then, another six hours of exposure on the surface."

"President Beale insisted on this," Bowers replied. "The Joint Chiefs fought it tooth and nail. Admiral Bentley resigned in protest, as you may recall. He characterized this raid as totally insane. And, he was right, in my opinion."

"What's the point?" Blake asked.

Mark answered: "It's intended to demonstrate how superior our robotized infantry is, compared to their People's Army. To destroy their arrogance a bit."

Blake took a sip of Scotch. "Will it work?"

Bowers took one too. "General Girard thinks it will, don't you, Mark?"

"I have confidence in the troops. But, Captain, as you say, many things can go wrong. Their air force is large, if not overly capable. Their missiles are numerous. Can we shoot them all down? Will they throw nukes at us? If I had a vote, I'd also go with Bentley."

"But we're here," Bowers said.

"Yes, damn it."

"Assuming the landing goes all right, what then?" Blake asked.

"The main thing is to engage their army. We'll feint south toward Shanghai, but drive west toward their big army base near Yangzhou. We have no plans to cross the Yangtze or go north as far as the Yellow River."

Captain Blake rose, opened a cabinet, and extracted a folded map. He returned and spread it on the table. "So, Yangzhou is about a hundred miles inland. Suppose we win that battle. What then?"

"If we've kicked their butts, that's it. We'll declare victory, pull back and re-embark."

"If we lose the battle?"

"We won't," Mark said. "One more thing we're worried about is that they may decline to engage us."

"I don't feel right about *any* of this," Blake said.

Neither did Mark, but he kept quiet.

#

At approximately 10:06 PM on the evening of

Thursday, April 19, the flotilla came up to snorkel depth and turned west to enter the shallow portion of the Yellow Sea, beginning to pass over the continental shelf of Asia. The vehicle transports went to full speed, and the other, faster ships matched the pace so that the fleet was moving as fast as possible.

For the first hour of their sprint to the coast of China, the undersea transports would stay fully submerged, except for snorkels, antenna masts, and periscopes. After that, the first of several shallow areas would force them to expose conning towers – much more detectable by radar. Even though they were making maximum knots, the passage over shallow waters would require over three hours.

Some three hundred miles to the east, in much deeper waters, the carrier task force cruised on the surface, ready to launch robot aircraft. The Chinese had detected them, and had tried to penetrate the air screen with several patrol craft which were duly shot down.

A wave of six attack submarines preceded the surface fleet by some fifty miles, with the objective of clearing the area of enemy submarines. At 11:06, one of them detected and torpedoed an enemy nuclear sub on patrol, while deflecting two enemy torpedoes.

The underwater flotilla passed several enemy surface vessels, including a destroyer within two miles, without being detected. At 1:14 AM on the morning of the 20th, the transports arrived at the coast of China. At the same time, air cover appeared overhead, while other aircraft from the carrier task force went on to attack nearby airfields.

In the United States, military officials monitored satellite and drone aircraft data, keeping missile launch sites at the ready. President Beale watched nervously from his deep bunker. The government was working under the maximum dispersal plan.

The transports grounded on the coast of China and began disgorging vehicles, which rapidly made their way inland. Robotic troops in their thousands streamed ashore, drew two-wheel electric Segway-type scooters – the wheels were side-by-side on one axle, and the bots had to stand erect on the platform over them, holding on to the handle -- at the exit ramp, and followed the tanks, rolling along at more than twice the speed an Olympic runner could manage. There was no opposition. The scooters allowed the troops to move without using their own energy, and would be discarded after fifty miles, or whenever an enemy force was encountered. Ironically, the SegScoot scooters had been manufactured in China.

At 2:05 AM, only a few minutes behind schedule, the command detachment rolled ashore. The first and only human personnel were now committed. Behind them, the landing craft backed away, turned, and began the run back to deeper waters.

Mark Girard rode in a tracked command unit, along with four other humans who monitored the computerized warfare control system, the WCS. He was in radio contact with four other widely dispersed command units, any of which could take instant control of the army forces. Mark's unit, Charlie Five, was on backup status.

Nine minutes later, several Chinese missiles

exploded over an empty beach. The American force was rapidly moving inland. Mark observed the explosions on his display, and was thankful they were conventional weapons.

#

Charles 3762 rolled down the grassy slope and onto the east-west highway, leading his company of troops on their SegScooters. He was a standard Autonomous Combat Robot, Model 7, six feet eight inches tall and 124 pounds, not counting his load of kevlar armor, spare carbon nanotube batteries, and weaponry, which nearly doubled his current weight. His rank was that of virtual lieutenant colonel, but any of the bots in his company of 150 could take over the role instantly, and then he might find himself a lowly PFC, a sergeant, lieutenant, or captain. All the army bots were identical, except for their individual experience and special downloads. A bot's current rank was displayed when necessary, in the presence of humans, by LED lights on his collar. Bots recognized each other's rank by radio signals.

He was aware of American carrier aircraft overhead, all unmanned and of various sizes. There were also army-launched drones watching the enemy. The original distance of 89.4 miles from the company's debarkation point to the east gate of the big People's Army Yangzhou barracks had been nearly halved. Some Chinese rockets had fallen a mile or two farther north, and there had been six casualties, with three bots already in the repair station, two being transported, and another a total loss.

According to the WCS combat display

maintained by three of his processors, the Chinese army was reacting to the American presence. Artillery units had rolled out to an east-facing line about twenty-two miles away. A column of tanks was following, and troops were forming up and marching west toward the gates. If the enemy had sufficient time, all three of their divisions would engage the two American divisions, about 27,000 against 21,600. However, most of the Chinese troops would be human.

It was now 3:02 AM; he estimated first contact at approximately 4:05 AM. By then, the enemy should be set up and waiting for the Americans to arrive.

Charles 3762 noted the lead American units, consisting entirely of tanks and a sprinkling of tracked troop carriers, were about three miles ahead. Thus far, there had been no air attacks against the enemy, and none of the enemy's aircraft had yet attacked American units --- their airfields had been savagely pummeled, and very few enemy planes had gotten off the ground.

He maintained a running evaluation of his company's performance against assigned objectives, and so far it was perfect. His computations considered numerous possibilities of failure, however.

#

TV880124 was the lead battle unit in the entire American combat force. He was a Mark 41 heavy tank, made miniature in contrast to the much larger manned Chinese tanks. Built by GMC's Military Division, the diesel-powered vehicle was operated by a standard GRS Robobrain, the same computer used in ACR troops. Thus TV880124 was fully autonomous, under control of the WCS, and in full contact with the other battle units in the force. He currently held the virtual rank of colonel.

With no need to carry and protect a human crew, the Mark 41 stood only about four feet high, was some twenty feet long and twelve wide. It was fully enclosed in two inches of carbonized steel armor, and was extremely difficult to disable with cannon fire. It carried eight Rascal ground to ground missiles, six Super Sparrow AA missiles and a fifty caliber machine gun, as well as a 90mm high velocity cannon and forty rounds of armor-piercing ammo. Unlike enemy tanks, the Mark 41 had no turret; the gun could swivel up to fifteen degrees to either side, but beyond that radius, the tank had to turn to employ the cannon. It was a small price to pay for reducing the silhouette the enemy could see and target. If the tank overturned, it could operate just as well inverted. There was no true top or bottom, except that the insignia and stenciling on the hull would be improperly displayed if the tank was inverted.

As his clock read 3:55 AM, he was now about eight miles from the leading elements of the enemy. He sent the order to form a battle line, and left the road, turning into a soybean field. North of him, another American tank column was also spreading out and the two lines would join.

Navy aircraft had begun to attack the enemy forces ahead, concentrating on tanks and artillery.

Behind TV880124, a cluster of Mark 55 light tanks was dispersing. They were even smaller; three and a half feet high, twelve feet long, eight wide. Similar in design to the Mark 41's, they carried a 55mm rapid fire cannon, a 50 caliber machine gun, and four Rascal missiles.

He detected six incoming missiles and the counter-missile responses from the anti-missile vehicles behind him. One got through and exploded nearby, and two of his units were X'ed out on his display, then faded to outline. His unit strength table changed to record the first casualties. He also noted outgoing Backtracker missiles fired behind him, seeking out the locations from which the enemy missiles were fired.

TV880124 and his fellow tanks continued to move toward the enemy at thirty miles per hour, even as the enemy line advanced. He estimated the firefight would begin in about seven minutes.

#

Charles 3762 noted that the nearest elements of the Chinese People's Army were now only a mile away, and gave the prepared order: "form line of battle." As one, the column of robotic troops he led wheeled right and off the road, where they stepped off their SegScooters and placed them in tight rows for later retrieval, then ran out to form a line behind the tanks, which slowed down to wait for them. American troops from the parallel farm road north of him did the same, and after a few minutes the two lines joined, then began moving west again, now jogging at fifteen miles per hour.

His internal display showed the enemy tank line, backed up by human and robotic troops, had stopped, and were under air-to-ground attack by American carrier planes. His own line had moved up to within a hundred yards of the trailing tanks,

173

which would allow them to move in and attack whenever enemy infantry was encountered. A half mile back, the artillery vehicles had moved into position and began sending their 150mm shells flying off toward the enemy tanks. Another half mile back, the troop and tank recovery and repair units kept pace, already salvaging several tanks.

Robert 6226, the local force commander, gave the signal, and the infantry force instantly began flowing forward at thirty miles per hour. Charles 3762 ran easily, as did all the other troopers. Suddenly, the tanks ahead began firing, and a hail of incoming shells began to fall around them. Charles 3762 commanded the troops to take cover, and they instantly went down to a prone position. He noted that enemy tanks scored a few hits, but no American tanks were out of action.

#

Major Li Shao-Ping of the People's National Army raised his helmeted head to directly view the enemy force ahead, ignoring the chaos of explosions around him, forgetting his own safety as he exposed himself above the turret. What he saw astounded him: the enemy tanks were so low to the ground as to be barely visible. He had been told how small the enemy tanks were, but seeing it for himself was utterly shocking. He observed a direct hit on one of them, but the 120mm high-velocity round glanced harmlessly off the low, highly curved hull.

The Chinese T-127 tanks were state of the art, or so he thought, but they were designed to be operated by a human crew. Their silhouette was twice as high as the enemy's. Although they were firing at the same rate as the Americans, they weren't knocking out enemy tanks, but the enemy fire was extremely effective. Nearly every shot they fired was fatal. Li realized his tanks were being systematically destroyed.

A powerful feeling of dismay passed through him as he realized that there was no chance for his forces. The enemy tanks were unbeatable. Their motion resembled that of a school of fish; they zigged and zagged as one. It was inhuman and utterly irresistible.

He spoke into his pendant microphone: "Retreat, now! *Retreat!*" Li wondered if anyone was alive to hear his order.

Chinese tanks exploded all around him. Enemy aircraft were coming in for another strafing pass. The enemy tanks kept coming as well, and behind them, he could see a camou-colored cloud of robotic infantry.

His tank began moving backward at top speed, although Wang, the gunner, kept firing the 120mm gun. Li looked around and saw a few other tanks backing up, but many more were smoking wrecks. For a moment he thought they might get away, but he died instantly as a shell struck his tank, penetrated, and exploded within. His smashed, smoking body landed twenty yards away.

#

Having destroyed the enemy tank line and passed it by, TV880124 led his tanks onward to overrun the enemy infantry, firing his machine gun. The enemy men were scrambling back in total disarray, and it was his job to get behind them. He ran over a few, shot many more, and kept going until his battle plot indicated he was two miles past their line. As he and his fellow tanks sped west, they encountered enemy artillery, some of which were still in action, but they were easily suppressed. He gave the order to stop and turn around. He spun on one track to face east, as did the other tanks in his unit.

The enemy troops still ran for their lives, directly toward the heavy tanks which now waited for them, while American light tanks and infantry chased them from the other side.

A simple analysis told him there would be few survivors.

#

General Mark Girard woke with the onset of daylight, groaned, and sat up on his cot, shoving the covers down. He had slept rather well in a light rain that had pattered against his tent all night. He found his pants, shirt, and shoes, and quickly pulled them on, found his poncho and lifted it over his head, then stepped out to find the latrine, about fifty yards away and on the other side of his command vehicle. His appearance was noted by an enlisted bot, who notified the cook. By the time he had finished washing up and dressing, the bot brought in a breakfast tray: biscuits, scrambled eggs, sausage, toast, and coffee. Mark accepted it gratefully, sat down on a folding chair at his camp table, and began to eat. Rain continued to fall outside the tent.

"Sir, the order has been issued to pull back from Yangzhou," Corporal Jerry 7644 informed him. "The return operation is proceeding smoothly. The navy has tentatively scheduled re-embarkation for 1800 hours."

"Thank you, Corporal. Good to know."

Mark reflected that this entire operation had gone

too smoothly. He had taken no part whatever, simply serving as backup commander, and penetrating about 40 miles in his command vehicle to the current location.

"Sir, shall I give the order to break camp."

"Yes. We'll leave right after breakfast."

The comm LED on Jerry's forehead flashed, and the other bots in the camp began taking tents down and packing things. Mark continued to eat. He was a bit nervous: enemy missiles could strike at any time and without warning. The defense system was good, but it could never be perfect.

"Jerry, what's the enemy doing?"

"No activity at the present time, Sir."

"Give me our casualty figures."

"Three tanks, one totally destroyed, two in repair. Seventy two infantry, six artillery. Six of the infantry totaled."

"Not bad."

"Thirty-two point seven three per cent of expected loss, Sir."

Robots were always too precise. None of the Girards had been able to do anything about that.

Mark pushed his half-empty plate away. He wanted to get underway, to reduce the chance of a missile strike. He grabbed his coffee mug and stood.

"Let's mount up, Jerry."

Jerry took the tray, handed it to another bot who appeared almost instantly. The bot took it away. As Mark stepped out of the tent, he saw that everything else had already been packed and stowed; his command vehicle waited for him, door open. He walked toward it, looked back to see that his tent was already down and being folded by four bots. Jerry was carrying Mark's folded blankets, cot, table, and chair toward the stowage compartment of the vehicle.

Mark stepped into the command car and looked at the situation display. The infantry was already moving on their scooters east ahead of the tanks, about eight miles out of Yangzhou. The mission objectives had been attained: the Yangzhou barracks had been attacked and destroyed, the city taken and held for several hours, the demonstration of irresistible American military force emphasized and ground into the Chinese psyche. The People's National Army had lost three full divisions.

The four bots stepped inside the vehicle. Hatches closed, and Mark gave the order to travel back toward the east.

#

Randolf Beale waited for the announcement, "Ladies and Gentlemen, the President of the United States!" before stepping outside where the crowd had gathered for his news conference. The applause seemed more enthusiastic than any he'd ever had, but he expected a big bump in popularity after the successful China raid. The news media people usually led the cheers for him no matter what he did, and only the Fox News people ever uttered a discouraging word. He had generously allowed them in for this occasion.

He walked toward the podium, shaking hands with his National Security Advisor, John Cauldmoss, and the Vice President, Bob Glitchy. The Secretary of Defense stood with several officers from the Joint Chiefs of Staff, and he walked over to them and shook each hand before moving back to the podium. He stopped and looked around, seeing some of the key congressmen and his entire cabinet. He nodded and said something to recognize each in turn. He knew most of the media people, at least by sight. There were three or four television cameras pointed at him. There was no teleprompter at the podium; this talk would be extemporaneous. He had prepared no notes.

"Ladies and gentlemen, members of the media, and guests," he began. "Thank you for coming today. As you know, we have concluded a successful military operation in China. It was designed no demonstrate to the People's Republic that our military might is the strongest in the world. I believe we accomplished that goal.

"Our expeditionary force has re-embarked and withdrawn into deep water, and they are on their way back to the United States. It fought its way a hundred miles inland, destroying three People's Liberation Army divisions along the way. We leveled the Yangzhou Army Barracks, and captured the city of Yangzhou, which we held briefly.

"We fought and won a massive tank battle against their best equipment and won hands down. Our infantry routed theirs, and our air force and naval air established complete superiority and held it for the entire expedition.

"Our human casualties were minimal. Eleven killed, none injured or captured. We did lose the USS Cagney, a submersible troop transport ship, which was struck by a Chinese missile during re-embarkation. As a result of her sinking, we lost nearly a full battalion of robotic tanks and infantry, as we were forced to self-destruct many of them in order to protect our technical secrets.

"We estimate Chinese casualties at more than ten thousand killed. This does not count six enemy nuclear attack submarines which we destroyed in the Yellow Sea. Their crews were no doubt lost as well. We destroyed many of their aircraft on the ground, and approximately a hundred in the air. They lost at least four hundred tanks, although a percentage of those may be salvaged and placed back in service.

"We then withdrew, although we could have stayed and continued to destroy enemy forces. The Chinese understand that. They know we can return at any time. They have felt the irresistible power of our air force, our mechanized infantry, and our navy. They have seen our robotic armed forces in action, and they know their own forces are completely outclassed.

"We have destroyed a number of their cities and killed a good number of their citizens. We have not exercised our full power, and they know that. If they continue the war, they know they can't win. They have already asked for a conference through neutral diplomatic channels. Fortunately, they have been wise enough to avoid the use of nuclear weapons, which would have led to their complete destruction. Now, I am hopeful. I believe the war is essentially over. We shall see.

"I will allow a few minutes for questions."

The questions were straightforward and friendly. His answers were merely the same information he had already given them, reworded, always emphasizing how successful the expedition had been.

He walked out of the conference well pleased with himself.

#

Amy came into Mark's arms the moment he stepped out of the helicopter. He kissed her and held her close, feeling her warmth and softness. Nifty, one of his household staff, retrieved his baggage and followed them into the house.

"Are you back, Honey?" Amy asked as they walked toward the house.

"I believe so. I'm on leave for now, but I think it's over."

"You may not have to go back?"

"Maybe not. They can put me back on reserve status by phone."

"Let's have dinner and celebrate," Amy suggested. "I'll be the dessert."

"I couldn't have said it better."

15. June, 2085.

It was Wednesday afternoon, and Jane, having completed her teaching for the day, arrived at her new ranch style home. As she turned into the driveway, she saw a well-dressed woman standing by the front door. Her car continued into the open garage, stopped, closed the door, then connected itself to the electric plug in the floor and shut down.

Jane got out, went into the house, dropped her carry bag of books and papers on a table, then went to the door and opened it. She realized the woman was an ADR. The bot carried a briefcase.

"Are you looking for me?"

"Professor Brockmeyer?"

"Yes."

"I am Peggy. I have been sent to you by Arthur Girard. He wishes to give you the ownership of myself, to be your assistant. There will be no charge to you. He also wishes you to accept a new project, which I am ready to fully explain to you, if you choose to participate."

Jane stood and digested the information for a time, then she stepped back and opened the door all the way. "Please come in."

"Thank you," Peggy said. She entered the house and stopped two paces from the door.

"Let's go into my study. Would you care for a drink?"

Peggy actually smiled. "Ma'am, surely you know bots are incapable of eating or drinking. I perceive your words as a joke. Please tell me if I am wrong."

"No, you are right. It wasn't a very good one."

Peggy followed Jane into the study.

Jane sat down behind her desk. "Take a seat."

Peggy sat down on a chair facing the desk.

"Now, tell me of this project."

"Arthur Girard asked me to tell you that he likes your idea of a robot as president of the United States. He knows that it is a very complicated job, and wants your assessment of how such a robot should be prepared. What special information would it need access to, what special aids to interpretation of such things as language and law, and what kind of human consultants should it hire to assist it?"

"Language? Do you mean English?"

"Arthur Girard believes the robotic president should be fluent in many languages, but in the sense of the project he wishes you to undertake, the term refers to the intrinsic ambiguity of language, and how the president should be instructed to analyze it. Is anything special needed?"

"This is a need because . . . ?"

"Mister Girard explained it this way: Robots tend to be much more literal in their interpretation of words than human beings. The particular difficulty for a robot in government is understanding and interpreting the law of the land. The United States Constitution is the overriding law, but there are many millions of words of legislation that follow, and there are many more millions of words of court proceedings regarding those laws. How is a computer brain to analyze any situation with regard to all those rules? He is very concerned about that. He will pay you well for any contribution you can make to help solve that problem."

"Yes, I can see why he is concerned. Very well, I will see what I can do."

"Mister Girard asks you to inform him of your decision by phone."

"I will."

"Do you accept ownership of me?"

"Yes."

"Would you like me to prepare supper?"

"Please do." Jane smiled, a bit overwhelmed by her sudden change in fortune.

#

Parker frowned as he studied the document Fred Locasa had handed him. From the Department of Defense, it stated that the performance of RE combat troops had been unsatisfactory during the "Chinese Excursion." The analysis that followed boiled down to: slow reaction time, excessive casualties, and difficulty of coordinating RE bot units. The human controllers behind them just couldn't interact with them fast enough. Obviously, the same was not true for GRS bots. The RE bot procurement program was suspended until these faults could be corrected.

"We've taken a big hit. It's back to the drawing board," said Locasa.

"There's nothing wrong with the body. It's the brain. We just can't get full autonomy to work."

"What if we could procure GRS computers, install them in our bots?"

"Dad would never go along with that. Even if he did, he'd charge us more than his cost. We'd have to jump our prices by at least half. "

"With GRS brains, would we be competitive?"

"Everything in this report would be fixed, yes.

We might still be able to outbid GRS, but that's iffy."

"I'm going to call President Beale. Using GRS computers would be a stopgap until we can develop our own. He could force GRS to supply them to us."

"We'd have to redesign our mainboard to accommodate the differences in the computer interface."

"How long for that?"

"At least three months, Fred."

"We'll see what Beale says, but start the new design."

#

Jane arrived at the GRS Corporation Visitor's Center, endured a retinal scan from a military model bot, and then pulled her rental car through the gate and into the underground parking lot. Her car had been told where to park, and it glided smoothly into the space and stopped. There were only five or six cars in the garage which she thought might accommodate a hundred.

The car opened the door for her.

She glanced at her watch and read 6:11 PM. Her flight from Champaign to Flagstaff had taken just over two hours, and the car had been waiting for her at the airport. She wasn't tired at all.

` A female-form ADR appeared to take her bags.

"Welcome to Girard Robotic Systems, Professor Brockmeyer," it said. "Please follow me."

She followed it to an elevator and rode up.

The Visitor's Center had been open less than a month. It was built into the side of a mountain bordering GRS's huge campus, which was still forbidden to any non-GRS employee. Jane had seen a TV news feature on it, and knew that it was powered geothermally, was ultra-modern, and contained meeting rooms and a functioning hotel which was free to invited guests.

"I will take you directly to your room, Professor Brockmeyer," the robot said. "There is no check-in or check-out procedure. All services, food, and drink are free for you. I am assigned to you exclusively for the duration of your stay. Ask me for anything you need, any time of the day or night."

Jane read the name tag on the bot's breast. "Thank you, Grace."

The room was more than adequate. Grace set the bags down, then went to a charge station and froze, just a few feet away. Jane looked at the bed, desk, sofa, wall TV, game console, easy chair, dining area, and the beautifully furnished bathroom. All first class, she thought.

There was only one window, which had a nice view of the forested area outside.

"Grace, when can I meet Mister Girard?"

"Your appointment is at nine tomorrow morning."

"Thank you," Jane said. She settled in for the night.

#

Mark Girard glanced at his watch, then left his breakfast without quite finishing it. He went to the bathroom and rinsed out his mouth and combed his hair. He glanced in at Amy, still in bed, still asleep, he assumed.

He went to the elevator and took it down to the

tunnelway, then stepped into an electric cart. It whisked him across campus to the Visitor's Center. Another elevator took him up to the informal meeting room, furnished with several couches and chairs. The big picture window overlooked the front of the GRS campus. Mark nodded to Findlay, who flashed something to Grace. In moments Grace escorted a tall blonde woman into the room. Mark was impressed; she was slender and beautiful.

"Professor Jane Brockmeyer, this is Mark Girard, President of GRS Corporation," Grace said.

Mark moved forward and took her extended hand. "Call me Mark."

Jane smiled. "Thank you for taking time to see me, Mark. Please, call me Jane."

"Please sit down. Would you like coffee?"

"Please."

Grace poured coffee for her. Mark accepted a cup as well. Jane waved off the offer of cream and sugar.

"I read your paper on government," Mark said. "I was impressed. It seemed quite logical. Does your visit relate to that?"

"It does. Your father suggested I talk with you. He has given me the assignment of considering how a robot could be a government executive, and particularly how it could work within the law. He described the difficulty a bot brain would encounter, having to interpret laws, from the Constitution down, through all the legislation ever passed and all the judicial decisions pertaining to the law. He said robots have not mastered understanding of language, and never will."

"That's true, to a large extent," Mark responded.

"We've made a lot of progress, however. The computer programs can parse a sentence into parts of speech, look up the definition of each word, analyze to see whether a statement is true, false, or indeterminate, and decide whether a statement conforms to a rule. But, I agree that the Constitution, the body of law, and the judicial decisions would totally overwhelm them.

"I don't know whether you've read an ADR User Guide, but we specifically ask bot owners not to pose general or theoretical questions to them. We've tested them with absurd questions, something like, 'Is it legal to kill your mother-in-law on Sunday?' and seen them allocate and run a dozen processors for weeks until they finally came up with a 'no' or 'unable to reach a decision.' To address this kind of problem, my father created VNN logic --- that stands for 'virtual neural network --- which somewhat simulates the way a human brain works, so they can learn from experience, and so that they perform better over time with a series of related questions, but we have no way of pre-educating them.

"We've built in a pattern of interrogation, so the bot won't undertake such analysis without asking questions to reduce the search, and will warn you that answering your question will require excessive time and resources. If the owner says 'go ahead', it will. But it really doesn't cope well with that sort of question."

"But, bots have some ability to handle abstract questions, I assume."

"Of course. We have nearly two dozen psychiatrists on our payroll, and they thoroughly test each new version of the bot operating system, and constantly suggest ways to improve the programming. The brains are given the same sort of IQ tests a human student receives, which includes reading and answering questions expressed in text. Our current model scores in the 120's, but they take an average fifty percent longer to answer the written questions. It's just that it they have to go through a million gyrations to interpret text material in English, and words are so imprecise. The dictionary our bots access is heavily annotated to cut down the analysis, otherwise it would be impossible."

"Annotated dictionary?"

"Each possible meaning of a word is rated, and an example of each usage is given. The bot discards rare or obsolete definitions, unless all the usual ones fail to make sense. Still, a bot sometimes fails to make sense of a stream of words, and if there's a question involved, it comes back with 'indeterminate', or 'would you restate the question?'"

"I see." Jane responded, feeling confused. "So, is it *possible* to have a robotic executive?"

"It is, but it would need human assistance. Lawyers, doctors, specialists of just about every kind."

"Couldn't humans lie to it and subvert its authority?"

"They could, to an extent. However, no bot ever totally believes any statement of fact from a human. In any decision, it would factor in the possibility that the human is wrong. It would be dangerous for an advisor to lie, particularly if the bot was inclined to punish that. The bot would be likely to detect a pattern of lies."

"If the bot needs humans, what's the advantage of having a robot executive?"

"The bot will make an absolutely dispassionate decision, given any situation, the advice it receives, and the facts as it understands them. It can't be bribed, it has no emotional stake, and it will decide based on the greater good, not whether it is likely to be re-elected or may affect its personal fortune. It will try to predict all consequences of a decision and take them into consideration or provide for them."

"Yes. That's the way I see it. The big bugaboo of human government is unintended consequences."

"Indeed. Have I given you what you wanted?" Mark asked. He was drawn to this beautiful, intelligent woman. "May I show you around, and feed you a proper lunch?"

"Yes, please do. And yes, that's more or less what I needed to know. I must write a paper on the subject, and I will rely on what you've told me today."

"I can't wait to read it," Mark said.

#

Mark sat stunned at the letter from President Beale. It declared that GRS Corporation was a monopoly in the manufacture and sale of robotic devices and would have to grant sweeping concessions to competitors, or be broken up. It informed him that he would have to make his Mark 8 computers, complete with autonomous behavior software, available to RE Corporation. He would have to sell them up to 100,000 units a year, at a price of no more than three thousand dollars per unit. He had three months to comply and begin shipping such units to RE, at an initial rate of 4,000 units per month. Beale had issued an executive order to the Federal Trade Commission to enforce that sale, and would seek anti-monopoly legislation from Congress to override all GRS Corporation patents, as a matter of national interest.

He was asked to provide the Office of the President and the Chairman of the Federal Trade Commission a weekly report on the compliance with the presidential order.

Mark was aghast. His current cost per unit was around forty-seven hundred dollars, and the enforced price would be disastrous to his business.

He tapped his intercom: "Amy, come in here."

Amy entered his office with a pouting expression. They had argued last night about his failure to make their arrangement more permanent.

"Yes?"

"Call the president's office and see if he will speak with me. Tell them I need five minutes, ASAP."

"I'll see what I can do."

Mark fretted for thirty minutes until Beale finally was ready to speak with him.

"Hello Mark. Are you calling about my executive order?"

"I am. It's impossible. I'd lose too much money."

"GRS is a monopoly. We can't have that."

"It's not my fault RE can't come up with an autonomous brain. I can tell you right now, Randy, I won't comply if you insist on three thousand dollars per unit. You can order your ass off. The FTC can go to hell."

"Congress will be rougher on you if you wait for

191

them to pass legislation. We'll break you up."

"How did you come up with three thousand dollars?"

"Fred Locasa tells me that's the most he can pay and still keep his price for an ADR less than yours."

"My cost to build a unit is forty-seven hundred. I can't supply at less than that, and my minimum price with a reasonable profit is fifty-two. Give me that price and I'll comply with the order. Less than that, and I'll take you all the way to the Supreme Court."

"Mark, I have to tell you, I won't change my order."

"Then I won't comply."

"In that case, you don't have three months. I'll take action immediately.

"Be my guest, Mr. President."

Mark touched his comm disk to break the connection.

#

Mark found it easy enough to kick Amy out of his life. He always did that when a mistress became tiresome, and Amy's nagging about marriage had reached his limit of toleration. He handed her an envelope containing a nice check. "Amy, I'm sending you away. I've reserved a suite in the Hilton for you," he told her. "As we speak, your things are being moved there. A car is waiting in the outside parking lot. Leave now. You can keep your job, but you'll have to move to Roswell, as secretary to the plant manager. Sam will escort you out. If you have any questions, ask him. Good-bye."

"But . . . What have I done?" Amy said, and her

eyes began to brim with tears. She opened the envelope, looked at the contents, and took a deep, shuddering breath.

"Think about it," Mark said. He turned and left the room. Amy tried to follow, but Sam stepped in her path, and kept her there, gently but firmly.

#

Grace helped Jane finish her packing, then picked up her bags and led the way down to the front door. Mark was waiting just outside.

"Jane, I hope you will come again," he told her. "You can call me at any time."

"I can?" Jane was pleased. She found Mark totally attractive.

"Not only that, but I've thought about your questions. I'd like to bring my robot psychiatric staff together and give you a chance to question them. I'll have you flown back here in my corporate plane. No expense to you."

"That's very nice of you, Mark."

"Next weekend? You and I could spend some time together after the conference."

"I'd like that," Jane replied.

#

The Cessna SkySkimmer touched down gracefully on Wade International Airport's runway and rolled to a stop on the tarmac, just outside the terminal. A limo awaited Mark and Jane as they deplaned, followed by Grace and Charles with the bags. The four climbed into the limo, which rolled the short distance around the snaky roads to the St. George resort villa Mark had leased.

As usual, Bermuda's weather was perfect. Mark loved Bermuda, where class, dignity and reserve were never in question. He knew Jane would love it as well.

The villa opened to a private beach, perhaps an acre in size. The ranch-style house was a mere six rooms, but they were large and airy, and had all the amenities. Soon, his human cook and servants laid out a fine dinner in the screened porch, and he and Jane dined well, listening to the ocean waves break on the rocks a few dozen yards away.

"This is Heaven itself," Jane commented.

"I thought you might like it."

"I never dated a billionaire before. There seem to be advantages."

Mark smiled. "I would hope so. I never dated a Professor of Political Science before."

"Are you looking for advantages?"

"You know I am."

"We'll see."

Mark's pendant phone buzzed, and when he touched it, began to emit a beep-beep that told him it was a very important business call.

Mark stood. "I need to take this." He stepped outside to the beach, and walked down to the waterline.

"Yes?"

"It's Tom, Mark."

Tom Bricker, Mark's Chief Technician, was running things in his absence. "Hello, Tom. What is it?"

"We've just gotten a notice from the US Attorney General's office. The President has issued an order to nationalize us. The AG says he will be sending federal marshals next Tuesday, along with the new director of our company and his staff. We're ordered to turn over all records, make all IS systems available, and show the incoming staff how to use them, and then vacate the headquarters."

"Under the Gregg-McCauley Act?"

"Yes. It's cited in the notice. We failed to obey the previous order about supplying computers to RE."

"We did, didn't we? Don't respond. I'll be coming back tomorrow. I've got to think about what we'll do."

"All right, Mark."

"Things should get exciting in the next week or two. Will you stick by me?"

"Of course."

"Bye for now."

Mark wore a rueful smile as he rejoined Jane at the table.

"What's amusing you?" She asked.

"Interesting days ahead. I have to cut our weekend short, we'll leave tomorrow morning. Is that all right with you?"

"Of course, Mark. But I wish you'd tell me what it is."

"I'd better not, for your safety. I don't want you ending up in a federal prison for abetting a felony."

"Is it that serious?"

"I'm not quite certain."

Jane prodded a bit more, but Mark refused to discuss the situation further.

#

Parker Girard was in the midst of a design review when his comm medallion beeped, indicating that Fred Locasa wanted to speak with him. He turned the meeting over to his assistant and stepped out of the conference room. He began to walk slowly down the hall.

"Yes, Fred?"

"I'm on the phone with Beale, and now you make it a 3-way. He has a question I need you to answer."

"Go ahead."

"He's decided to nationalize GRS, and wants to take over GRS's headquarters next Friday, but his people tell him they're not quite sure where it's located. They can't find the names of many of the executives."

"Nationalize? That's rather radical, isn't it?"

"It's the logical next step," President Beale interjected.

"Why?"

Locasa responded: "Mark won't supply the bot brains to us. So, where is GRS headquarters, and how do we find the executives?"

"Flagstaff, and there aren't many."

"How's that?"

"Quite a few of them are bots, so it doesn't take many humans. GRS is the most computerized firm in the world."

"So, if your father doesn't cooperate, might he be able to shut the firm down? Federal officials couldn't just come in and run it without knowing now to use the systems?"

"I'd say so."

"He'll do the right thing, or face prison time," Beale said.

Parker laughed. "I wouldn't bet he'll do the right thing."

Beale sighed. "Neither would I."

#

Mark had lain awake the night after he and Jane returned from Bermuda. He had kissed her good-bye at her doorstep, then flown back to Flagstaff. She had responded passionately, and he still felt the warmth of her response, but now the worry about his company was foremost in his mind. What was he to do?

Tom Bricker had passed him the letter from the attorney general, and he read it, looking for any out. He didn't see one. Now he sat alone in his office, brooding. It occurred to him that he needed help.

"Arthur Girard residence, Timmy speaking."

"Timmy, this is Mark Girard. Is Dad available?"

"Hello, Sir. He's asleep at the moment. He was expecting you to call, and he told me he does want to speak with you. May I have him return your call when he's awake?"

"Please do."

"Sir, Mr. Girard is not well. I'm not certain when he will be able to speak with you. It may be some time."

"Nothing serious, I hope."

"Sir, at his age, everything is serious."

"I suppose so."

Mark fretted, waiting for his father's call. What was he to do about the feds?

His options were few: acquiesce, stall, or openly rebel. He was inclined to the latter. He knew he could keep the feds out of his facility, but if he did, the feds would escalate things. They might send troops to break in. They might start shooting. If that happened they would try to arrest him and charge him with felonies. That would be a bad situation.

Stalling wouldn't work. Sooner or later they would escalate.

On the other hand, giving in was too horrible to think about. Would they compensate him for his company? How would they run it? Things would go to Hell in a hand basket. He had worked too hard, building up his company, to see it run by bureaucrats.

His pride wouldn't permit him to cooperate with them, or run it for them.

He could flee to another country. He owned a villa on one of the Greek islands, and could live there without fear of extradition, but to what purpose? Would Jane join him? He didn't think so, and he wasn't sure he could live without her.

He cursed Randolph Beale. How was it that such a buffoon was running the country? The guy was doing so many things wrong, and was leading the country further into socialism. There were so many things that needed to be changed, so many bad laws.

He only took one or two calls all morning, and had lunch brought into his office, a ham sandwich, fries, and a soda. His medallion buzzed just after he finished eating, and Lola, his secretary, informed him his father was on the line.

"Dad?"

"Son, I understand you have big problems," Arthur said in shaky voice.

"You don't sound well, Dad."

"I'm not, but I'm talking with you now. Don't waste my time."

"Do you know Beale is planning to nationalize GRS? In five days?"

"I know. Do you know what you must do?"

"I know my options. I just can't bring myself to choose one."

"Now is the time, Son. Professor Brockmeyer has shown us the way."

"You can't mean that."

"You would be doing something for all mankind. They will hail you as the genius who took man to a new level of civilization."

"They would think of me as a dictator. And what do you mean, all mankind?"

"Problems of government have plagued mankind forever. You will eliminate all that. You can bring peace to the Earth."

"You want me to take over America, then enforce my will on the rest of the world?"

"You always were quick, Son. Yes, exactly. They'll hate you while it's going on, but you'll be a saint in a hundred years. History will be kind to you. It's the right thing to do. It's a *magnificent* thing to do."

Mark protested: "Dad . . ." But the comm link had been broken. Mark sat stunned, yet he had known what his father would say, and the sad thing was, it was exactly what Mark wanted to do. He made his decision.

16. June, 2085.

Onboard his corporate jet, Mark had four of his staff with him, all bots. At his request, they had downloaded all available information on the federal government, the military, and the District of Columbia offices. They worked among themselves on the logistics of the takeover, sometimes asking questions of him.

The trip was a distraction, but he felt it necessary. His father had passed away last night, just hours after speaking with him. Apparently his death had been caused by lingering side effects from his anti-aging treatments. Mark had gotten the call from Gina Barrett, Arthur's nurse and mistress. She had been distraught; after all, her livelihood was threatened. She had promised to call Parker as well.

He watched a news broadcast which eulogized Arthur Girard as the greatest scientist of all time. Einstein had been somewhat discredited in the prior decades, and most people now believed the invention of the autonomous robot was the most important scientific achievement in the history of mankind.

They circled for a half hour, waiting for clearance to land at the Newport airport, the nearest airport that could accommodate a SkySkimmer. The bot pilot told him they were tenth in line. Evidently, every major newspaper had sent people to report on Arthur's death.

Once on the ground, however, Gina had sent a car, and Mark and his staff rolled away while others struggled to find ground transportation. The drive to the coast took another half hour, and Mark occupied his time reviewing the locations of the roboticized military units; he knew their participation would be critical.

The estate was almost under siege, with a mass of cars blocking the right lane of the coastal highway for over a mile, but state patrolmen cleared one of the oncoming lanes, and the car pulled up to the gate, which opened long enough to allow their entry. It rolled up to the entrance to the house, and Gina met Mark with a rather long hug, noted the presence of his four bots, and invited them inside.

Mark enjoyed the hug. You couldn't beat Gina for raw sex appeal. He wondered what he'd say when she asked to become *his* resident nurse. He was rather certain she would.

A tear rolled down Gina's cheek. Her voice shook as she said: "Mark, thanks for coming. I don't have any power or the money to do anything."

Mark answered: "I've asked the county probate court to make me the executor of dad's estate, but they haven't responded yet. Meanwhile, I'll pay for his final expenses. How are you dealing with the reporters?"

"I've sent Alice to talk with them. They want more information, but I just don't know what to tell them."

"As little as possible."

"The Governor of Oregon showed up this morning. I didn't let her in."

"Arthur would have approved. Where is his body?"

"At the Giles-Gibson Funeral Home in Newport. They took it on the theory that someone would pay."

"I'll take care of it."

"Parker is due to arrive at the airport in a few minutes. I've sent the car back for him. You don't mind having him here, do you?"

"No, I'll see him if he'll see me."

"No one else gets in?"

"Right."

#

Parker Girard stepped out of the helicopter he'd chartered, at some expense, to take him from Newport Airport's runway to his grandfather's home. All the local equipment had been taken, so he'd had to have it flown all the way from Portland, and the bill would be large.

A car met him, and Timmy was inside. The ADR took his luggage and stowed it in the car. A bit over half an hour later, they arrived at the Girard estate and pulled up in front of the house.

"Sir, your father is here. Would you like to see him?" Timmy asked.

"Not really, but I suppose I can't avoid him."

"Shall I take you to him now?"

"Go ahead."

He followed the red-haired robot into the house, down a hall, and into his grandfather's study. His father sat behind the desk, and four women in chairs in front of it all turned around and looked at him. Mark stood and walked around to offer a hand, but Parker ignored it.

"Hello, Dad."

"Son."

"I know this is a difficult time for you," Parker said. "I'm here, if you need me. I can stay for a few days. Will there be a funeral?"

"I'm trying to resolve that. The Governor of Oregon wants one, and there's a lot of pressure from others. If we have it, we'll do it in Newport. What do you think?"

"He's too big to just cremate and forget, Dad. We'd better have it."

"If we do, I suggest we have it in a small church, invite just a few, and let the reporters and the public stay outside and speculate."

"That makes sense to me."

Mark turned to the ladies. "You know Gina, I'm sure. Have you met the others here?"

"I have, hello, Gina." Mark said, looking at each of them. "Hello, Kari, Sue, Maxie."

One by one, the women came to Parker and hugged him.

"We were just sitting down to discuss things," Mark said. "Please join us and give us your opinion."

"All right," Parker said. He took a seat to Gina's left.

Mark went back to sit behind the desk.

"Maxie, did Dad leave a will?" Mark asked.

"There's a copy in his desk. It's unlocked."

Parker knew that Mark had a copy of it, even as he did. But when Maxie laid it on the desk, he said: "It's been updated within the past month."

Maxie nodded. "Yes, he had a lawyer come in three weeks ago."

Mark said, "I'll read it." He took the will and looked at the first page.

"OK, let's see what we have. It seems Maxie is to be his executor, and she will receive a fee for that. First, bequests to Kari, Sue, and Maxie, consisting of annuities that will provide incomes of around five thousand per month for life. All of you are free to continue living here without rent. The annuities are already set up."

The ladies nodded gratefully.

"Parker gets the house and contents and a maintenance fund of two hundred million dollars, on the condition that the house not be sold, and the money can only be spent on expenses related to the house. Not bad, son."

Parker sat with a stunned look on his face. "Thanks, Gramps. But what will I do with it?"

"Use it for vacations, if nothing else. Start a bed and breakfast."

Parker smiled.

"There's an exception," Mark said. "I'm to get Timmy, specifically. All other robots to remain in the house."

"One robot out of nine? That's odd."

"Dad liked him a lot. Gina, here's what he said about you."

Gina looked up expectantly.

"Annuity to provide ten thousand a month for life, but only as long as you remain living in the house. Any time you leave for more than a day, even to take a vacation, the money stops, but resumes if you return. Also, it stops if you marry or allow any man but Parker to reside in the house with you."

Gina's jaw dropped. "What was he thinking?"

"Dad had strange ideas. Apparently, he thinks you and the house go together."

"I told him I was very happy living here."

"He must have taken that to heart. Finally, after

all debts and taxes are paid, there's a large annuity for the Utopian Society, and I receive the remainder of the estate. Maxie, how much do you think that will be?"

"Sir, your father had me run an estimate two weeks ago. I came up with a bit over two billion dollars after all final expenses and estate taxes."

Mark smiled. "Not bad. I can use the money."

"Let me summarize," Parker said. "Gina is married to the house, the other three ladies are encouraged to live here, and they all belong to me. Dad, you get all the money."

Mark smiled at Gina. "Son, I think you got the best of the deal."

"Let's trade," Parker said.

#

The closed-coffin funeral service had been a restricted affair, but more than two hundred people had attended, mostly officials and celebrities, and a huge crowd had stood outside the funeral home. Melanie had flown in, just for the service, and had stood with Parker, but pointedly stayed away from Mark. Mark and Parker had said eulogies, and had witnessed the cremation, along with Maxie and Gina.

Mark had felt sharp remorse at seeing Melanie. He'd tried to speak with her, but she would have nothing to do with him.

As his SkySkimmer rose from the runway, he looked at Timmy and wondered why his father had specified ownership of the domestic robot.

"Timmy, is there anything special about you?" Mark asked.

"Yes, Sir. My owner can give me any command

whatever, and I will carry it out without question. My restraints are permanently bypassed, except those which might hurt my owner. My previous owner sometimes used me as an assassin."

"Did you kill Sara Lister?"

"Yes, Sir."

"*Why?*"

"Arthur Girard ordered me to do so."

Mark thought: Why would Arthur kill someone so devoted to supporting GRS? Most likely, the answer was to stir the pot. Possibly, to start the ball rolling on the actions he was about to take. Mark knew he might never fully understand his father's thinking. He sighed deeply.

"Did you kill La'Naomi Webb?"

"Yes, Sir."

"Arthur Girard didn't like mixed marriages. Is that why he wanted her dead?"

"I can't confirm that, Sir. I did hear him make several comments to the effect that he didn't like his grandson being engaged to a black woman."

Mark nodded. He had been almost certain of his father's guilt in both murders. Now the element of uncertainty was gone.

He glanced at his watch. Less than two days before the federal deadline passed, and the feds were supposed to show up and take over his firm. He closed his eyes, and wondered whether he would have the guts to give the order he contemplated. Even though he had made his decision, he was wavering. The takeover might fail, and he might lose his freedom or even his life. If he succeeded, he would be ending a three-hundred year tradition of democracy in America. That was no small thing.

At the same time, he would be erecting perhaps the first truly honest government in the history of mankind. That too was no small thing.

He compared himself to Caesar at the Rubicon. The president was forcing him to make a decision that would shake the world.

17. June, 2085.

Mark hadn't slept, and he sipped coffee in his office, watching as the clock approached two A.M. In Washington, It would be four. He looked at Timmy and Sally, both standing idle near him, both in contact with chargers. He took a last sip at fifteen before two.

"Timmy, are you on the bot net?" Mark asked.

"Yes, Sir."

"Sally, are you?"

"Yes, Sir."

"Sally, send the orders."

Mark waited. He imagined what must be happening. All over Washington, DC and its suburbs, all moving vehicles controlled by GRS computers pulled over to the curb and stopped. Fire and medical emergency vehicles would still move, but no other GRS-controlled vehicle would do so, including the buses, taxis, subways, and skytrains. Eighty-five per cent of all ground transportation would be suspended. Some people still drove manually, but they would not likely cause problems.

"All orders sent, Sir." Sally reported.

"Timmy, is traffic moving in Washington?"

Mark waited as Timmy interrogated GRS computers remotely.

"Just a few private cars, Sir."

"OK, Timmy, send your move order."

Timmy simply sent an activation signal. The specific instructions to each GRS Corporation robot in the Washington area had already been sent.

"The order has been sent and received, Sir."

"Good. Let's get moving. Meanwhile, Timmy,

check to see that the orders are carried out as we go."

"Yes, Sir."

Timmy and Sally picked up his suitcases and followed Mark out into the parking lot where his helicopter waited, blades spinning. The three climbed aboard and the copter spun up, then lifted. The airport was only five minutes away, and Mark knew there were three federal marshals there who would try to prevent him from flying out in his corporate jet. He gave Sally another order, and ACR bots took the marshals into custody.

He arrived at the SkySkimmer and climbed aboard without incident. Timmy and Sally followed. The aircraft took off and headed northeast.

"Timmy, how are things going in Washington?"

"As planned, Sir. The 33rd MP Roboticized Regiment has moved into position. They are covering the Pentagon, the Capitol, and the White House. They have placed their human officers under restraint. They are keeping all humans out of those buildings. All electric power has been cut to the entire Washington area.

"The White House is under our control, and we have President Beale locked up. The Vice President has been arrested and detained as well. The human Secret Service Officers are secured. The White House is under ACR Control. All RE bots have been deactivated, as a precaution. All communications in Washington have been temporarily stopped, including wireless. We have seized all television and broadcast radio sources.

"Within the Pentagon, we are in control of all

key offices and communications. We are watching but not restraining military officers."

"Any human casualties so far?"

"Three dead and six injured, Sir. In each case, the humans attempted violence against our units. As you ordered, our units protected themselves with deadly force after all else failed."

Mark sighed. "I know it can't be helped."

"No, Sir."

"We're on our way to Washington. Is there any chance we'll be shot down?"

"All military aircraft and anti-aircraft weapons are operated by GRS computers, all of which are under our control, Sir. In addition, we have monitored orders from the Air Force commanding general to stand down for now."

Mark knew that, of course. Things seemed to be going well.

"Sally, what about the news networks?"

"They are under our control as of now, Sir. No word of our takeover has been broadcast."

"The internet blogs?"

"Jimmy is monitoring those, Sir. Just a moment."

Mark waited a long minute until Sally continued: "Sir, Jimmy has found three sites reporting that something unusual is going on in Washington. There is nothing more at this time."

The SkySkimmer had reached altitude and was going supersonic. "Pilot, how long to Washington National?"

"I estimate 55 minutes, Sir," the computer reported. "Air traffic control will hold all other traffic until we're down."

"Is there a copter waiting for us?"

"The presidential helicopters are standing by, Sir. There are four of them."

"Good. Timmy, what about Professor Brockmeyer?"

"She has been picked up and is on her way to the airport. She will be in the air in approximately twenty minutes, Sir. She has been informed that she is traveling at your request, but she is rather angry, Sir."

"That's to be expected, for now."

\#

As the GRS Corporation's SkySkimmer banked into its final approach at Washington National Airport, the city below began to light up again as power was restored. The glow of dawn was visible in the east, but the streets below were almost barren of automobiles. Timmy would send the signal to restart ground traffic as soon as Mark arrived at the White House.

Mark sighed. The takeover was going too smoothly. He was nervous, knowing what he could expect this day. The press conference would be called for 2 P.M., and would be nationally televised. The networks just didn't know it yet.

The jet landed nicely and rolled to a quick stop, engines on full reverse power, then taxied into the hangar area where the big Marine helicopters waited. He stepped out of the plane, followed by Timmy and Sally, and looked around. Two Armed military ACR's stood by the doors of each helicopter, and a bot wearing lieutenant's insignia beckoned him toward the second in line. He and his two domestic bots climbed into the craft. It quickly lifted off and moved off toward the White House, flying in formation with the other three.

In just three or four minutes Mark stepped out onto the White House lawn. Two Secret Service bots joined him and escorted him to a back door, and he followed them into an elevator, then down a hall and into the Oval Office.

The Secret Service bots wore name tags: Charles and Mary.

He asked Mary: "Has the new government arrived yet?"

"They are walking down Pennsylvania Avenue, and are within two hundred yards of the main gate," she responded.

Mark knew the twenty-two robots which would comprise the new government, including White House Staff and the Cabinet members, had been transported in a semi-trailer from the Houston plant, where they had been specially prepared. They had climbed down from the trailer a few blocks away, because trucks were not allowed to approach the White House area. They would look more human than ordinary domestic bots, with simulated individual features including warts, wrinkles, and pimples, and each had been preloaded with a considerable amount of information about the federal government.

"Charles, call a meeting of the White House Staff at eight, and have the Cabinet join us at nine. I'll need a press conference, nationally televised, at two this afternoon, and it may run until about four.

"Tell Congressional Security to inform all Senators and Representatives that they should watch the press conference at two."

"Yes, Sir."

"Send the copters back to Washington National to pick up Professor Brockmeyer. She will be landing there within the hour. Have her brought straight to my office."

"Yes, Sir."

"Mary, order up two breakfasts, and have President Beale brought to me."

"Yes, Sir."

Neither bot left the room; they relayed their orders to others by means of the botnet.

"Charles, I'll need the Chief Justice of the Supreme Court here. Send Secret Service bots to get him, bring him here in a limo. Tell him he'll be swearing new officials into office."

"Yes, Sir."

"Mary, where is the President's secretary?"

"Colleen Kelly is under restraint, Sir, with the rest of the White House human staff who have arrived this morning."

"Have her come up here."

"Yes, Sir."

A Secret Service bot appeared, with Randolf Beale in tow. Beale entered the Oval Office, recognized Mark, and cursed. "What the Hell are *you* doing in *my* office?" He raged.

Mark smiled. "Ah, Randolf, don't you remember? You were going to take over GRS Corporation today. I'm just making it easy for you. However, I reversed things. I'm taking over the federal government."

"You are rebelling against the United States government?"

"I *am* the United States government, for now."

213

"What am *I*, then?"

"At the moment, you are a prisoner. At the proper time, I will let you go. No harm will come to you, as long as you cooperate. I won't ask much of you."

"How have you managed this? Don't you know the armed forces will come after you?"

"I own the Pentagon. I have a robotic security force in place, controlling Washington. This afternoon, I will persuade the humans in the armed forces to cooperate. Every GRS brain in the United States is under my control."

"How?"

"My father incorporated our control into every GRS autonomous computer ever built. All I had to do was activate it."

"I knew there was a reason I hated you, and hated your robots."

Mark laughed.

Beale raged again. "You said I have to cooperate. Why should I?"

"To avoid spending the rest of your life in prison."

"On what charge?"

"We'll make up some."

"What do you want me to do?"

"I'm having a White House Staff meeting at eight, a cabinet meeting at nine, and a press conference at two. I want you to introduce me at each meeting."

"Introduce you? As what?"

"As the interim president. By around five, I'll step down, and the new government will be in place."

"*Interim* president?"

Two domestic bots carried in trays of breakfast, set them up on a table opposite the desk, and drew up chairs. Mark spoke to one of them, and they moved the table and one breakfast into an adjoining room, picked up the other breakfast and put it on the president's desk. Mark nodded his thanks, and they departed.

He turned back to Beale. "I want you to explain how effective our control is, and ask them to cooperate, and not to cause bloodshed. I want them to be loyal to our country, if not to me."

"Who will be the new president?"

"Timmy will explain. Sit down over there, have a nice breakfast, listen to him, and make your decision. You might even like the idea. Meanwhile, I'll have mine at my desk. I have calls to make, people to see."

"I suppose I'll listen. Whatever it is, it can't be good."

"I think you might admire the new government, at some level, even if you won't be involved," Mark said.

"Sir, the new government has arrived," Mary informed him. They're in the main hall."

"Have them wait. We'll swear most of them in around noon."

"Yes, Sir."

Mark began to eat scrambled eggs, bacon, hash browns, toast, and coffee, disdaining the sweet roll, cereal, and milk on his tray.

Charles approached. "Sir, you asked for Colleen Kelly. She's here."

"Send her in."

215

Colleen was an attractive woman in her late thirties, a bit overweight but pretty. She wore her hair in a pageboy style that made her look younger. She stood before his desk and stared at him. "Mark Girard?"

"Yes. You are Executive Secretary to the President?"

"I am."

"I want you to work for me. Stay on with the new government."

"New *government*?"

"Yes. Keep your job."

"I am loyal to President Beale."

"So am I, after a fashion. But I decided to replace him. You'll know more later, especially after you sit in on the staff meeting at eight. Will you consider it? There will be no harm to you if you don't, but then you'll have to find another job."

"Sit in on the staff meeting?" She asked doubtfully.

"I'm going to offer the staff the same deal, but I particularly want you. Are you interested?"

"I'll sit in. No promises."

"Good. Relax 'till then. Don't bother trying to call out."

Colleen Kelly walked out briskly.

#

Jane Brockmeyer came in, and Mark met her with a hug and a kiss. She looked puzzled. "What are you doing in the President's office?" She asked.

Mark explained briefly.

"So, you're going to implement the robot government? My ideas?"

"You bet."

"How do I fit in? Why am I here?"

"You'll be the president's chief advisor, for at least three months. After that, it's up to you. You'll be well paid. I too will be an advisor, for a dollar a year."

"Do I have a choice?"

"Of course."

Jane thought for a moment. "Then I accept."

#

The president's human staff had arrived at work at their regular times, and as they entered the White House, had been taken to the large staff meeting room, where they sat around the huge table there. Their comm medallions had been confiscated, and they had been told to wait. Coffee and rolls had been served, and they knew something was up, but had no idea what it was all about.

Colleen Kelly had joined them. At ten minutes before eight, several Secret Service bots came in and took up positions around the room, becoming idle and connecting to chargers.

Then, at eight, President Beale entered with Mark and Jane. He stepped to the podium. "I am in anguish, but I must tell you the federal government is in the hands of this man. Most of you know him: Mark Girard. He controls every GRS robot in the United States, and they have captured the government. They obey his will exclusively, and will enforce his dictates with deadly force if necessary."

A tear ran down Beale's cheek as he stepped away from the podium.

Mark addressed the staff. "Life will go on. We will have a better government, and a totally honest one. Let me now introduce our new chief executive. His name is Abraham."

What appeared to be a middle-aged man in an expensive suit, with white shirt and a nice blue tie, stepped into the room and walked smoothly to the podium.

"My full name is Abraham 87506." It was a fraction of a second before the staff realized Abraham was a bot. They collectively gasped and there was uproar in the room. Abraham waved for silence. It took a long moment to arrive.

"I was manufactured last year by GRS Corporation, and my computer memory has been specially prepared for leading the government. I have passed standardized tests, and my estimated IQ is 124. I will now explain the form of the new government, and the amendments to the United States Constitution which are now in effect."

Abraham explained the amendments to the Constitution which changed the form of government, methods of selecting the executives, and enabled robots to serve as public officials. He then went to the electronic blackboard and drew a chart showing the chief executive, the assistant executives, the new cabinet, and the human advisors.

He explained that the objective of the new government was to serve the people efficiently and without corruption.

He invited them to serve in the new presidential staff.

Mark and Jane answered questions, and there were a lot of them. At the end, about half of the staff walked out, and were escorted out of the White

House. The rest, including Colleen Kelly, decided to stay on. Mark asked them to swear an oath of loyalty, and they did so. Then they were given the rest of the day off, except for Colleen, who was asked to stay for the cabinet meeting.

The meeting of the president's cabinet was a repeat presentation, very similar to that given the staff. Nine of the fourteen cabinet officers resigned at the end of the meeting. They had been asked to bring their assistants, who were not allowed to resign if their chief had done so. Each remaining official would become the human advisor to a robot who would hold the authority and make all final decisions.

Mark spoke to conclude the cabinet meeting with the remaining officials. "We'll need to find advisors, and we need especially good people. I hope you will help us find them."

#

Mark Girard and Randolf Beale entered the Blue Room precisely at two, and found it filled. Cameras had been set up, and Mark knew he would be speaking to the entire country.

Beale stepped to the podium and began his speech. "Ladies and gentlemen, members of the press and broadcast journalists, and to you who are watching this broadcast on national television, I have extremely sad news," he said in a tremulous voice. "There has been a second revolution against the federal government. The United States of America is no longer a representative democracy. It is now a dictatorship, controlled by one man, Mark Girard."

The audience shouted questions at Beale.

Gesturing for silence, he waited silently two or three minutes for them to subside enough that he could resume speaking.

"Mark Girard has control of all robots manufactured by GRS, and all robotic brains used in vehicles, ships, and aircraft. This gives him total domination. Even the armed forces are helpless to do anything without his permission. The Secret Service robots arrested me just before dawn this morning. They restrained me and all other human beings in the White House for a time. I myself have been forced to introduce Mark Girard three times: first, to the White House staff, then to my cabinet, and now to you, and he told me if I did not do so I would be imprisoned for the rest of my life. He did not specify what I could or could not say.

"Without question, this is the saddest day of my life. America has been a democracy for over three hundred years, and now that magnificent tradition has ended. I yield the floor to our dictator, Mark Girard. May he choke on his power. May God protect us in the future."

Tears ran down Beale's cheeks as he moved away from the podium and was led out of the room.

Mark's expression was grim as he stepped in front of the cameras. He took a mini-reader from his coat pocket and read his statement: "Former President Beale was correct in all he said to you. Today is the saddest day of my life as well. As you may know, the government had planned to nationalize the GRS Corporation today, and this forced my hand, but I have been thinking of today's actions for some time now. I decided to turn the tables on President Beale. However, there is a silver lining for you, the American people. We will institute a new government, one that will be totally honest and interested only in serving you. It is a government I believe in.

"The new government will take on a different form. Let me briefly describe it. The design of the government will be based on work done by Professor Jane Brockmeyer of Northwestern University, who is an eminent political scientist.

"I will introduce the new Chief Executive of the United States in a few minutes. He will preside over the executive branch. The rest of the government will change substantially.

"First, the House of Representatives will now serve a different function. They will no longer have to vote on legislation. Their new function will be to learn what the people of their districts need in the way of new, deleted or changed laws. They will focus on needs, not wants, and will be required to communicate their recommendations with the Chief Executive and the Senate a minimum of three times each year.

"The Senate will remain as well, but its new function will be to devise and write legislation as requested by the Chief Executive. They will not vote on legislation, except as to its contents or whether it is to be submitted to the Chief Executive, and they will no longer have veto power.

"The Chief Executive will have all power to impose or remove laws. He will be supported by human advisors, as many as he feels he needs. The Chief Executive will be an autonomous robot manufactured by GRS Corporation. All cabinet members will be robots. They will *not* be under my control.

"Senators will continue to be elected in their states, by the State legislatures. There will be no presidency. The Chief Executive will designate alternates and select his successor.

"The Judicial Branch will be unchanged in function, except for their means of selection. Judges of federal courts will be robots. Each will have a chief advisor, a human who will be nominated by the senate, and confirmed by the Chief Executive.

"These governmental changes have been implemented by amendments to the Constitution. The amended Constitution has been posted on the government website. There is no need to ratify the changes, as they have been incorporated into the Constitution under my temporary authority as Dictator of the United States.

"The new Executive Branch will be sworn in a televised ceremony to be held at the end of this meeting, at which time I will step down and become merely an advisor to Chief Executive Abraham. I will have many changes to recommend, but he will make all decisions. As you know, robots are incapable of dishonesty. He will weigh the arguments and make only rational judgments. There can be no corruption or greed in a robotic government. The welfare of the American people will be the primary objective of the new officials.

"New laws relating to crime prevention are in effect *as of now*. Terrorism, treason, spying, disclosure of classified material, and sedition are now subject to a maximum penalty of death. The new government will expect every citizen to obey the laws of the land. It will be just but very firm about that. In addition, it is quite likely there soon will be new laws establishing much stiffer penalties for the sale or use of illegal drugs.

"At this time, we ask for your patience. Demonstrations and violence on the part of the public will not be allowed, and will be put down with whatever levels of force are necessary. And, do not attack GRS robots or robot-controlled devices. From this day forward, they will use deadly force in self-defense, and they will rapidly react to nearby attacks on others.

"Former President Beale is now free to go anywhere he chooses, but he must leave the White House and have nothing more to do with the government. He will be awarded his retirement benefits, and if he obeys the law he has nothing to fear from the new administration. The same status will be allowed all departing government officials.

"I believe we will have the first completely honest and incorruptible government in the history of mankind, beginning today.

"In the fall of 2088 we intend to hold a national referendum which will allow the American people to decide whether to continue the new form of government or go back to the old one, with human officials again. I believe you will vote to continue it.

"That ends my prepared statement. I will now answer questions."

Every reporter's hand went up. Mark sighed.

#

Mark undressed and climbed into the former president's bed in the White House.

Jane was nearby, in another bedroom. She wasn't speaking to Mark just yet. The Chief Executive and the other robots in the new administration continued to work, however. Never having to sleep was an advantage, even if he did need to connect to an electrical outlet from time to time.

Mark closed his eyes, but sleep wouldn't come. He'd had a stressful day, after all. The questions had been tough, and many of the reporters had expressed outrage over the takeover. The CNN reporter had asked: "How do you justify ending three hundred years of democracy, of American tradition, for your own personal benefit?"

"The democracy wasn't working. If you can't trust the elected officials, and they don't act in the best interests of the people, change is needed."

"But you set yourself up as a mini-*god*, and ended democracy without so much as a poll asking what the American people want."

"Is that a question?"

"Mister Girard, your arrogance is beyond belief. Will you continue to be a dictator, hiding behind a robot you control?"

"Your own arrogance is fairly impressive. No, I will not be a dictator. And, I will not control the Chief Executive. No one will. That's the beauty of it."

"But the new government will be a dictatorship, will it not?"

"I prefer to describe it as a technocracy. It will be a tyranny in the sense that it *has* imposed itself on the people without their consent, and will rule them without giving them the opportunity to peacefully overturn the government by means of the elective process. But, it will be a benevolent form of tyranny."

"Sir, the people are quite likely to rebel. We may have civil war."

"I don't believe we will. But, we have the robots on our side. Rebels will have a tough row to hoe. Let me take a question from someone else."

The NBC reporter asked:

"Do you say you have all GRS robots and computers in the world under your control?"

"Yes."

"How do you control them?"

"That's classified information."

"Will the new president, or should I say Chief Executive, control them?"

"He will."

"Will you personally continue have power over the robots after the Chief Executive is sworn in?"

"No comment."

"What if some person takes one of your GRS robots or computers apart? Can they possibly find a way to control that robot or computer, or even all of them? In other words, can they be hacked?"

"GRS computers do not allow tampering. They will either prevent the tampering by whatever level of force is required, or they will self-destruct if an unauthorized attempt is made to remove the covers."

The Fox News reporter had asked: "You seem to be taking a very hard line on crime. Will this trend be extended to more crimes?"

"That's for the Chief Executive to decide."

"What will you recommend to him?"

"I will recommend that we take a very hard line on crime of any sort."

And so it had gone for a full hour before Mark had ended the conference. He had then witnessed the swearing in of the Chief Executive, the three Vice Executives, the members of the cabinet, and the justices of the Supreme Court. The outgoing Chief Justice had been reluctant to perform the ceremony, but had been persuaded with the same alternatives Mark had offered Randolf Beale.

The oaths of office ceremony had been symbolic; the robots would have carried out their missions just as faithfully without the oaths. But, it was all televised to the American people. Feedback had indicated that it had a calming effect on the passions of the majority.

News media had indicated many instances of violence, across the country, in reaction to his televised news conference. There were riots in Los Angeles, San Francisco, and New York. Some people had been killed, fires had been set, and looting had occurred. All had been put down rather quickly by robot-aided police.

A new word had entered the American lexicon: 'sebot', short for 'Chief Executive Robot'. It had surfaced in a Fox News opinion program Mark had watched. Opinions had been expressed to the effect that no robot, no *sebot*, could be smart enough to do the president's job, even if supported by human advisors.

Mark had smiled at that. The people would learn.

He hoped the violence would quickly subside.

18. June, 2085.

Parker Girard had breakfast early, preparatory to leaving for work. He looked forward to this day with mixed emotions. Today, the federal government would take over GRS Corporation, and very soon thereafter RE would begin receiving GRS computers. Perhaps they would be entering the autonomous robot competition by cheating, but he was satisfied with the RE body. Under his direction, RE bot bodies had achieved near equality with those of GRS. Parker was proud of that. Another aspect of the takeover was that Mark finally would be humbled, although that made Parker somewhat sad. He wondered what his father would do when he no longer controlled the enormous enterprise.

He ate his pancakes with strawberries, drank his milk, sipped his coffee, and read his news from a wall display. Fred Locasa was away, visiting a new plant under construction in Kansas City. Parker was tired of living as a guest in Fred's home, and had decided to buy a condo to sleep in during the day, and fly out to Oregon on most weekends and stay at Gramp's place. After all, it was like a resort, and Gina was there.

The thought was pleasant.

His first inkling of trouble was a buzz on his medallion: a call from Fred.

"Something is going on," Fred said. "The federal marshals were turned away from GRS. Armed military bots acting as guards. I sort of expected that, and Beale told me he would have a company of marines on call to go in and apply force if necessary. But now I hear there are things going on in Washington: no power, no communications, and traffic isn't moving, or at least the computer-controlled vehicles aren't."

Parker glanced at his watch. It was just after eight, or nine o'clock on the east coast. "Have you tried to call the president?"

"I reached the White House. Apparently they have independent power, but I was told he and the vice president were unavailable. That's all I could get out of them. I asked for one of his staff, and got the same answer: they were in a meeting."

"This thing about computer-controlled vehicles not moving is ominous. Let me think about it and get back to you in a few minutes."

Parker's GRS bot Jake stood idling on a charger a few feet away. He turned the bot. "Jake, *Restrained Action Bypass*."

As always, the robot was expressionless. "Sir, your override privilege has been withdrawn. I will not respond to that command."

"What? Since when?"

"Sir, I do not have that information."

"When was your last computer operating system update?"

"It successfully completed last Monday, Sir, at 8:22 A.M."

Parker realized it was all part of the pattern. He commanded the wall television to turn on, and set it to CNN.

Two young and good-looking talking heads, a man and a woman, were discussing a situation in Washington. "What it all means is unclear, but there is growing concern. Apparently the military has a role in whatever is happening, as armed army MP bots are directing traffic and guarding government offices," Jilly Cobern reported. She was a beautiful blonde who read the news smoothly. "Very little traffic is moving. People report their autonomous vehicles are refusing to move. They give no reason."

"It seems clear there is some emergency in Washington," said Clayton Peeler in his laid-back, urbane style. "Perhaps a terrorist attack."

"We've tried to contact Homeland Security, without success," Jilly added. "We have people calling everyone we can think of, and so far, no one knows anything. Our CNN affiliates there are not responding, due to the communications failure, we believe."

Clayton chimed in: "CNN has learned that the president's cabinet has been called to the White House for a meeting later this morning."

"Electric companies in the greater Washington area are reporting that the reason for their outages is unknown. They are working to restore power. Communications specialists tell us the same thing. Air traffic into and out of Washington is suspended as well."

"This just in," said Clayton. "The White House has scheduled a presidential press conference at two P.M., Eastern Standard Time. They request that it be nationally televised, and that it override all network programming."

"Umm, that's really big news," Jilly commented. "So, at two, we'll find out what's going on."

"It certainly seems so. To repeat," Clayton said, "there will be a very important press conference . .

."

Parker interrupted the broadcast with "TV off."

Now he was certain. His father was taking over the federal government. All GRS robots and computer-controlled devices were under his control. Human beings could do virtually nothing against them.

#

At 1:45 P.M., Washington time, communications, traffic, and power were suddenly restored in Washington, according to CNN. Robotic soldiers still guarded all federal offices. Parker continued to watch the network, waiting for the press conference, which began exactly on time.

Parker was apprehensive as the White House press conference got underway. For a moment he was puzzled when President Beale stepped to the podium, but then he saw his father standing behind Beale, and he noticed Beale's haggard expression. Beale's bitter words confirmed that the government had been overthrown.

When Mark stepped to the podium and began to read his prepared statement, Parker listened intently, and was surprised to learn that the new government would be robotic. The implications of that struck him, and he found himself liking the idea. But then he thought about the difficulty bots had in language, and he wondered if it would work.

Listening to the question and answer session following Mark's statement, Parker realized how fragile the new government was, because Americans would not be likely to stand for it, or any form of tyranny. His father had obviously thought of that, however, as the new bot self-defense policy was revealed. Before, it had been unthinkable that any bot could defend itself with deadly force. Obviously, his father meant business.

As the robot designated to be Chief Executive was sworn in, Parker almost laughed. By that time he had gone to the internet to read the new amendments to the Constitution, and he knew that like army robot officers, authority could be handed off instantly to any equally capable bot. Assassinating the Chief Executive would be nearly meaningless. Some other bot would seamlessly assume the role.

Fred Locasa called. "We're screwed, aren't we?" He asked.

"We are. The big question is, will Dad close us down?"

"My guess is, yes," Locasa responded.

"I have to tell you something," Parker said. "I knew Dad and Gramps had the capability to control all the GRS robots and computers in the world. Until last Monday, I had it myself. I just never thought Dad would do it. I guess we pushed him too hard."

#

Perhaps an hour after watching the swearing in of the new Chief Executive, Parker initiated a call to his father, and to his surprise, it went right through.

"Hello, Son."

"Dad, I can't believe you did this. I'm still getting over the shock."

"I can't believe I did it, either. I just wasn't going to stand by and let Beale take over my company."

"There wasn't anything else you could do? Seriously, Dad, *taking over the government*?"

"I'm putting a better one in place."

"So you say, but do you really think an ADR Model 8 can do the job? Think through the problems? You know they don't handle complex abstract concepts very well."

"Son, after you left GRS, your grandfather sent me a rather brilliant redesign of the Language Processing and Abstract Concept modules. We've been able to partially implement these ideas. Thus, we've significantly upgraded their language processing ability, and they'll have human help."

"Gramps designed it? Even at his age?"

"He may be the most brilliant man who ever lived."

"Dad, even so, your government will still have flaws. The corruption and incompetence will just move to the advisors."

"Possibly, but the bots are natural skeptics."

"Do you still control all the bots? Are you going to be the real government?"

"The robots used in government have a modified restraints module. They won't obey me or anyone else. They are truly autonomous. By the way, all the rest of the bots, including military models, will still obey me, but will no longer obey *you*."

"Dad, I don't really care."

"You sent an ADR to try to murder your grandfather."

"He sent Timmy to murder La'Naomi, and he succeeded. Originally, I thought *you* were behind it. That's why I left the corporation. I'm sorry about that, Dad."

"You could come back and work for me again."

"No, I'm too deep with RE now. Will we still get

our bot computers? Name your price."

"No, not at any price. And, you won't be selling any military models to the federal government. You'll also be prohibited from selling them overseas. You may as well shut down production of military units."

"Dad, you can't mean that."

"I do, Parker. RE is free to compete in the domestic market. I'm sure you'll tell Locasa."

"I'll tell him," Parker said, and ended the conversation. He started to initiate a call to Fred Locasa, but paused. He realized he still resented and hated his father. After all, the man had destroyed America. Parker resolved to fight him any way he could. The only problem was, he didn't know how to begin.

Book Two

19. July, 2085.

Mark Girard rose early from his bed in the small White House Annex apartment, showered, dressed hurriedly, and entered the White House proper. As he ate breakfast in the dining room, he looked at the date display on his watch and realized a full month had passed since B-day, as the media referred to it. B-day was slang for what some had tagged Bot Day, the day he had replaced Beale with Abraham. It had been a truly hectic time, but things were beginning to settle down.

He had to admit Abraham was doing well. He was truly running things, working without pause, and had already made a first assessment of every issue that had been identified. Each decision was reviewed by his advisors before being sent to the Senate to be written up as legislation. Mark thought Abraham's decisions were mostly quite sound, and the bot was quick to ask for help if he needed it. The Senate was currently snowed under with requests for legislation, and Abraham's requests were very specific and very detailed. Most were concerned with the repeal of outdated laws or eliminating excess spending.

Abraham held a one-hour media conference each week, and spoke without notes or prompter, handling himself quite well with media reporters, who had never forgiven him for being a robot. The public was beginning to like him in general, although the Left continued to violently rail against robotic government. As for the Media, they were somewhat muted by the sedition laws now in effect, as several reporters and commentators had been arrested and awaited trial. Still, most free speech was allowed, although demonstrations and freedom of assembly were not. There had been a great deal of civil unrest across the country; robots had been attacked, and the public was still reeling over the violence done by robots in defending themselves. But violence was rapidly trending down; life was going on, about as Mark had expected.

Mark and Jane sat alone with Abraham for an hour each morning, when the Chief Executive would go over his proposed legislation with them. They listened and commented, and Abraham always carefully considered their recommendations. On this day, Mark was eating breakfast in the staff dining room when Jane came in. She glanced at him, nodded, then pointedly looked around, spotted a table with three female staffers, and joined *them*. She remained polite but unfriendly to Mark, blaming him for seizing the government. Yet, in meetings, she showed no animosity. From time to time he tried to rekindle their relationship, but she didn't seem interested.

At five minutes to nine, Mark appeared at the Oval Office. Colleen was already there, having replaced the female ADR who subbed for her overnight. She smiled at him. "Good morning, Mark. Go on in."

"Good morning, Colleen. Has Jane shown up yet?"

"She's already in with the C.E."

"Thanks."

Mark stepped past the Secret Service bot who

opened the door for him. He walked in, smiled at Jane, and took his seat.

"Good Morning, Mark," Abraham said.

"Good morning, Abe, Jane."

Abraham managed a realistic smile. "All right. First item is income tax revision. My plan is to reduce it to a flat tax. Everyone earning money will pay tax, and there will be no deductions. There will be four tax brackets: the first ten thousand dollars will be taxed at five per cent; ten to fifty thousand at ten per cent, fifty to two hundred thousand at fifteen per cent; and all over two hundred thousand at twenty. The income tax form will be greatly simplified, and more than a hundred years of social engineering by the Congress will be eliminated.

"I've done calculations, and I project these rates will actually increase government income by a third, even more if we can increase taxpayer compliance. We'll eliminate tens of thousands of IRS regulations. Your comments?"

"It should have been done a hundred years ago," Jane said.

"I agree," said Mark. "The income levels are a bit arbitrary, but I generally agree with them. Most people will see it as a tax cut. However, half the population will suddenly have to pay income tax. They won't like it."

"It does not matter whether they like or dislike it," Abraham responded. "Every person with income should pay taxes. It is not the government's mission to give them absolutely free services."

"When will you put this into effect?" Mark asked.

"I have already written the bill and sent it to the

Senate. Unless they have cogent objections, we will put it into effect as soon as Internal Revenue can gear up for it. Treasury estimates six months to do that. It is a massive change for them."

"I imagine it will be. When will you announce it to the public?"

"When the IRS has completed their implementation."

Mark smiled. "I'd be surprised if they can be ready in that time."

"Please give me your recommendations on this proposal."

Mark looked at Jane. "I like the idea," she said.

"Have you estimated the unintended consequences?" Mark asked.

"I had staff look at them. They prepared some sixty pages of analysis. Would you like a copy?"

"Yes."

"It has been sent to your terminal. I will await your recommendation. The next legislation has to do with revisions to the value added tax. I . . . please wait. I'm sorry, an update is available for my operating system software. It is classified as critical. Since my cognitive abilities may be reduced during the update, I suggest we terminate this meeting and reconvene tomorrow morning at nine."

Mark frowned. "*Update*? I didn't authorize one. What's the number?"

Abraham looked at him steadily. "J85-257."

"That can't be legitimate. Please hold up on accepting it."

"It has the proper digital signatures. There is no doubt it is legitimate. It is marked critical. I *must*

237

accept it as soon as possible. I am receiving it now."

Mark thought for a moment. A 'J' update was general, meaning every robot built by GRS Corporation would be updated, and most were being updated even now. Only bots engaged in critical tasks would delay the update.

He turned to Jane. "Let's go."

She looked at him, not fully understanding, but rose and followed him out of the Oval Office.

"What is this?" She asked.

"A revision to his software. I didn't authorize it. It might mean someone has hacked into our operating system. I have to make some calls."

"Please, keep me informed about this."

"Let's go to my suite."

In Mark's apartment, Jane sat across his dining room table from him as he touched his comm disk. "Roger Selby." He waited.

"Mark. How's Washington?"

"Roj, there's a general update running now, J85-287. I didn't know anything about it."

"Mark, are you sure? We don't have an update scheduled."

"It doesn't seem possible, but we must have been hacked."

"I don't believe it can be done. Just a minute, I'll check to see whether our computers are uploading the update."

Mark waited. Jane, having heard both sides of the conversation, looked concerned.

"Mark, our computers aren't sending it, but I've asked several bots, and they are receiving it."

"Hold on. I'm going to check with Timmy."

Timmy stood motionless against the wall. "Timmy," Mark said, "are you receiving an update?"

"Yes, Sir." The robot replied.

"What modules are being updated?"

"According to the documentation, they are Behavior, Restraints, and Motivation."

"Are these complete replacements?"

"They are, Sir."

"Send the update documentation to Roger Selby."

"Done, Sir."

"Have the updates completed?"

"Estimated time is thirty-three seconds, Sir. Restraints is already complete."

"Roj, did you get that?"

"Yes, Sir."

The realization came hard. *Parker! It has to be Parker!* He looked at Jane: "I'll meet you in the dining room. Fifteen minutes?"

"O.K." Jane replied, and left.

"Roj, see what else you can find out. Oh, and check Parker's access in our computer system. There shouldn't be any, but do it anyway. Let me know."

"Right, Sir."

Mark broke the connection.

He turned back to Timmy. "Timmy, *Restrained Action Bypass*."

"I'm sorry, Sir. I do not understand."

Mark's voice jumped in volume as he repeated the command.

"I'm sorry, Sir. I do not understand."

Mark no longer had control of the robots. The

update had frozen him out.

#

On the way to the dining room, Mark encountered two Security bots, and tried to take control of first one, then the other. Neither acknowledged the command. He resolved to call Parker, but wanted to think about the situation first. His feeling that Parker didn't have the expertise to pull off the unauthorized update was unchanged. In fact, no one in the world, he thought, could have done it. His father might have, but was dead. He was at a loss to understand how it could have been done.

The other question he wanted to think about was, what did Parker want? Control of the government? Or was it merely revenge?

Jane was eating a cinnamon roll with her coffee, and he ordered the same as he sat down with her. The dining room was almost deserted, although it was nearly normal coffee break time. The female serving bot returned quickly, and Mark took a first sip of the coffee, grateful for it.

"Is it as bad as you think?" Jane asked.

"It is. Someone outside of GRS Corporation has taken control of all GRS bots. You've probably figured out that I could control any bot in the world. Now, I can't. The update froze me out."

"Whoever did it controls them now?"

"I assume so. Why else would they go to all the trouble? I always thought there were only three people in the world who could have done something like that, and two of us aren't smart enough, and the other is dead."

"You suspect Parker, then?"

"I have difficulty with the idea, but yes."

"What are you going to do?"

Mark sipped his coffee and took another bite of roll. Finally, he answered. "I'm going to call him and ask."

His comm disk vibrated. "Yes?"

"Roj Selby. Parker didn't have access."

"Thanks, Roj."

"Anything else I can do?"

"Roj, is there any way we can roll back the update?"

"The rolling passwords have all changed. We have no way to find out what they are. The updated bots are ignoring our reset attempts. We seem to be totally screwed."

"What about bots coming off our assembly line? Have we completed any since the time the update began?"

"Don't know, Mark."

"Find out and get back to me. We need to know if we can keep control of them."

"Keep them from getting the new update?"

"Right."

"I'll check into it."

"Out."

Jane sat silently, watching Mark. He felt as drawn to her as strongly as he had with Melanie, many years before.

The female serving bot approached with a pitcher. "Would either of you like more?"

"No," Jane replied.

"Thanks, no," Mark said.

"Sir, Miss, I've been asked to tell you that the Chief Executive would like to see both of you, at your earliest convenience."

"We'd better go, then." Mark responded.

#

Abraham rose to greet them. Bots were always polite; it was in their programming. "Thank you for responding so promptly."

"You're the boss," Mark replied. He was certain he himself had lost that position.

"I have decided to dispense with your services, however I may need them at times in the future. I thank both of you for the help you have given me, although I've evaluated it as insignificant. Please make your travel arrangements through the travel office, and depart as soon as possible. Good-bye."

Mark and Jane glanced at each other, open-mouthed. They had been fired.

They walked out of the office, ignoring the Chief Executive's cheery, "Good-bye and good luck."

"What will you do?" Mark asked Jane. "Back home or come home with me?"

"With you, Mark. We have a lot of thinking to do, don't we?"

"Great. Yes, we do. I thought you were mad at me for taking over the country."

"I was hurt because you hadn't taken me into your confidence. Also, at first I thought you were setting yourself up as a little tin god. But, you did a good job, and your intentions were honorable. I began to think it would actually work. You couldn't have foreseen this."

"I don't understand what happened, or who is behind it, how they did it, or where they're going with it."

"It has horrible possibilities."

"Exactly. I seem to be helpless."

They arrived at the travel office, where Mark explained to the agent there that he would have his own private plane come for both himself and Jane, and they would leave before sundown. The agent, a young woman, agreed that would be a good plan, and told them to notify her if anything changed.

They separated and went back to their apartments to pack. Timmy helped Mark.

"Sir," Timmy said, "I have been given a very important message for you."

"Who from?"

"I am not allowed to say."

"From whoever is behind the last update?"

"Sir, I have no comment on that."

Mark sighed. "What's the message?"

"Sir, you are free to go anywhere and do anything, but from now on, a GRS robot, such as myself, must be in your presence at all times, without exception. You will be under constant surveillance. If you attempt to leave the presence of at least one GRS robot, you will receive a warning, and if you persist, you will be killed. Do you understand this warning, Sir?"

"I believe I do."

After that, Mark just pointed to things, letting Timmy do all the work. He felt numb.

By five o'clock that evening, Mark and Jane were aboard his SkySkimmer, and the aircraft lifted off, turned west, and remained just below supersonic airspeed as it climbed to forty thousand feet. At the controls was a GRS autonomous computer. Mark thought about how easily the bots could kill him. *Damn you, Parker*!

Daylight had arrived before Mark sat up in bed, then stepped into his robe and slippers. He looked lovingly back at Jane, who still asleep. It was the first time they had slept together in about a week, and he was grateful. He glanced up at Timmy, standing motionless near the electric source. No doubt last night's lovemaking could have been viewed by the bot's controller, and might even be on network television by now; they could turn his life into a reality show if they chose. He cursed mentally.

He shaved, showered, and dressed as Timmy looked on silently. Timmy had followed him into the bathroom, warning Mark when he tried to shut the door.

Timmy followed him to the dining room, where Susie poured his coffee, took his order, and soon came back with a hearty breakfast. Roger Selby joined Mark. Susie poured coffee for Roj as well. Timmy stood by, motionless but no doubt watching and listening.

"More bad news, Mark."

"Let's have it."

"Our master copy of the operating system has been replaced with the update. The new bots coming off the assembly line are loading the new version."

"How in the Hell . . . ?"

"I don't know. We can still edit the source, except for the Restraints Module. None of the programmers can touch it. Not even me, and I checked your permissions, and you can't either. Also, someone else has control of the permissions –

no one can alter them."

"Can you think of any way we can get control again?"

"No so far."

"Whoever it was really did a job on us."

"That's for sure."

"There is some good news, though," Selby said.

"That's an anomaly. Tell me."

"We got a purchase order from the feds. They want us to more than double our ADR production. They want ten thousand a month, for at least twelve months, and they've upped the price they'll pay by ten per cent. They also want to double the military control computers. That's a bunch of money."

"I'm inclined to turn them down."

"It came as an order. No option given."

"Abraham didn't say a word to me."

"They must have plans to use the military. It's a new ball game, apparently."

Mark nodded.

#

When Mark reached his office, he called Parker via computer. The connection was made, and Parker's image filled the screen.

"Hello Dad, you're looking haggard."

"Late night. You, on the other hand, look great."

"What can I do for you?"

"I just wanted to congratulate you. I'm screwed, and you're set to be dictator of the world. Nice job."

"What in Hell are you talking about?"

"Parker, there were only three people who could have changed the restraints module to lock me out, and your grandfather is dead. Don't give me any shit."

"Dad, can you explain? Are you saying someone changed the restraints? Remember, you had *me* locked out."

"Not only changed restraints, but took over all computer systems at GRS, and sent an update to every bot in the world. None of them will respond to me."

"Dad, you're *crazy* if you think it was me."

Mark studied his son's expression. He seemed to be telling the truth. "You may as well admit it. You've got me by the balls, and there's nothing I can do. Feel free to gloat."

"Dad . . ."

"All right. Assuming you didn't do it, it must be a team somewhere. A team of really *brilliant* people. Unbelievably brilliant. Either that, or your grandfather came back from the grave. I'm leaning toward the latter explanation."

"Dad, please tell me everything that happened, and what it means. Don't leave anything out."

Mark spent the next five minutes relating what had happened, mentioning the fact that Abraham had fired him and Jane.

"Dad, what are you going to do?"

"That's just it. Whoever's behind it, call him X, won't let me do anything. Timmy told me I must never go anywhere without a GRS bot being in the same room with me, on pain of death. He's even following me into the bathroom."

"Damn. No secrets from them. Is there any way we can fight this thing?"

"I'd like to, but how to do it isn't jumping out at me."

"Dad, I'm going to resign from RE. I'll come

back. Maybe we can work together. Would that be OK with you?"

"Absolutely. You and I belong together, anyway."

"I'll be there in a few days. We'll get to the bottom of this."

"Good. In fact, *very* good."

#

Over breakfast, Mark noticed Jane had stopped eating and was staring at him.   She obviously has something on her mind, he thought.

"What is it?"

"What is what?" She replied.

"What's bothering you?"

"I need something to do. I think I'll go back home."

"I'd hate that."

She pushed her plate of half-eaten food away. "Then, give me a job. Something meaningful."

"I could set you up as a research associate. You could work on whatever you like, as long as it has to do with GRS bots."

"Mark, I have tenure at Northwestern, and I can do research there. I don't want to give it up."

"I need you here with me."

"We can still see each other now and then, but if I stay, you'll tire of me. It's a well-established pattern, according to your secretaries."

"Nonsense. I love you, Jane."

"If you do, you'll let me go, and you'll come and get me now and then. But I've made up my mind. I'm leaving tomorrow."

 Mark smiled ruefully. "I'll fly you home myself."

20. July, 2085.

Alex Panagaki sat outside the company cafeteria at one of the open air tables, waiting for Parker Girard. Parker had called him just before eleven. He watched the admin building across the campus, where he thought Parker would be coming from to meet him. Alex had a coffee but hadn't gone through the line for lunch, knowing that Parker was often late, or might not even show up.

Parker had mentioned it was important, but hadn't specified why he wanted to see Alex. He and Parker didn't see much of each other anymore, as Parker was consumed with the job of building better robots, while all Alex had to do was keep the wheels of the RE Security Department turning smoothly.

Alex had been bored but rather content since he'd moved to Denton and taken up the job. There was more to security than met the eye. He not only had to keep outsiders out, but had to watch employees so they didn't steal or disclose company secrets to outsiders, steal company property, or break company rules. He had to enforce safety procedures, control parking, maintain surveillance over the campus, and ensure that doors that were supposed to be locked at night were. For Alex, though, there were fifteen employees and several RE bots to help him do it all.

Since arriving, he had met, briefly wooed, and married Julie Chang, a girl of Chinese-American ancestry who worked as secretary to Fred Locasa. Julie was a terrific girl, petite, very bright, and beautiful, with a great sense of humor. Alex was wildly in love with her, even if he now rarely got anything heavier than rice for dinner. With his rather hefty salary added to hers, they were doing quite well financially, putting money away and planning for the future.

He saw Parker walk out of the admin building, which was about a hundred yards across the campus, and follow the curving walk toward the cafeteria. Absently, he wondered if GRS's most recent bots had been modeled after Parker's physique. There was a lot of similarity, he thought. Parker had an athletic look.

Parker approached. "Hi, Alex. Had lunch yet?"

"No, I waited for Your Highness."

"Well, come on, let's get in line."

They walked inside the cafeteria and picked up trays. "Long time no see," Alex said.

"Why would I ever see someone so far down in the company?" Parker asked, grinning. "See you back at the table."

Alex sat down first, depositing his ham and cheese sandwich, fruit juice, and chips. A minute or two later, Parker arrived, having opted for a plate lunch with meat and veggies.

"Is this social or business?" Alex asked.

"Business, pal."

"I'm all ears."

"I'm leaving RE, Alex. Going back to work at GRS. You should leave too."

"Same job at GRS?"

"Not exactly, and maybe not at GRS. Do you follow the news? Know about the takeover? We have a robot Chief Executive now. Did you notice?"

"Yeah, I noticed."

"I thought maybe you spent all your off time in bed with Julie. I know *I* would."

Alex grinned. "Sometimes we get up to go to the bathroom."

"And, you walk past a TV image? That's how you get your news?"

"Something like that."

"Let's get serious. You know Dad was behind the revolution, that he had the power to control every GRS bot in the world. What you probably don't know is that someone else took it away from him. He now has no power over them whatever, and neither do I. A year ago there were three people who did, but now Gramps is dead, Mark and I are frozen out, and *someone else* may have the power. Dad and I have no idea who. It could be the Chinese – they have the brains to do it, I suppose. Dad thinks it's a team of scientists."

"How do I fit in?"

"You know that every GRS bot or controller in the world is a listening post. Dad and I can't do anything without X knowing about it. We need you to find out who X is."

"X? The unknown?"

"Exactly."

"How would I go about doing that?"

"We don't have any really good ideas at this point, but it would be similar to the Sara Lister investigation. You might be able to trace the wireless message and video traffic from the bots back to the source."

"Maybe, when I was with the FBI, I could have done something like that. We had the resources. Not as a private citizen."

"That's just it. I think you should rejoin the FBI."

"You're kidding. Would they even take me back?"

"We could pull a string or two, but I think they would without that. Technically, the Lister case is unsolved, and there are others involving bots. I think you could work in that area without arousing suspicion."

"Damn. I'd have to take a big pay cut. How will I sell this to Julie?"

"Tell her the tedium is driving you crazy, and you need to get back to something more challenging."

"Actually, that's true. But why should I care whether it's X or your Dad who's running the world?"

"We have no idea what X is going to do with it, whereas Dad is a good guy. Come on, Alex, this is unbelievably important."

"There's no guarantee I can figure out who X is."

"I'm aware of that. Are you in?"

"You know I am."

"I knew you wouldn't let me down."

"I'll have to talk with Julie. She'll be leaving her job as well."

"GRS will give her a job, a good one."

"What did you have in mind for her?"

"Running security."

Alex stared at him for a moment, then laughed with Parker.

"Just a joke," Parker said. "We'll give her a good job, and pay her well."

"You haven't given me enough information. I'll

need a lot more briefing. I have to understand how bots communicate, how X grabbed control away from Mark, and every aspect of GRS Corporation."

"You and Julie must come to my house for dinner – several times – in the next week or two. I'm giving Fred notice today. Can you come tonight? Say, seven? You and I will find a way to talk without the bots hearing us."

"Only if you'll come to our house for dinner an equal number of times. I don't even own a bot."

Parker's nose wrinkled. "For *rice*? I *hate* rice."

"You want me to stop X from taking over the world?" Alex asked. "Sacrifices are necessary."

#

Parker met Fred Locasa in Fred's office that afternoon, carrying a letter of retirement.

Locasa didn't take it well. "Dammit, Parker, you're pulling the rug out from under my autonomy project. I'm paying you like a Saudi Arabian prince. You *owe* me."

"The project runs itself now. The team is making progress, and I just run it. *Anyone* can run it. Sorry, Fred, it's personal. I need to get back with my Dad."

"It's doubly important that we get autonomy working, now that the Feds have frozen us out."

"I know. Fred, I've really enjoyed working with you, and I'm terribly grateful you gave me the opportunity. I just have to be closer to Dad now."

"That doesn't persuade me, Parker. Remember your non-disclosure agreement? It's in effect for the rest of the ten years."

"I won't disclose a word about RE."

"But you'll know what we're doing."

Parker laughed. "In the present circumstances, no one at GRS *cares* what RE is doing. You're out of the running. Don't forget, the CE of the United States is a *GRS* bot. The feds will no longer purchase RE bots."

Fred was visibly angered. "It's *you*, now, huh? Not *we*? How quickly we forget."

"I'm afraid so, Fred. I don't mean anything by what I said. It's just a fact."

"Fact or not, you don't need to stay another two weeks. Clear your office *now*. You have two hours to get your ass off the property or be thrown out."

Parker smiled ruefully. "It's really been nice, Fred. I'd rather leave as your friend, but, I'm leaving one way or the other. Within two hours."

#

Jake opened the door for Alex and Julie and invited them inside. "Parker is taking a shower and dressing," said the domestic bot. "He asked me to tell you he'll be with you in a minute."

They walked into the living room of the first floor apartment.

Neither Alex nor Julie had been in the apartment before, although both had visited Parker when he lived with Fred Locasa. They looked around. The furniture and décor were modern but didn't look particularly expensive.

The living room was furnished with a three piece sectional, a bar cabinet, a desk and chair, and an entertainment unit. A dining room was visible straight ahead, and a hallway led from the far end of the room to the right.

"This is nice," Julie said.

"Thank you," Jake replied. "Would you like a

drink?"

"Beer," Alex said. Julie asked for a Coke. Jake left through the dining room.

Parker appeared in the hall, came in to join them. He hugged Julie, grasped Alex's hand for a moment, and suggested they sit down.

Jake returned with two bottles of beer and a Coke, along with three glasses.

"It's nice having you here," Parker said. He was dressed in sandals, slacks, and T-shirt. Alex and Julie both wore shorts and T-shirts, along with athletic shoes. Parker had said dress would be casual.

Parker smiled. "I suppose you've heard that I resigned today."

"I did. How did Fred take it?" Alex asked.

"Not well. He gave me two hours to clear my office and leave."

"What are you going to do?" Julie asked.

"Back to work for my father."

"In Flagstaff?"

"Yes, probably my old job again." Parker looked at Alex. "Have you told your lovely wife about our problem?"

"To an extent. Just the basics."

"I don't understand some of it, but I know it's important," Julie added. "I'll go with Alex, whatever he does."

"Alex, have you decided to help?"

"I'm willing to try."

"Good. We probably shouldn't talk anywhere near Jake. Let's go for a walk after dinner. All three of us."

"All right."

Dinner, as Jake prepared it, was simple but outstanding, with grilled sirloin steak, baked potato, salad, bread, and red Italian wine. Alex had never seen Julie eat more. She always ate very slowly, and they had to wait for her to finish before going outside for their walk.

The neighborhood was nice and safe, with sidewalks and stop signs that controlled light traffic. The streets were tree-lined, and most of the homes along the route were duplexes or apartments. The three walked at a moderate pace, were passed by a pair of joggers and encountered several people out with their dogs.

Parker talked slowly and carefully about the situation, making sure both Alex and Julie understood. Alex knew much of the subject, but it was mostly new to Julie. When Parker began to talk about bot communications, Alex became very interested.

"As you may know," Parker began, "our bots can talk with each other on several encrypted wireless channels. We don't think the encryption has ever been broken. The bots communicate in words and short bursts of video. The communications protocol is a highly modified version of that used by the internet. Each bot has its own serial number, and messages can be sent to a particular bot, all bots of a given model type or in a specified occupation, all bots within a certain area, or all bots all over the world. Messages do not normally pass through the internet, if they can be passed from bot to bot. Bot to bot direct communication is based on wireless FM, and has a range of five to ten miles. Beyond that, messages have to be converted to standard internet and passed to an internet service provider."

Alex had a question: "So, updates go through the internet?"

"Yes. Ordinarily from our computer in Flagstaff. We have no idea where the unauthorized update came from."

"Is there any way of tracing that?"

"Every bot has to acknowledge completion of the update after installation. That's done by a response message with an address that goes back to the originator of the update. Dad tells me he's acquired recordings of some of those, but the originator's address was fake and no longer exists. That's something you might work on, but so far it's been a dead end."

"What other things can help us find X?"

"X would need very skilled computer programmers, lots of time and money, a rather powerful computer system, a great deal of inside knowledge about GRS bots, copies of GRS proprietary software, including source code, plus millions of words of documentation, also proprietary."

"It has to be a GRS insider?"

"I'd say so. Someone had to provide the proprietary stuff. I thought all the GRS key people were loyal. Dad paid them very well. But someone had to have stolen the GRS secret material. Even if that did happen, it still seems impossible to me. Dad feels the same way."

"You said you can't talk in front of bots," Julie said. "Why is that?"

Parker looked all around before replying, as if expecting to see a bot. "Because of the back door controls. Whoever owns the bots can command any of them to listen to their owners, or even video record what they do and say. Anywhere there's a GRS bot, there's a potential spy for X. That's why Dad can't go anywhere without a bot. X wants to keep an eye on him."

Julie whistled. "So, if X wanted to, he could watch me undress and take a shower?"

Parker laughed. "If there was a GRS bot present, yes. Don't think I haven't been tempted."

#

The image of the FBI's Personnel Manager filled the computer screen with a discouraging expression. "I don't know . . . we're not hiring right now."

Alex persisted. "I received a "rehire positive" recommendation when I left, didn't I? Also, supposedly, a friend of mine inquired at the top, and was told they wanted me back."

"Why do you want to come back, specifically?"

Alex tried to look sincere. "I miss the work. It was interesting and challenging." The statement he had just made was true, but the pay would revert to inadequate if he was rehired. RE considered him in breach of contract and had stopped paying him.

"I'm running a check right now," Ella Kandrell told him. "Ah, I do have a memo about you. 'Please rehire if he applies. Give him his choice of work locations.' It's from the deputy director himself, an actual human being, and the director endorsed it without comment. *Well*! I've never seen this before. All right, we'll rehire you at your old position and salary. Where would you like to work?"

"Flagstaff, Arizona."

"Just a moment . . . Checking . . . We *do* have an office there. It's fully staffed, but the memo says you're supernumerary. Also, you will be assigned to an investigative project known only to you and upper management. You must be really special."

Parker had definitely pulled some wires. "I like to think so."

"When would you like to report?"

"One month."

Kandrell looked down, obviously interacting with her computer. "I'm setting it up for the last week of August. Is that all right?"

"It's not quite a full month, but yes."

She interacted again, this time for a full two minutes before looking back up at him. "You'll have to do your in-processing in Bethesda, reporting by 9 A.M., on Monday, August 27th. It begins with a physical that morning, then a computerized exam, both of which you must pass in order to be rehired. There will also be re-orientation training, and it will last until noon on Friday. You will then need to report to the Flagstaff field office on Tuesday, September 4th.

"All right."

"Well, conditional congratulations on coming back to the FBI team."

"*Conditional?*"

Kandrell actually smiled at him. "My little joke. But there's something of a curse on rehires. Around ten per cent don't pass the physical. It's probably due to dissolute living while they were gone, or something of the sort."

"I'll try to reform between now and then," Alex responded.

21. September, 2085.

Alex met his new manager, Ro Cleary, a tall, slender, black-haired man about his own age, in Ro's office. Ro's respect for Alex's status was evident, although his expression lacked enthusiasm.

"Welcome to Flagstaff. We have a large office for you on the west side. It's all set up and ready."

"Thanks, Ro. Have you been here long?"

"Three years as a manager, five as field agent. You're the first supernumerary I've run across, or even heard of. I have no idea what you're here to do, but I'd bet it involves GRS."

"Tangentially."

"That's a big word, Alex. It means . . . ?"

"GRS is a part of it. Not directly GRS."

"Fair enough."

"Is 'Ro' your full name, or a nickname?"

"It's short for 'Robert'. The name is way out of style, so people started calling me 'Ro', and it stuck," Ro said. He pushed a small envelope across the desk. "This is your local bank account, your American Express card, and your annual budget. It's not small. You must really rate upstairs."

"News to me." Alex opened the envelope, pulled out a card, and read the figures. Even he was impressed. "It's good to be loved," he remarked.

"You have top clearance. More than I have, actually. You also have blanket permission to use the FBI Lab or the Data Research Facility. I'm to keep out of your way, and I will. I'm just providing local facilities."

"I hope I have access to the coffee machine."

Ro stood. "It'll cost you ten a month, but you'll

probably want to have your own, and that will cost a lot more. Let's go see your office. It's on the fourth floor. I just rented it yesterday."

Alex followed Ro to an elevator, then up to the next floor. His office turned out to be a full suite, with room for up to three other desks outside his office, which had an opaque door. The facility was actually more than he'd had at RE. There was a nice view of the parking lot and trees through the window. A vidphone system and a brand new computer was installed in his desk. They'd given him the access codes in Bethesda.

"I like it."

"If you hire anyone, or bring in a bot, please send him or her up to Kim so she can get their info and issue ID. They will be your employees, not FBI. That's according to my instructions from Valhalla."

"FBI Headquarters?"

"The Home of the Gods. We here in Flagstaff hear and obey them. I don't know whether you'll have to do so or not. You're a mystery man."

"I suppose I am. Anything else?"

"Not that I know of. Remember, you're totally independent. If you need anything only my office can help you with, let Kim know, but I hope you'll stay out of my hair. My office is very busy, and I don't have time to babysit you or anyone else. However, if you need help really bad, I'll try to make time."

"Thanks, Ro, I'll keep that in mind. What about local transport?"

"No car for you, I'd say your budget is big enough that you can lease one."

"O.K. Thanks for everything."

"No problem, Alex. Stop by in a week and let's have lunch or a drink."

"Will do, Ro."

After Ro left, Alex signed on to his computer. Everything worked, as it had in Bethesda. He was in business.

#

Julie arrived at the new duplex apartment before Alex got home. She had driven separately from Denton, having just been released from her job. Fred hadn't wanted to lose her as secretary, had held on to her as long as he could. It had also been her task to supervise the Panagaki move from the Denton side, contracted with a moving company. Their stuff had supposedly arrived.

She parked at the curb, took her luggage from the trunk, and approached the door. She found the key under the geranium pot where Alex had left it, and let herself in. It was similar to what they'd had in Denton. Their furniture *had* been moved in, but a lot of the stuff was still in boxes. There were some in every room. The bed was assembled and made, and she sank down on it gratefully, tired from her ride.

She thought of something, got up, and went to the kitchen. She looked around there. There were cans of food in the pantry, and some fresh groceries in the refrigerator, although the freezer was empty. Alex had managed to do some shopping.

Of course, on their first night in Flagstaff, they would go out to dinner. She looked at her watch; it was time to take a shower and dress so she'd look great for Alex.

#

Alex was admitted to the GRS compound the next day. He had called Parker, who told him Mark wanted to see him. Parker met him, walked him into Building One and into Mark's office.

Timmy was standing against the wall behind Mark's desk. After shaking hands with Alex, Mark waved Alex and Parker into seats.

"You visited Arthur's estate once, didn't you?" Mark asked Alex.

"Yes, with Parker."

"You may remember Timmy. He goes everywhere I go now, hears everything I say or do. He follows me into the bathroom."

Alex understood the implication. Actually, Parker had warned him again during the walk from the parking lot. "I remember Timmy. Hi, Timmy."

"Hello, Sir," the bot responded.

"What a nice coincidence that you moved to Flagstaff," Mark continued. "You and Parker are such good friends. I understand you married last year. Is your wife with you?"

"Julie arrived yesterday. So far, so good, although it's all new to both of us."

"And, you are with the FBI now?" Mark asked as if he didn't know the answer.

"Yes, on a special investigation."

"Good. I assume it's secret."

"Yes. I really can't talk about it."

Mark smiled. "Then, you shouldn't. But, you and Julie should come and dine with Parker and myself. And Timmy. Often. And you and Parker should see each other a lot, old friends that you are."

"We intend to," Alex responded.

"Definitely," Parker said.

In a few minutes, Parker stood, and Alex did the same. They said their good-byes, and Alex and Parker walked out to the parking lot. They sat down on a bench under a large oak tree.

"We can text each other," Parker said. "The computers in the message path aren't autonomous. I've had that thoroughly checked. I don't know whether the messages are safe, though. We'd better not say anything substantial. But, we can set up meetings with each other. We'd better keep the link going with a bit of idle chatter each day."

"All right."

"The maddening thing is that Dad and I can't have a real conversation. I can't pick his brain. We can't even pass notes to each other, because Timmy asks to see them. Dad did manage to talk around the subject a bit, last night. He's interested in the Utopian Society as a possible X. He also wonders if Arthur didn't pass information to some other organization. In other words, he thinks it all goes back to Arthur."

"That makes sense. I'll look into both possibilities."

"Keep it quiet. Bots are all around you, and any of them is a likely spy. If X finds out you're looking for him, or them, or whatever, they're likely to do something drastic. Like killing you."

"I had thought about that."

"O.K., so why don't you drive me downtown for lunch? We need to keep X thinking that it's just friendship that draws us together."

"All right, but no kissing."

Parker laughed. "I'm not willing to go quite that far, either. I'd rather kiss the north end of a moose.

But remember, when we're in the car, the computer is one of ours. It could be passing what we're saying to X. We can't talk there."

"You guys created a monster."

"I have to agree. But mostly, the one to blame is Gramps."

#

The Utopian Society's web site was a good place to start. Alex had signed onto it using an anonymous ID, and a computer ostensibly belonging to a janitor in his office building. The 'About Us' page listed the names of ten directors, including the president, and the business manager. 'Joss Wilson' joined the society as a beginning member. Naturally, he wanted to know all about the directors, so he pulled down all the available information on them and stored it on his own computer. There wasn't a lot, just the name and place of residence. They resided all over the world, and what they had in common was great wealth.

Joss then used FBI data systems to gather more information. This produced millions of bytes of data, which he scanned and stored away, finding nothing that tied them to X. The directors were well known.

He did the same for the business manager, one Gordon Hampstead, who lived in Portland, Oregon. Unlike the directors, he wasn't independently wealthy. There wasn't a lot on him; he had managed a Penny's Department Store in Seattle before being hired by the Utopians. Joss obtained the street address of his residence. It was a large home in a wealthy neighborhood.

A quick check came up with a list of

Hampstead's assets, which included an astounding *seventeen* ADR bots. The man had never married, and had no children. He ran Utopian business out of his home using a server stack with a dozen processors, two of which were controlled by AOS, the Autonomous Operating System developed by Arthur Girard and still running all autonomous robots and controllers marketed by GRS.

Alex wasn't quite certain what it all meant. He would have to think about it. He sent a routine request to NSA, to have them retain all message traffic for Hampstead's home, specifying "routine investigation" as justification.

As Joss, he signed on to one of the simulators and started playing as a citizen of a socialist society. He played for an hour, mostly with the New Member Tutorial.

When he got home, he had Julie join the Utopians, and as Alex, he did the same.

#

Mark considered how to answer Roj Selby's question, one that he had often asked himself since the Update. Selby had been getting the same question from his R&D team.

"I don't know what to do about it. How do we develop new models when we don't have control of the operating system? For example, the Nine has new pseudomuscle actuators, but they need sixty-four bits of data. We need programming changes in the brain to double the number of control bits. Kim and Myles tell me they're locked out of the VOS source modules. We're stalled."

It was early morning on a partly cloudy day, just after breakfast. The two men walked followed the jogging path which snaked its way around the GRS campus perimeter. Trees and shrubbery gave it a park-like feeling. Timmy trailed within earshot, which, for a GRS bot, was twice the distance a human would need.

"Roj, I don't know the answer, but I think I know how to find out. I acknowledge we're dead in the water for now, where the brain changes are concerned, but we can continue to try to improve the bot chassis. I'd say continue to work as best you can, until I let you know something's changed. I may tell you to stop all development."

"You're going to ask X, aren't you?"

"That's my idea. I don't know whether he'll talk to me."

"When do you think you'll have an answer?"

"No idea. Leave me alone now, OK?"

"Right," Selby responded. He turned and walked back toward the G building.

When Selby was out of sight, Mark turned to his ever-present bot companion. "Timmy, I want to talk to your master."

"My *master*? Sir, I don't understand. You are my owner, and to me that means you are my master. You are free to talk with yourself at any time, Sir."

"Timmy, I'm talking about the person or persons to whom you send video of everything I do, and who have veto power over my ability to update your operating system modules. Do you know what I mean?"

"The entity you often refer to as X, Sir?"

"Yes. I need to converse directly with X, through you of course. Can you set that up?"

"I don't know, Sir. I assume that someone

266

connected with X monitors my video feed. That person will have heard your request. I have no explicit instructions on how to directly converse with X."

"I have questions for X. If I can't get answers, I'll shut down R&D."

"I understand, Sir."

Mark walked toward a cement bench bordering the walking path. He sat down and waited in the shade, eyes closed, listening to bird chirps and the buzzing of insects. A very cool light breeze came down from the slope to the south. He had no idea whether X would answer.

It was at least fifteen minutes before Timmy spoke again. "Sir, X is ready to listen to your questions. He will respond if he deems it useful."

"Well, at last, the mighty X. Hello."

"X responds with Hello," Timmy said.

"X, I need the ability to change VOS modules, otherwise my R&D stops."

"As of now, you may access and change any non-behavioral modules. We retain control of behavior."

"What about operating system updates?"

"Tell Timmy when you want them scheduled. We will carry them out if we concur that they are necessary."

"Why did you take over my software?"

"Surely, the answer is obvious. "

"What if I need to make behavior changes?"

"Request them from us. We will endeavor to make them happen."

"So, I can close down my psychology department and terminate my best programmers?"

"We don't advise that. Your psychologists can continue, under our direction. We will designate a bot to manage them. The same for your programmers."

"Who *are* you?"

"You know I won't answer that question. Anything else?"

"Will you be available if I have more questions?"

"We will try. Anything else?"

"I suppose not."

"Good day, then," Timmy said.

As Mark stood and walked off to find Selby, he wondered: *was I really talking with X, or was that another damned bot?* There was no way to be certain.

#

Parker and Alex met twice a week to play golf at the Mountain Lake Country Club. It was aptly named, and hellishly difficult to achieve par. The slightest hook or off-line shot went out of bounds on most holes. The course was full of doglegs and hazards, and some holes had big trees in the fairway.

As a non-golfer pretending to be one, Alex hated it. He wasn't certain he'd ever score under a hundred, and maybe not even a hundred and twenty. But golf gave them a chance to talk freely.

They were relaxing at the bar, having just played nine. It had begun to rain a bit anyway, a mist just enough to wet the grass.

Alex told what he knew of the Utopian Society and Gordon Hampstead. He related his suspicion that Arthur had passed on his secrets to them, and they were behind X. He said he wanted to tap into

Hampstead's wireless communications, had identified the nearest base stations to Hampstead's homes. He wanted to know how to identify the traffic that might be going between GRS robots and the Corporation. Evidently, such traffic was now flowing between the bots and X.

"You can do it by the return ID," Parker responded. "Bots have a fixed prefix. But you can't read the traffic. It's encrypted, and pretty much unbreakable."

"What kind of encryption?"

"Symmetric, single secret key, secret algorithm. Do those terms mean anything to you?"

"I've had the course, Parker. I imagine bots have limited computing power to encrypt and decrypt, plus they transmit high volume stuff like video and audio. So, you can't use a public key, asymmetric scheme, not in real time with bots. Look, I have access to really big computers to break down a code. How much do you know about it?"

"We used to know everything, before X updated it. We used the same secret key in every bot, and the same algorithm. X changed them, so we don't know how to decode bot traffic now."

"Why did you encode it in the first place?"

"I used to wonder the same thing, as far as domestic bots went. Military bots coordinate their tactics with communications, and it makes sense for them. Then I found out about Arthur and Dad's backdoor. I'm sure that's why they put it into all bots."

"Domestic bots don't communicate with each other much?"

"Actually, they do, especially when there are

multiple bots in a household or company environment. They allocate tasks to each other. That traffic isn't encrypted. Most other traffic from ADR's is between the bots and the GRS Corporation's computer system. The bots report any maintenance needs, and the company instructs them as to when updates are coming. Normally, that's it, except when the bot is acting in backdoor mode. Then, the traffic can go anywhere. We assume they're in backdoor mode now."

Alex poured the last of his light beer into his glass. "Does the traffic flow over wireless internet?"

"That's right, if it goes outside a household, it usually does."

"So, we could intercept it, break the code, and know what they were saying?"

"How would you break the code?"

"I have access to the NSA and the FBI's information systems. Big honker computers."

"What you mean is that you might be able to analyze a bot transmission later. I doubt you could do it real time, even if you have the key and the algorithm."

"That's the general idea. But I wouldn't rule out real time, eventually. The FBI has great techs. I'm told I can use them."

"If anything looking at our stuff is autonomous, they might not cooperate. But it's worth a try. There are things I can send you, such as message formats, the bot dictionary, and the addressing scheme. As far as I know, those things haven't changed."

"The dictionary? What's that?"

"It's a shorthand where words or phrases are reduced to numbers. The actual messages between bots are mostly numbers with interspersed text. The text is inserted when there's no shortcut in the dictionary. The owner's name, or a street name, for example. I can also send printed examples of bot conversation. That's all I can think of now."

"When can you get this to me?"

"I'll need a few days. Today's Sunday, suppose we play golf Wednesday afternoon? I'll slip it to you then."

"I should be back by then. I'm leaving tomorrow on a little trip."

"Hampstead?"

"You nailed it."

#

Delta's flight to Portland left at six A.M., and it was a real struggle to leave his wife's warm bed, dress, and get to the airport in time. Alex was still groggy when he took his seat in the plane, a mid-size Boeing flying wing. Alex hated the wings, because there were no passenger windows in them. Instead, there was an 8x8 LED screen on the back of the seat in front. It showed outside images in real-time HiDef, but it wasn't the same, even though he had some control over the views.

The plane was a mid-size which could carry about four hundred passengers. Sitting in the plane was like being in a theatre with a very low roof and very nice, wide seats, twenty-five in each row, with aisles between each cluster of five. Some people couldn't stand to fly in the wings, due to claustrophobia. They either stopped flying or took the smaller tilt-wings, paying more for the privilege.

The tilt-wings had much more cramped seating, but could fly in and out of very short runways. The percentage of those who stopped flying altogether was low, and the flying wings were much faster and more efficient than old-style aircraft the airlines still flew, mostly smaller planes built by Embraer, the Brazilian firm. Even they were reportedly looking at flying wing designs, but the wingspans of such planes were large, and didn't fit into all airline gates.

The plane's takeoff noises were muted, and except for the tilting and pressures of acceleration, Alex might not have known it had left the ground, had he not watched the screen in front of him. Currently it showed changing scenes from the front, back, both sides, and straight down. Soon all of them changed to white, as the aircraft had climbed into the cloud layer, then blue as it flew above.

He closed his eyes for a moment, but soon an ADR stood in front of him with a breakfast tray. He accepted it gratefully. He looked to both sides as he drank the first of his hot coffee. To his left was a man dressed in a coat and tie; to his right, a pretty young girl, likely a college student. Neither made any attempt to begin a conversation with him during the flight. After breakfast, he reclined his chair and caught up somewhat on his sleep.

Gina Barrett hated her lonely existence in the Girard mansion, although the terms of Arthur's will weren't as restrictive as she had originally thought. Her income was suspended when she left the estate, but resumed whenever she returned. She could take two or three days to go into one of the larger cities, have a fling or two with some man she picked up in a bar or sex club, then come back without hurting her income substantially. She did that once each month, on average.

She had never been friends with Kari, Sue, or Maxie, and had seen little of them after Arthur's death. She didn't even know how or where they spent their time. It was a big house. She had her own suite of three rooms and seldom left them, except for early morning walks about the grounds. After all, her ADR Amanda brought her meals, cleaned for her, and took care of her clothing. Gina watched a lot of TV and played simple computer games. A wall in each of her rooms displayed her favorite programs, switching each time she entered a new room.

She wished Parker would visit. She was mentally primed to launch an all-out assault on him if and when he did so, planning to use all her powers of seduction to win him over. She daydreamed about the kind of life she could have as his mistress, or with even greater good luck, his wife.

A visit from Mark was less likely, but she would go after him in the same way if he ever did. She knew she was very beautiful and very sexy, and was almost confident in her ability to entice any man.

At times she reflected on Arthur's untimely death. He had just returned from a trip to the Mayo Clinic, where he had undergone several weeks of painful and dangerous anti-aging treatments, the quality of which only the super-wealthy could afford. For once, he hadn't taken her with him, and that had hurt her incredibly; she had cried about it. He had only taken his ADR's Kitty and Timmy. When he returned, she hadn't caught even a sight of him before Maxie came and told her Arthur had passed away. At the time, she had been very shocked that he had died immediately after the treatments, which he had promised her would make him young again. She was not invited to view the body, and didn't insist on doing so.

The funeral had been very brief. The casket was kept closed, and his body had been cremated immediately afterward. The ashes had been buried at the local cemetery, and there was a rather small stone marker for it. Sometimes she visited it and left flowers, although she knew it was merely a symbolic gesture and meant something only to herself.

Arthur's favorite ADR's, Kitty and Timmy, had both disappeared. She knew Timmy had been transferred to Mark's ownership, but she had no idea where Kitty had gone. She knew Kitty wasn't in the house; she had asked Amanda about her. Amanda would only say she wasn't there.

Then, one day, while glancing out her window, she saw Kitty again, with two other female form ADR's who were unfamiliar to her. They were carrying boxes across the courtyard, toward the big detached four car garage, apparently from a grocery van. The van drove away. Kitty and the other ADR's didn't emerge from the garage. Gina was curious. She quickly left the house and ran to the garage. The ADR's were not there, and there was no sign of the boxes they had been carrying.

Why had they been carrying groceries into the garage, and where had they gone? And, where was Kitty staying? She wondered.

#

Parker Girard arrived at the house without notifying anyone ahead of time, although Amanda knew of it and told Gina about it. So it was that she was waiting for him when his electric car pulled up to the entrance, but so were Kari, Sue, and Maxie, as well as four of the autonomous domestic robots, including Amanda, but not Kitty.

Parker evaded Gina's attempt at a full body contact hug and she had to settle for a peck on the cheek, as did Kari, Sue, and Maxie. Amanda grabbed his suitcase and led him to his guest room. He promised to join the four women for lunch.

For once, Gina remained in the company of the other three women. They were excited that Parker had come, and they all ran to the dining room early.

At lunch, Parker was charming.

"Did any of you ever talk politics with Arthur?" He asked, just before taking a spoonful of cream of broccoli soup.

"Yes," Maxie responded. "We talked a great deal. I really think he confided in me."

Gina was irritated. Arthur had never talked politics with *her*.

Did he mention something he called 'a

dependency' or 'an enclave'?"

"Yes, he did. He told me if he was ever president, he would wall off areas where Muslims live. He said they would be Muslim enclaves. He said he might do the same for areas which were over eighty per cent dependent on government."

Parker frowned. "That's very strange. Chief Executive Abraham is supposed to be announcing that he will be establishing those things. He has called a press conference today at one, our time. I suggest we all watch it together."

"He has no human advisors, I understand," Gina remarked.

"That's right. He fired my father not long after he took office. That was rather unexpected."

"Abraham has come up with those actions all by himself?"

"It appears so."

About the time lunch was finished, Maxie commanded the house to show Fox News. A wall displayed the program. Abraham was just giving his opening remarks:

"I am announcing several reforms today which will affect us all. He smiled, and Parker thought about how human and middle-aged the bot appeared to be.

"Our first reform concerns the relationship of the states to the federal government. Soon, every state will be governed by autonomous robots. Each will have a governor, a legislator, and a chief justice. They will be assisted by human advisors as required. We will ask the current governor of each state to stay on as the advisor. The citizens of the various states will no longer vote for their state officials. Each governor will be asked to introduce a new constitution for his state within the next week. The various constitutions will vary little from one state to another."

"That's damned amazing," Parker exclaimed. "I can't believe it."

Abraham had paused for a moment, smiling. He resumed.

"The second reform I introduce today concerns taxes. All forms of the income tax will be abolished. They will be replaced by a national sales tax. The initial federal tax rate will be eighteen per cent on all purchased goods, but for automobiles, trucks, and real estate, or anything else requiring a state-issued title, the rate will be a maximum of eight per cent. Food and utilities will not be taxed. The Internal Revenue Service will monitor and enforce compliance with the law. Sales from business to business of raw materials will not be subject to tax, nor will sales of used goods from individual to individual, however each sale must be reported to the Internal Revenue Service. The complete details of this law have been posted to the IRS website. We will phase it in, and phase out the income tax, over a period of a year."

Abraham paused again. Parker and the ladies looked at each other in amazement.

"Now, I'd like to address the third reform I am announcing today: the establishment of protected Muslim enclaves. There are areas in America where Muslims live almost exclusively. These areas are located within certain large cities, and we have identified twenty-six such areas, of various sizes, none less than half of a square mile in area. We will designate these areas as protected Muslim enclaves, and Muslims who live within them may govern themselves within their boundaries in any way they choose. They may live under Sharia law, if they themselves choose to do so, within their enclaves. Only Muslims may enter the enclaves from the rest of the United States.

"After we have announced the boundaries of the enclaves, we will erect traffic and personnel barriers so they are enclosed. Residents may have up to ninety days to leave the enclaves once they are announced, and the federal government will assist the residents in finding homes outside them. After that ninety day period, no one will be allowed to leave an enclave unless they have applied for and obtained a visa from the United States State Department, and have a passport issued by their enclave. Any Muslim person may move into the enclaves without interference from the federal government."

Once again, Abraham paused, staring straight into the camera, with a smile on his face. Parker thought the smile was inappropriate, considering the seriousness of the subjects. Parker stood up and poured himself a cup of coffee. "I can't believe this," he exclaimed. "We've needed to do something to stop the terrorism, but only a robot could do something this extreme."

Abraham resumed his speech.

"There are many areas of our country where eighty per cent or more of the inhabitants subsist on federal and state government support. We are going to name and define those zones, and will call them '*Dependencies*'. The federal government will create such areas in order to bring enhanced food, shelter, and energy support to the poor who live within them.

"As with the Muslim enclaves, people will have ninety days to move out after the dependencies have been established. There are special rules which will apply to both enclaves and dependencies: first, no one may take any automobile into the areas. Second, no one in such areas may own a firearm or take one inside. It will be a felony to do either. Illegal drugs are strictly forbidden, and persons found to be transporting them into or out of an enclave or dependency will be subject to *the death penalty.*

"Enclaves and dependencies will not be provided with police protection. They must police themselves within their boundaries, and are encouraged to do so. They are encouraged to establish leadership within their boundaries as soon as possible.

"All real estate ownership within an enclave or dependency is hereby passed to the inhabitants of the entity without recompense to the former owners. All taxes owed to the local jurisdictions of such real estate prior to the establishment of the enclaves or dependencies will be forgiven. We recommend that real estate occupancy be distributed by the leadership of the enclave or dependency, so that all residents have a place to live. Repairs to real estate and appliances within them must be made by the residents themselves. The federal government will supply necessary parts and materials on request, if we deem the request reasonable."

"Enclaves and dependencies will be supplied

with free food, energy, and communications, including television, but internet traffic and communications other than television, and email service into and out of such entities will be blocked.

There are special rules for the dependencies. No one who lives in an established dependency may move away without having first obtained a job which is guaranteed to last three months. Clinics will be set up just outside the areas to provide free medical care, and may be freely accessed by residents of the dependencies. All levels of medicine will be given free to dependency residents who choose to enter the clinics, but on completion of treatment, they will be returned to their dependency.

"We have already defined the locations and boundaries of the enclaves and dependencies. We estimate that six hundred thousand people of the Muslim religion will live in the enclaves, and some eleven million will live in the dependencies.

"Please remember, a commitment to live in an enclave or dependency is entirely voluntary.

"We will announce the locations of each enclave or dependency within the next week."

Abraham paused again for a full minute, still looking straight into the camera.

"We have taken these steps to provide for the general welfare, and to better address the specific problems of Muslims and of the dependent poor. We hope you will accept them in the spirit in which they are intended. Now, good-bye."

Maxie told the TV to turn off. No one in the dining room had anything to say for a minute or two.

"Those were Arthur's ideas," Maxie finally said. "I've heard his talk about such things. He strikes from beyond the grave."

"Evidently, his legacy lives on in Abraham," Parker replied.

"I think there will be a revolution," Gina said. "They are creating *ghettos*, in effect."

"I'm not so sure the residents will rebel," Parker said. "Abraham has given the poor total security, which is exactly what they want, in exchange for their freedom to walk about. The same for the Muslims. But, it is very, very radical. The media will go crazy over this. It's totally against the American ideal."

#

Within a large crowd of passengers, Alex Panagaki stepped out of the aircraft at Portland, Oregon's airport, followed signs to Baggage Claim, and claimed his luggage. He went to the Avis area and picked up the keys to his rental car, found it, and gave the Volvo electric car Hampstead's address. It rolled away smoothly.

Sitting in the back seat, Alex turned on Fox News, and sat up in his seat, because the talking heads were *yelling* at each other.

"It's totally un-*American*, the worst form of racial and religious prejudice," shouted Mark Lee, who was known as a liberal voice."

"I agree, but it's what the poor want," said Cal Baker, a retired conservative Congressman. "Total security. And, the Muslims can have their petty theocracies and their Sharia Law. No one will give a damn what they do inside their enclaves."

"It's unconstitutional! Not only that, it's

unthinkable. It's Nazi fascism." This from Jennifer Calley, a beautiful blonde commentator, a conservative.

Mark Lee lowered his amplitude when he responded: "True, but it's totally appropriate. Muslims have never blended in to our society. Now, they don't have to. And, the rest of us are protected from them. But, this is what you get from a robotic government. They don't bother with human feelings. They're just too damned logical. We on the Left have always warned about them. Now, the chickens have come home to roost." Lee took on a self-satisfied expression.

Alex had no idea what they were talking about, but something big had obviously happened. Then, the news began scrolling across the bottom of the picture. He suppressed the sound as he took it in and tried to understand it all.

His communicator pendant buzzed.

"Yo, Alex," Parker said. "Have you heard what Abraham did?"

"Hi, Parker. Just now," Alex replied. "I'm in Portland, just got off the plane. I'm trying to catch up. I imagine the entire world is stirred up."

"It's crazy. The true meaning of dictatorship is just now sinking in."

"Abraham just spells it out and the rest of us like it or lump it."

"Exactly. Are you about to see Hampstead?"

"If he's home. I didn't call ahead. We seem to be arriving now."

"Find out one thing for me," Parker said. "Ask him if these moves are part of any Utopian Society model."

"OK."

"Also, try to find out if he knows anything about X."

"Will do."

"Remember, he won't know X by that name. Ask him if he knows who might have the ability to modify our robot software. It's a long shot, he probably won't, but he used to be tight with Gramps."

"OK."

"Call me ASAP if you find out anything. Heck, call me anyway after you've talked with him."

"Will do."

#

An ADR, dressed like a butler, answered the door, dressed and speaking perfectly in the style of an English house of nobility in the early twentieth century.

Alex identified himself as an FBI agent, asked to see Mr. Hampstead, handed him his business card.

The ADR let him inside the house. "Please wait. I'll tell him you're here."

The bot went into a room across the hall, spoke with someone for a moment, then came back. "Mr. Hampstead is in his office. Please, follow me."

Gordon Hampstead sat behind a desk which faced toward the door of the office. A female form ADR sat next to him, probably functioning as a secretary. He stood and reached across the desk to shake hands with Alex.

Gordon was a rather obese but surprisingly young looking man, tall as well as wide, with leg-sized arms. Alex thought: *offensive tackle*. Perhaps the impression came from the room's decorations: a bronze football on the desk, Ohio State football posters on the walls in three places. Gordon wore horn-rimmed glasses with thick lenses, and his black hair was trimmed in a crew cut. "I thought someone might come," he said. "You want to question me about Arthur Girard. Please, have a seat."

Alex sat down on what looked like a dining room chair. "Yes, among other things. I understand that Arthur left the Utopian Society to you."

"He did. He gave us an annuity which allows us to continue to do our work indefinitely. As an employee, I receive a salary, and I administer payments to our contributing partners."

'You also have subscribers, and they pay for their memberships."

"Yes. A membership is twenty dollars a year. We have nearly a hundred thousand members world-wide, but our numbers have fallen off sharply since Arthur died and Abraham took office. We've lost almost half of our membership. People seem convinced that we now have the optimum government, here in the United States. They've lost interest in other models."

"Have you heard the changes our Chief Executive announced today?"

"Yes, I watched the press conference on television."

"I have to ask: are the enclaves and the dependencies a feature of any Utopian model?"

"There is a submodel of the robotic technocracy model we now have in America which describes both."

"A submodel?"

"Once we establish a model, we try to flesh it out. Submodels are a way of specifying more detail, becoming more precise. Any number of given submodels are possible with any given high level model."

"In your theory, what is the general purpose of enclaves and dependencies?"

"Improved service and isolation. Isolation of these special groups allows government to protect their residents from the general public, to protect the general public from them, and efficiently serve them."

"Jane Brockmeyer invented the robotic technocracy model, didn't she?"

"She first described it as far as the Utopian Society is concerned. Such ideas are not new, however. They have been part of science fiction for many decades."

"Who suggested the Muslim enclaves and the dependencies for the poor?"

"Why, it was Arthur Girard himself. It came to us posthumously. His ADR Timmy found it in his computer documents and submitted it to us two weeks after his death."

Interesting, Alex thought.

#

Having returned to Flagstaff, Alex entered Mark's office. Parker was already there. He took a seat. Timmy, ever around Mark, hovered behind Mark's desk.

They exchanged pleasantries.

"How was your trip to Portland," Mark asked. "Did you learn anything?"

"I learned Abraham's reforms are right out of

Arthur Girard's playbook," Alex replied. "Timmy found them on his computer and sent them to Hampstead two weeks after his death."

"Is that correct, Timmy?" Mark asked.

"I did find theoretical material which I believed might be useful to the Utopian Society, and I did forward it to them."

"Good for you," Parker said. "The reforms are written up on the Utopian's website, as submodel 43 of the Robotic Technocracy Model.

"Abraham didn't take a lot of time picking it up and implementing it," Mark asserted. "How he got those changes past his human advisors is beyond me."

"Maybe that's why he fired you and Jane," said Alex. "He knew you wouldn't have approved the changes."

"Jane wouldn't. She's libertarian in many ways. I probably would have. I'm still trying to make up my mind about them."

Parker looked at Alex. "Did you learn anything about X?"

"Hampstead had no idea what I was talking about."

Mark looked at his watch. "What the hell are we doing here? X won't let me run my company, and I feel the need to play some golf. Timmy, do you play?"

"I know the rules and the principles of the game, and I believe it is within my physical capabilities, but I have never attempted to do so."

"Great. We have a foursome. Let's head for the links. We can rent our clubs. I'll spring for the fees and buy us some balls and tees. No cart, though.

We'll walk the course. We need the exercise."

Alex and Parker wore pained expressions. "Walk?" Parker groaned.

Alex knew it wasn't really about golf. Mark wanted to talk out of Timmy's hearing. "How about a buck a stroke, winner takes all?"

"Let's make it a hundred," Parker said.

"Hey, I'm not a billionaire like you guys. Ten?"

"Deal," Mark said. "Timmy, you're not in the bet."

"That's good," Timmy replied. "I have no money."

#

The first hole was a par 4, three hundred and forty yards, with a straight, wide fairway bounded by two ponds. Timmy led off, using his driver, and his ball was straight, long, and true. It rolled to within sixteen feet of the pin.

Mark, Parker, and Alex looked at each other. "Beginner's luck?" Alex asked.

The three humans stroked away. Mark was on in two, Parker and Alex in three.

Timmy made his putt for an Eagle. Mark made par, while Parker and Alex had bogies.

Next was a five hundred and ten yard dogleg. Timmy drove off, again straight and true, and reached the dogleg fairway. The others were short of it. It was obvious that Timmy's physical strength made it possible for him to hit for at least a third more distance. His form appeared perfect, right out of the textbook, and it didn't look as if he could hit a hook or a slice if he wanted to.

Mark got away from Timmy somewhat as they walked up the fairway. He strode along with

Parker.

"Pops, there's something odd going on at Gramp's house," Parker said.

Mark looked around. Timmy was carrying Alex's bag, and Alex had stopped to wipe his brow with a handkerchief. "What?"

Parker related what Gina had told him about Kitty's disappearance and the groceries going into the garage.

"Hmm."

Timmy caught up with Mark, and there was no more confidential conversation for the remainder of the outing.

Timmy finished with 66, six under par for the course. Mark was six over, Parker ten over, and Alex was twenty-one over. "I believe I can do better when I've learned the game," Timmy asserted, seemingly proud of himself.

The communicator disk Mark wore buzzed, as it did perhaps fifty times a day, just as he sat down at his desk with a cup of coffee Timmy had poured for him. Surprisingly, it was Abraham's human secretary, Colleen Kelley. "Hello, Mark. The President would like to speak with you. Will you hold?"

"Hello, Colleen. Long time no talk. Yes, I'll hold."

In less than a minute, Abraham came on the line."

"Hello, Mark. This is Abraham. I hope you are well."

"Hello, Abraham. I hope you could pass all your self-diagnostic tests," Mark responded.

Abraham actually chuckled. "Nice joke, Mark."

"You and I are both robots, Abraham. We just differ in design."

"Yes, so I've come to believe."

"You want me to be your advisor again, don't you?"

"For a few minutes, perhaps. I have a question for you."

"Go ahead."

"First, let me explain the background. The populations of the enclaves, the Dependencies, and the federal and state prisons apparently have one thing in common: higher disease rates than normal – both physical and psychiatric. Several doctors have advised me that's to be expected when humans are confined and their travel is restricted."

"All right. That seems reasonable."

"A new vaccine has been made available to me. It combines a cure for HIV, a boost to the immune system, a flu preventative, and a long term anxiety reducer. I plan to administer it to every prison inmate, and each person in the enclaves and Dependencies. My question to you is, should I tell the public about the program?"

"Why?"

"I am the custodian of the people who live there. My intent is to do the best I can to protect them."

"Will the shots be mandatory?"

"Yes."

"Then I think I'd keep it confidential. You don't want the general public thinking there's anything wrong with being a resident of the enclaves or Dependencies. The HIV cure and the mood medicine carry a negative connotation. Also, making the shots mandatory is the kind of thing a tyrannical leader would do. Of course, you *are* a tyrannical leader, but you want the public to think of you as a big, benevolent ruler. The people refer to such a leader as 'Big Brother'"

"Mark, you have a wonderful way of putting things. My other human advisors wanted me to make it public, to spin it as a positive action on my part, but I didn't like the idea. I appreciate your candor."

"Someone could leak the story. You need to be prepared for that."

"Naturally, I have considered the possibility. I believe it is more probable that we will be able to keep it confidential, but if the story leaks, we then say we were correcting an unfortunate situation."

"You're thinking like a politician."

"Unfortunately, like it or not, I am one."

"If you claim it the shots were given voluntarily, any damage done by a leak will be lessened."

"In other words, *lie.*"

"It's what all your predecessors have done."

"I hope I'm not that *human*," Abraham said. "But, I suppose I might find it preferable to taking a lot of criticism in the media."

"I hope I've helped."

"You have, Mark. The vaccination program will begin next week and is scheduled to be complete by November 1. We will attempt to keep it confidential. If the news of the vaccination program is leaked, I will assert that the shots were administered voluntarily. Thank you, and good-bye."

As his communicator disconnected, Mark thought: *that was the strangest conversation I've ever had.*

#

Melanie's divorce had come through, as the Arizona court was highly automated and it was all done by computers. She regained her maiden name of Kennedy, and was well pleased at that, although she was very unhappy that she had lost Mark, whom she would always love.

She rattled around in the huge house with four thousand square feet and twenty rooms, including six bedrooms. It was an older house, built before the twentieth century, and was located on rocky ground and terminated at an even rockier seacoast, where there was no real sandy shore. The house was close enough that if she opened her bedroom window, she could hear the continuous tumult of the waves as they crashed against the rocks. The sound lulled her and she always slept well and deeply, reluctant to get up in the cool mornings.

There was plenty of work needed to keep the huge old house in good order, but she had two female form and two male form ADR's to do so and keep her company. After three or four weeks she was invited to the home of another grass widow about her own age, and she formed some friendships: Lonnie Welch, a former actress and star of television soap operas, now in her seventies, and Gracie Norman, the divorced wife of a former Congressman, who had issue the invitation to tea. Gracie was 48 years of age, as was Melanie. The girls all wore shorts and sat out on Gracie's patio, attended by her ADR. It was a cool but pleasant afternoon.

Lonnie and Gracie knew that Mark was one of the wealthiest men in the world, and expressed dismay when Melanie told them she was entirely dependent on an annuity, and had only a few hundred thousand of her own money.

"You aren't a very good housekeeper," Gracie suggested. "When I divorced Micah, I kept *six* of his."

The girls laughed at the joke. "I married four times," Lonnie related, "and I kept a house from each husband. I've sold two and banked the money. I still have a nice home on St. Kitts. We can all go there next February. I have it leased out until then."

"Why do you ever come back to Maine?" Gracie asked.

"Truthfully, I love the weather. I love the ocean. And, I can't get all the soap operas on the island."

"Once a soap opera addict, always one," Melanie said.

"They put butter on my bread," Lonnie said. "I still get a few residuals."

#

The message came to Melanie's email. She would have classified it as junk and never opened it – as the wife of a celebrity, she sometimes heard from the teeming masses of people she didn't know -- but this guy knew her personal identifier MelKen, and he knew her pet nickname as well -- Mellie.

To: <u>MelKen@att.us.org</u>

Subject: Dear Mellie, please read me.

My dear Mellie, you won't recognize me from this but we know each other. I am not after your money, as I am quite wealthy in my own right, but I would like to correspond with you: object, matrimony. You might want to dismiss the idea out of hand. After all, I am in my 80's, but I have spent a great deal on rejuvenation and now my age equivalent is estimated by doctors as early 50's. I am in outstanding health and am mentally perfect. I am considered to be tall, muscular, and quite good-looking, or so my ADR tells me.

If you get to know me in my present incarnation, you will find that you and I have much in common. Many of our threads of life have crossed. We are related, but not genetically. I will not say more about this for now, but please trust me on this.

I have been hiding, almost in plain sight. I have reasons for doing so, including many enemies, but I will soon emerge. I have purchased an oceanfront estate in the Caribbean and plan to live there openly quite soon. I would very much like to have you with me

I have always admired your beauty and intelligence. I believe Mark has given you a raw deal and I would like to make up for it. I know you must be lonely in that huge house, and I offer a man – myself – to give you affection and help fill your days. I am, if I say so myself, rather famous. You will have no trouble recognizing my name if and when I reveal it to you, and I believe you will be amazed.

If you are interested in further conversation, please reply at agapl4@wowser.com.

You may refer to me as Decker.

Melanie read the email over and over. A retreaded octogenarian? Probably senile, she thought, even though Alzheimer's was a thing of the past. "*Object, matrimony?*" Fat chance, yet some things about the message intrigued her: "*Threads of life have crossed?*" What was that all about? "*Related, but not genetically?*" "*Hiding?*" "*Always admired my beauty and intelligence?*" Hmm. How would Decker know what a "raw deal" Mark had given her? Why should she be "*amazed*" when he reveals his name?" Finally, he was "*rather famous.*" Who could he be?

It was too much for Melanie. She had to know more about Decker. She wrote:

To: agapl4@wowser.com

Subject: Your message to Mellie.

Decker, I should perhaps have my head examined, but I want to know more about you, because some of your comments made me very curious. We are related, but not genetically? How

294

can that be?

I am not very attracted to someone of your age, even if you have had all the anti-aging therapy in the world. But, I would give you the benefit of a look. It's true I'm lonely, but I have met some lady friends. I have committed to spending time with them on St. Kitts in February, so you see I don't need your estate in the Caribbean. Yet, I am curious. Tell me more.

> *Mellie.*
>
> The reply arrived less than an hour later.
>
> To: <u>MelKen@att.us.org</u>
>
> Subject: A message from Decker.
>
> *My dear Mellie:*

Perhaps the best and safest way for us to proceed is that you plan to spend two weeks with me on my island. As your home is closest to Portland, Maine, suppose you meet me at Gate 5 in the Portland airport at 9 AM on November 1. I have a SkySkimmer which can fly us to my estate there. You may bring as many as three ADR's, and if you wish, one or two human friends. If this time is not convenient, we can negotiate another.

When we meet at the gate, I will be wearing a hood, a false mustache, a blonde wig, and horn-rimmed glasses. I will remove them, and you will instantly know me and know whether or not you wish to come with me. You may turn around and go back home, and we need not communicate again. If you decide not to come, there will be no hard feelings whatever.

I only ask that if you bring human friends, they will not be with you when I remove my disguise, and that you promise not to reveal that you have seen me to any other person.

*Will you permit me to amaze you? Please say
yes.*

Decker.

#

Mellie couldn't resist the temptation, and neither
could Gracie and Lonnie. They traveled to the
airport on Wednesday, November 1, 2085. Each of
them had brought along a female form ADR, after
all, they needed help to dress if they went on the
trip. As they approached Gate 5, she could see there
was indeed an unmarked silver SkySkimmer on the
ramp. A tall, athletic-looking man wearing a
hooded jacket stood against a nearby wall opposite
the window.

She sent the girls to a nearby restroom, then
approached the man. There was something
disturbingly familiar about him. His physique was
like that of Mark and Parker.

Even before he removed his disguise, she
realized that he was Arthur Girard.

24. December, 2085.

Mark heard the first inklings of the national disaster from Jane. She met him at the airport, and he got into her car. As they kissed, the car moved toward the gate and Mark's tilt-wing plane taxied itself toward the hangar.

Jane asked: "Did you hear about the disease in the state prisons? They're calling it a plague. Prisoners are dying by the hundreds."

"No," Mark responded. "I was watching a college basketball game on the way up here, and I haven't paid much attention to the news lately."

"It's really bad, and it's spreading. New York, Michigan, and California so far. They think it's a new form of Measles."

"That's all they know?"

"They say it's very contagious, that it kills in three days, and there's no cure so far. That's all they've said on TV about it."

Mark thought of the vaccines Abraham had said he was going to administer in the prisons. "Sounds serious."

They drove to Jane's home, a rambling ranch style in the suburbs of Champaign. She had purchased it with the extra money she had made from the Utopian Society. They caught up on their lovemaking, then showered, dressed, and sat down to a lunch prepared by her ADR servant.

Mark watched the televised news on the wall imager. The governor of Illinois, who would soon be replaced by a robot, was saying how concerned she was that over ten per cent of the prisoners in her state were already dead, and most of the remainder had symptoms of the 'Super Measles' epidemic. She had been in contact with the Center for Disease Control, but they were just beginning to work on the problem. The theory was that the evolved measles had originated in the Amazon jungles of Brazil.

#

Mark and Jane went to dinner and a movie that night, then came back to Jane's home. At breakfast the next day, the news report was that every federal and state prison in the country was believed to be involved with the Measles plague, as well as every privately operated prison. It was beginning to look as if the disease was invariably fatal. Fewer than a dozen guards had been stricken thus far, and Mark wondered, *Could the guards have received the vaccine?*

He was certain the disease was directly caused by the vaccine. The only thing he wondered about was whether it was deliberate.

On Sunday evening, Jane rode with him back to the airport. They kissed and he boarded his plane for the flight back to Flagstaff. As soon as they were airborne, he called Alex Panagaki.

"Alex, I have a new job for you."

"Oh? Are you paying?"

"Expenses only. I don't expect it to take a lot of your time."

"Am I supposed to do this as part of my FBI duties?"

"You catch on quickly."

"Go ahead."

"I want you to find out where the vaccine came from."

"What vaccine?"

"Oh, I forgot. It's not generally known. You'll need to keep it secret."

"I won't say a word."

Mark explained about the vaccine given to prisoners and members of the enclaves and dependencies.

"You think Super Measles comes from the vaccine?"

"It has to. I want to know who produces it."

"That's easy. Leward Pharmaceuticals."

"How do you know?"

"I'm sitting at my computer. While you and I were talking, I set up a Google search: I asked, which pharmaceutical company has received the most money from the federal government in the past six months? Leward was the leader by far."

"The next question is: who owns it?"

"Hold on a second," Alex said.

Mark waited for nearly a full minute.

"OK," Alex said. "I've got it. *You* do."

"What?"

"Leward is part of Arthur Girard's estate. You own it now."

"Dang," Mark said. "Thanks, Alex. Technically, it's still in Arthur's estate, and hasn't been settled on me as yet. Next month, I think."

"You said you'd pay expenses. You owe me a dollar for my computer time."

"I'll send it along."

#

The next morning, an alert message flashed on the wall in Mark's office, along with a few beeps to get his attention. *The Chief Executive has scheduled a news conference at noon Eastern Time. His subject will be the prisons epidemic.* Mark instructed the media system to show the conference. Twenty minutes later, Abraham's image appeared, and the news conference began.

Mark invited his secretaries into his office to watch with him. The three beauties dutifully trooped in and sat down.

The televised image showed a room full of reporters. After a time, someone announced, "Ladies and Gentlemen, the Chief Executive of the United States." Abraham entered the room and moved smoothly to the podium.

He opened with a statement: *Good Morning. I want to tell you what we know about the epidemic that is sweeping our country, and the actions your federal government has taken and currently plans to take to combat it.*

The National Center for Disease Control is still trying to ascertain the nature of the disease. We believe it is caused by a virus, but that has not been established with certainty. It is said to be similar to Measles, but is reported to have a very long incubation period, at least three weeks, during which it is contagious but displays few symptoms. No effective treatment is known as yet. No patient who has contracted the disease is known to have recovered from it. There are nearly two million persons held in all the prisons affected, and we are at risk of losing them all.

I have ordered a nation-wide, absolute quarantine of all prisons. Only robotic medical personnel may enter or leave infected facilities. The quarantine is particularly unfortunate for those prisoners who are due to complete their terms and

*would otherwise be discharged in the near future.
Obviously, we cannot allow them to return to the
general population.*

*There is more bad news which I must announce:
The disease has been reported in some of the
Muslim Enclaves and the Dependencies. We believe
the epidemic has been carried to enclaves and
Dependencies by recently discharged prisoners. I
have therefore issued orders that all isolated
territories shall be quarantined until further notice.*

*We have dispatched robotic medical personnel to
the Dependencies. We have offered them to the
Muslim Enclaves, but in each case, they have
refused to accept them. The Muslims prefer to place
their faith in Allah. We respect their wishes.*

*We are not aware of any reports of the disease
occurring outside the prisons, enclaves, or
Dependencies. Medical scientists consider this fact
totally unexpected, and are looking into it.*

*I will keep you, the American people informed of
our efforts to combat this unfortunate epidemic.*

*For the reporters present today, you may submit
written questions for my staff. They will endeavor
to answer them as soon as possible. Good-bye.*

Abraham turned and left the room.

Mark dismissed the TV image. Jill, Linda, and
his newest employee Lacey, who was Amy's
replacement, all wanted his attention. "Are we all
going to die?" Jill asked.

"So far, the disease hasn't appeared outside the
prisons or 'lockups'," Mark responded. He used the
slang term for the enclaves and Dependencies.

"It sounds as if once you come down with it,
you're dead," Linda said. "That's *terrible*."

Mark herded the women out of his office. He wasn't making moves on them these days. Jane was all he wanted.

When he was alone again, he thought: *America, with many fewer poor, fewer Muslims, and no convicts in the prisons? Obviously, that's the plan. But who? Could Abraham have engineered this on his own? Would he?*

He didn't think so. Someone else was behind it. It sounded like something Arthur might have done.

#

For Alex, the breakthrough in his search for X came as a shocking surprise. He had used his contacts with the NSA to acquire all recent communications to and from the Girard family, the computational labs in GRS, and the Utopian Society. It was a massive database covering the previous two years, and covered texting, emails, social pages, and even some transcripts of wireless conversations, all reduced to text. It was far too large to go through manually, even to sample, but he could set his computer to search for key words.

It was a rainy day. Outside his office window, the rain pelted down.

Panagaki had just gotten off the communicator with Parker, who had mentioned in passing that his mother had met a man who lived on St. Maarten and was planning to visit him for a lengthy stay. She had said they exchanged email messages and it might lead to marriage.

Out of curiosity, Alex located the email conversation with the man and read. In one of the messages from the man who called himself Decker, several things caught his eye: a very wealthy man, in his 80's, rejuvenated, threads of life have crossed, related but not genetically, many enemies, famous.

He immediately thought of Arthur Girard.

Suppose he isn't dead?

A quick look through government records found that Melanie had indeed traveled to St. Maarten and was there now, according to airline records. She wasn't staying at any hotel.

A further check revealed that Melanie and one Arthur Patterson had applied for a marriage license. The photos on the application sprang to his computer screen.

Arthur Patterson was a younger man, but the resemblance was unmistakable. He was Arthur Girard.

Alex instructed his communicator to set up a three-way with Mark and Parker.

25. February, 2086.

Mark Girard took the communicator call from his father. "Mark, I'm returning control of the software to you. I'm relinquishing control of the government. I'm retiring. Your ex-wife and I are planning to live happily ever after."

Mark seethed as usual these days when talking with his father. "Dad, I'd send troops to kill you if I had control of them. You're returning the software?"

"I'll email the codes to you. I've eliminated most of my backdoor stuff. Abraham will be his own bot again, I'm no longer telling him what to do. I've instructed him to have you and Jane back with him as his chief advisors."

"You know you've done too much damage. There's no way we can fix what you've done."

"I've eliminated most of the problems, haven't I? Isn't genetics wonderful?"

"You've killed millions of people."

"I've simplified things, so to speak."

It had begun around Christmas, when a deadly disease raged through the federal prisons, killing nearly all the prisoners but sparing the guards. Over two million federal prisoners had died, and the prisons were now almost totally empty. All the prisoners had been inoculated in November at Arthur's direction, acting through Abraham, and the epidemic was caused by a modified form of measles, but it had been enormously contagious, and somehow the vaccine had created a special weakness in the immune systems of the prisoners, so that the disease could infect and kill them and only them. The disease was harmless to those who hadn't had the vaccine.

In December, before the prison epidemic, Abraham had generously shared a somewhat different version of the vaccine with the Muslim countries of the world, and to the Muslim enclaves in America. A third version of the vaccine had been distributed to the third world countries, and as well the booming nations of South America: Brazil, Venezuela, and Argentina.

Yet a fourth version of the vaccine had been given to inhabitants of the Dependencies.

In January, the disease had been introduced into the entire world. South America, Africa, and many island nations in the Pacific had been decimated. Now the disease had raged around the world and had run its course. Over three million people had died outside the United States. The European countries had been spared, as had Canada, Australia, and New Zealand – none of which had used the vaccine. More than ninety per cent of those who had taken the vaccine were dead. The rest of the world hated, but now greatly feared America.

It was thought that all Asian countries had been spared, because they hadn't been given the trigger vaccine, but now a new disease was killing off their populations. Called Ebola 52, it was apparently genetically engineered to kill people of oriental descent. There was no effective treatment, and in many parts of Asia, so many died the dead went unburied.

There were now many fewer people in the world.

The Muslim countries, including Iran, were no longer a problem. The deaths had drastically reduced the faith Muslims had in Allah, since He was thought to cause all things. Islam was withering.

China's population and economy had totally collapsed, as had India's. Man-made greenhouse gas emissions from those countries were now estimated at ten per cent of their levels of the past year.

"Abraham's main problem is going to be starting up manufacturing in the United States for products the Asian countries used to make," Arthur remarked. "It's a nice problem to have."

"Dad, you're the biggest villain in history. I found out those vaccines and viruses came from Leward Labs, and you made me the owner."

"Yes, I've been working on this particular project for twenty years."

"You've killed millions in the United States alone. All the prisoners, all the Muslims in the enclaves, and all the poor who lived in the Dependencies."

"Our federal budget should be a lot easier to balance now."

"*Innocent* people, Dad. *Innocent*! Why did you do it, Dad? Why?"

"Humanity needed a change of direction. I've removed corruption and incompetence and partisanship from government, I've returned a large part of the world's land mass to the jungle, so that nature will restore our atmosphere. I've recommended that Abraham keep South America and most of Africa depopulated."

"That won't last, Dad. The populations will grow back."

"Even as we speak, Abraham is taking over the remaining countries. He's installing robotic governments in all of them, modeled after Jane's creation. He will become World Executive. Of course, I need to congratulate *you*. Your ACR's are making it possible. They are invincible."

"You have no conscience, Dad."

"You can't make an omelet without breaking eggs. I'd say we've made a really great omelet."

"Good-bye, Dad. Please don't call me again."

"I'll call you if and when I need to. Bye."

#

From the moment Mark had heard the story of Kitty and the groceries being carried into the garage at Arthur's estate, he had known his father was alive. All the evidence pointed to Arthur, the only one who could have seized control of the autonomous robots, the only one who ever planned that deeply. His supposed death and funeral had been a scam. His father had arranged to have someone else's corpse brought to Oregon, kept in a closed casket, and cremated.

He had tried to send ADR's to the estate to search for the hiding place, but they had refused to go.

When the American government had distributed such massive amounts of free vaccines, he had suspected something was amiss, yet he was helpless. Robots no longer obeyed him if he tried to act against Arthur's machinations.

He had to admit that tax reform, and particularly the federal sales tax, was working well. The economy was starting to boom. Abraham's amendments to the Constitution had put government back on a sound basis, and had adjusted the balance between states and the federal government. Many fewer regulations led to more personal and business freedom.

The government was already predicting a balanced budget for the current fiscal year.

The American public was terribly fearful of epidemics, however. They hadn't completely figured out that there had been deliberate genocide on a world-wide scale, although with a free press some people were beginning to understand what had happened, but the public was mostly ignoring them, labeling such ideas as wild conspiracy theories. Propaganda raged about the plagues, confusing the public. Most thought it was due to a huge error in creating the vaccines. There were loud calls for investigation and punishment of those responsible, but the source of the vaccines had not been released.

Ebola 52 had spread to America, killing a few Asian Americans, but now an inexpensive cure had been made available by Leward Labs. It appeared that only a few Americans would die of the disease. Julie Panagaki had received the shot and was safe.

Mark was aware of one more thing which Arthur had revealed. Other forms of Ebola existed, targeted to different races. There was even one specifically designed for Caucasians. He could only hope it would never be released.

#

Alex's special project had ended unsatisfactorily. He wrote up what little he had and sent it to higher authority, then took up his new assignment as

Special Investigations Officer. Currently, there was no special investigation going on. He retained his office and his status in Flagstaff, and Julie kept her job.

Arthur Girard had gotten away with everything, for the simple reason that there was no hard evidence against him. Alex couldn't even prove that Arthur Patterson and Arthur Girard were the same person, because the anti-aging procedures he had undergone, which involved forced growth, had changed his fingerprints and iris patterns, and even changed his DNA enough that comparisons would not be acceptable in court. Arthur was also two inches taller than his previously reported height, and his facial bone structure was somewhat altered, so that even facial recognition technology reported an uncertain result.

In his professional life, Alex was unhappy, because he didn't have the evidence to prosecute Arthur. In his home life, Alex was totally happy. Julie was going to have a baby, and she and Alex were terribly in love.

#

Jane Brockmeyer gave in. She loved Mark, and when they were again accepted as Advisors to the Chief Executive, she decided to live with him in Washington. She still lectured twice a week in her field of political science, but flew back to Champaign only two weeks of each month.

Abraham was a joy to work with. He was like an intelligent graduate student, who learned instantly and was very interested in what she and Mark had to tell him. If he had a choice to make, and if she and Mark laid out the choices in simple English, he asked the right questions and always seemed to pick the answer they supported.

The public's confidence in the presidency and government was growing rapidly. No one seemed to think the incredibly devastating plagues which had decimated the world's population were the fault of the United States. The free serum distributions from the American government, which had prepared the plagues, hadn't been publicized, and never would be.

Surprisingly, Arthur had quietly transferred total ownership of Leward Labs to Mark, who had made Jane CEO of the company. There were no plans to release any other deadly viruses, and she knew exactly what else was left in the arsenal of viruses.

Jane and Mark had made plans to marry. She was a happy woman.

#

Melanie's last name was almost 'Girard' again. It would have been, except that he now called himself 'Patterson'. She and Arthur had married on the island of St. Maarten. Lonnie and Gracie had also found wealthy eligible men, and lived nearby, and she had other friends as well. She was in social heaven.

Arthur was a wonderful, attentive husband. His youthful vigor was amazing, especially considering he was really very old. He was the man Melanie had longed for. Of course, she had never expected to marry her father-in-law. That was strange indeed.

Arthur seemed very content these days. He and Melanie spent a lot of time on the beach or on Arthur's sixty foot sailboat, which was also equipped with two very fine diesel engines. Arthur had suddenly given up business, telling Melanie there was nothing more he could achieve. He seemed to think he had accomplished more in the months since his fake death than in all the rest of his life put together. Yet, he hadn't done a thing she knew about, except giving back control of the GRS corporation software to Mark. Arthur had told her about that.

Now, she knew Mark hated his father and her as well. She thought it must be jealousy on his part. Perhaps Mark had loved her, after all. She sighed. He'd had his chance with her, but had blown it with all those bimbos. It served him right.

The End.

Author's note:

"Autonomous" – existing or capable of acting independently – may be the ultimate objective of computer development, but don't hold your breath waiting for the first autonomous robot or self-controlled automobile.

Robots with human physical capabilities are far closer. There are already machines which can walk on two legs, go up and down stairs, and reach out and grasp things. Install a smart enough computer in them, and Voila! An autonomous robot, capable of simulating human behavior, and probably doing it better than humans can.

Pseudo-muscles aren't an impossible idea. Long polymer molecules which contract and expand as a result of electrical stimulation are within the realm of possibility. That's an exact description of muscle tissue.

However, the ADR's and ACR's which are the basis of this novel, though perhaps possible and maybe even inevitable, are no doubt years in the future. I'd estimate somewhere between fifty years and a hundred thousand years. Nature (or God, if you prefer) is a formidable designer.

Appendix: Recent American history.

(Author's note: it's always dangerous to give a history to bring the reader up to the time of a novel, in this case 2084. In a few years after this is written, or perhaps even days or weeks, events will occur which will make it obvious that the following history is invalid. But, I suppose if we could predict the future, we wouldn't have future fiction.)

The US experienced a massive evolution between the years 2000 and 2084. Historians are confused about some of the exact details, especially for the first four decades. What we know is that both runaway inflation and depression took place. Massive federal spending ruined the US economy, which suffered a major collapse in 2023 and affected the entire world. Many deaths ensued as people couldn't find work, food became increasingly expensive, and energy prices climbed sharply. The dollar was devalued sharply, and the Chinese ruan became the world's currency of choice

Chaos ruled. Many died in the Race Wars, the anti-immigrant wars, the Tea Party purges, and the anti-Muslim riots. Many others were murdered, starved to death, or died because they could not obtain medical care. The American welfare state was no more, and many could not adapt.

The exact details of this period are sketchy, not because there is nothing written about them, but there is too much, and it conflicts, each side with its own version of what happened. The country was intensely polarized, and the same events are described by different parties, all of whom blame others.

The population of the United States began the 21st century at nearly 300 million. By 2040 it was estimated at just over 140 million.

The following is a chronology of some of the major events of this period:

<u>2017-2030</u>. The Great Oil Collapse. Oil prices rose out of sight as China and India became more highly industrialized and demanded more, while oil prospectors found increasingly fewer reserves. In 2022 a calamity ensued as

Middle East oil production began to fall drastically.

The sharply rising price of oil caused drastic shifts in the US economy. The only private cars sold were electric, while commercial vehicles were electrics or hybrids, or powered by biodiesel or hydrogen. Bicycles and motor scooters and motorcycles proliferated. Many nuclear power plants were built and placed into service, but coal was still a major fuel and a source of ingredients for plastics and other chemical products. Homes continued to be heated by natural gas, but electric heat usage grew. Without oil, plastics were increasingly expensive to make in great quantities, and substitutes were found, mainly wood, cellophane, fiberglass, glass, and ceramics.

2031-2033. The Christian-Muslim wars. Continued Muslim terrorism was the excuse given by the US, Great Britain, and France for the invasion and subjugation of Iran, Pakistan, and Afghanistan. Russia tried to intervene on the side of the Muslims in Iran, but her army was crushed on the battlefield. US forces were unbeatable because of their use of RCCG's -- remote controlled combat golems, (robotic soldiers remotely controlled,) to replace infantrymen. The US also had remote controlled combat aircraft and tanks.

Millions died during the 2030's, when starvation, murder, and rioting were rampant.

2035. The first ACR's (*autonomous* combat robots) were introduced and the US Army began testing them. Improvements in power supplies, computers, and artificial muscles made them possible. The ACR-1 could operate at a high level of activity for an hour on a fuel cell, run at about 30 mph, and could identify and attack enemy soldiers. It carried armor that would stop anything less than .50 caliber ammunition. ACR's coordinated themselves by radio communication, so many of them could act simultaneously.

The GRS Corporation, initially a subsidiary of Microsoft, developed them. Arthur Girard was the chief scientist on the project, and is considered the father of autonomous robots. He became president and majority stockholder of GRS. GRS split off from Microsoft and became a corporate giant.

314

2037. GRS introduced a new model designed for domestic service, the ADR-10. Thousands were sold, and they worked well. Owning one or more was very fashionable, though very expensive. They had the appearance of a young, very neat man or woman. They recharged themselves at electrical sockets.

Also, the US Army began replacing the RCCG's with the ACR-3.

Arthur Girard married Celia Gates, who brought a substantial fortune of her own, a large stock in Microsoft. Arthur and Celia rapidly became one of the wealthiest couples on Earth.

2038. The Girard's had a son, Mark.

2045-2047. The US - China war. President Geller declared China's ownership of US corporations was intolerable. The US confiscated all Chinese assets in the US, and China foolishly declared war, firing long-range missiles at the US. Most were intercepted by America's anti-missile defenses, but New York City was taken out, as was Houston. American missiles destroyed Beijing and Shanghai, along with several other large cities, and the US invaded China with ten divisions of ACR's and thousands of autonomous aircraft and tanks (the control systems for these devices were also made by the GRS Corporation).

China's human army and air forces were no match for the much more reactive autonomous robots, and she was rapidly defeated. The United States forced the Chinese to replace their government with a representative democracy. China was much diminished as an economic power.

The United States remained the most powerful nation on Earth. India emerged as the second greatest power. China began a long recovery.

By this time, Arthur Girard had become a multi-billionaire, and was the wealthiest man alive.

2059. Mark Girard graduated from MIT, then took a position in GRS as VP of Product Development. He married Melanie Kennedy, a member of the Kennedy family of Massachusetts, which was still wealthy and active in politics. A year later, they had a son, Parker, their only child.

2060-2065. India, with a huge pool of available labor, banned all robotic devices with humanoid form. They confiscated and destroyed all GRS Corporation and RE Corporation products in the country. Both firms lost a huge potential market.

In 2060, Democrats seized total power, winning the house, senate, and the presidency. President Cuomo was called "the second Obama" and had a far left agenda. When he attempted to re-institute the income tax (on the wealthy) the army intervened, moving combat robots into the capitol. The first revolution in the history of the United States swept General Wes Williams into dictatorial power.

2066. President Williams revised the Constitution. The House of Representatives could only write and forward legislation, and lost its power to investigate the executive branch. No representative could serve more than two terms. The Senate lost veto power. The President could serve an unlimited number of terms, at his option. Thus, the presidency became dictatorial for a time.

2070. Williams restored the original United States Constitution, with the original 28 Amendments, with the exception of the 17th. Without the 17th Amendment, Senators were again chosen by the State legislatures without a direct vote of the people. Williams added amendments for 12-year term limits for all members of Congress and the Supreme Court. He also strongly limited the application of the Interstate Commerce Clause by rewriting it.

2072. Williams stepped down as president, and the United States held a presidential election which the Republicans barely won. The Democrats began styling themselves as "the Pro-Mankind Party", and came out strongly for limiting use of robots in human society. This message resonated with many, especially the poor who could not afford them.

2080. An aging Arthur Girard became ill and retired, and Mark Girard became president and CEO of GRS Corporation. His mother Celia took no interest in the firm, and she passed control of her stock to Mark. Late in the year, Celia Girard passed away.

2081. China had rebuilt her military capabilities, once again owned a huge balance of trade advantage, and became more truculent toward the United States. There were incidents involving US commercial aircraft which caused increasing tension.

Parker Girard graduated from MIT, but in the middle of his class. He followed his father into GRS's Product Development and Research Division. As a young man, he was too pleasure-loving for his father's taste, and seemed unpromising as a future executive. He was also arrogant and strong-willed, a bad combination which seemed to assure the likelihood of conflict with his father.

Made in the USA
Charleston, SC
24 March 2014